Ac

ER!

"Ric

"Be

"An

"On
of a

"U

"I

i

h

core
o

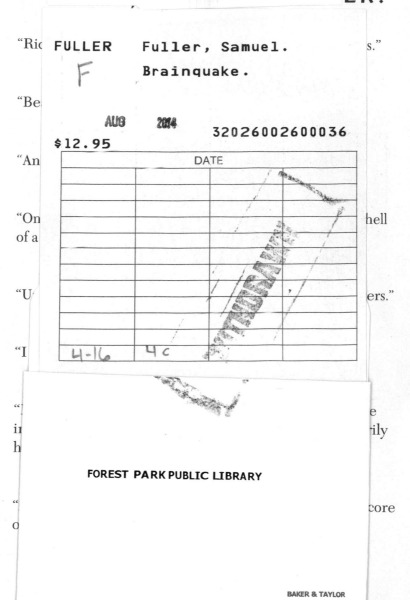

s."

hell

ers."

She studied his blank face. Eyes, nose, mouth, chin, contours normal like millions of people who have faces easily forgotten. Paul had not a single distinctive quality one could describe.

She was frustrated because parsing bagmen was like juggling smoke.

What did it take to be the most trusted men in the most dangerous business in New York City? What gave them that incredible, dependable virtue of loyalty and trust? What made them so impervious to money? To all that cash they carried every day and every night?

Bank tellers steal. Bank directors embezzle. Cashiers steal. Bartenders steal. Politicians steal. Government officials embezzle. But when one of them was caught, he didn't face a bullet in the brain.

That bullet in the brain didn't keep a bagman honest.

Their honesty was something that she could never figure out, no matter how often she tried. A bagman made good money but never in the class of other jobs; never a fortune.

Bagmen carried hundreds of millions without opening the bag to borrow a few thousand. Rarely had a bagman that vanished with his bag got away with it. The ones that tried it were caught.

Looking at Paul she finally suspected how his father had learned about the job, and about the qualifications for it. Some retired bagman who played the horses, placed bets with Barney, must've got drunk, run off at the mouth, told Barney that she was the boss of all the bagmen in Manhattan.

That son of yours, he must have said. What a bagman that boy would make...

BRAINQUAKE

by **Samuel Fuller**

A HARD CASE   CRIME NOVEL

A HARD CASE CRIME BOOK
(HCC-116)
First Hard Case Crime edition: September 2014

Published by

Titan Books
A division of Titan Publishing Group Ltd
144 Southwark Street
London SE1 0UP

in collaboration with Winterfall LLC

Print Edition ISBN 978-1-78116-819-6
E-book ISBN 978-1-78116-820-2

Design direction by Max Phillips
www.maxphillips.net

Typeset by Swordsmith Productions

The name "Hard Case Crime" and the Hard Case Crime logo are trademarks of Winterfall LLC. Hard Case Crime books are selected and edited by Charles Ardai.

Printed in the United States of America

Visit us on the web at www.HardCaseCrime.com

To Christa Lang
and our daughter, Samantha

*Love makes a bagman
a poet or a madman.*
—AL CAPONE

I

Sixty seconds before the baby shot its father, leaves fell lazily in Central Park. Sparrow-weight with bulging jugular, the balloon peddler shuffled past the man sitting on the bench near the path bend, saw nothing to remember in Paul's thirty-year-old cipher face. Paul was half-hidden behind a book of poems. Reading and re-reading Emily Dickinson's *If I can ease one life the aching*, Paul relived the ten-year-old Paul suffocating his mother with a pillow. She didn't struggle. He lifted the pillow. She weighed 97 pounds dead.

A leaf fell gently on the poem.

Paul heard the music box playing *Frère Jacques* without knowing the tune's name. He'd heard it first a day ago. He didn't look at his wristwatch. She was on time. Music or no music, she had pushed the carriage around that bend every morning at 9:30 for two months.

A bad thought flashed through his head. He had a ten o'clock appointment with Dr. Adson, arranged by the Boss. The doctor was to examine Paul, try to cure his brainquake. But Paul was going to be late.

For two months he had lacked courage to speak to her. This morning he had the courage.

The sun made the big, black carriage nosing round the bend shine like wet tar. He would write a poem about it. The red rose he'd left at her apartment door yesterday was clipped to the top of the carriage hood.

Suddenly he was slammed by an emotion he had never felt. Jealousy. For two months she was alone. Now the blonde, blue-eyed, ivory-faced girl—his girl, his Ivory Face—was with a stranger, pushing the carriage past the two cops. One cop younger, one older. Paul had seen them every morning for two months at the bend. They were smiling at the baby in the carriage.

The baby was hypnotized by the toy monkey dangling from the wire clamped to the top of the hood between the music box and Paul's rose.

The balloon peddler stopped shuffling. Only the cluster of his balloons was moving in the gentle breeze. His amused eyes followed the hypnotized baby who believed that the monkey was making the music.

It stopped.

The baby, having learned the magic way to make the monkey play the same music again, pulled the monkey's long tail.

The music box began playing *Frère Jacques*. The gun fired from the carriage. The bullet shattered the stranger's throat. His blood splattered the baby. The stranger fell. Ivory Face collapsed beside him. The baby cried. The balloon peddler hurled his soprano shout:

"The baby shot him!"

The two cops streaked past the peddler holding onto the cluster of balloons, his finger pointing at the carriage and the crying baby. Paul jumped to see if Ivory Face was hurt but his jump didn't take place. He was nailed to the bench. The nutcracker squeezed his brain. Shouting in silence with excruciating pain, he heard the music of the flute. The tidal wave of blood drowned his brain. Paul jerked, shook, rumbled.

The brainquake came.

The explosion turned everything pink. The epicenter cracked his brain open, registering 7.7 on the Richter scale. Blood cells fell into the crevice. Fleeing blood cells were sucked into it. Paul ran naked. Another tremor. 7.8. Paul was chased by the toy monkey playing the flute. The monkey was chased by the two naked cops. The young cop was cranking blood cells out of the music box. The older cop swung the crying baby tied on a rope like a bola. The baby smashed into Paul who fell into the crevice. The rope coiled around Paul's throat. Blood cells sucked them down toward death…

The brainquake was over.

Sound of flute, color of pink gone. *Frère Jacques* still playing on music box. Baby crying. Green grass blinding. Blue sky beautiful. White clouds lovely. Sitting on the bench with book still in hand, the sweating Paul was a trip-hammer staring at the darker blue blur rising from the unconscious Ivory Face.

"Just shock." The blue became sharper. The young cop left Ivory Face on the ground.

His older partner, now in razor-sharp focus too, was still checking the dead stranger. The young cop reached into the carriage for the blood-covered crying baby.

"Don't touch it!" his partner boomed. "Don't touch a goddam thing in that carriage!" The old harness bull grunted, forcing himself to his feet, his back killing him, his hip knifing him. "Get Homicide and an ambulance."

He left a trail of blood to reach the closest eyewitness, sitting on the bench with a book of poems. He jerked Paul to his feet, thumped Paul's arms above his head, frisked him for gun, seized wallet, plucked the book from his hands, checked the book for a gun, tossed book on bench, checked bushes behind bench, turned trash bin upside down, dumped bottles, plastic bags, condoms, trash on ground, kicked around for the gun, pushed down Paul's upright arms.

"Where'd that shot come from?" he thundered.

A scraping sound from Paul's mouth. With effort he forced out each word.

"I was reading."

"That why you're sweating?"

Paul nodded.

"I didn't hear you."

"Yes."

The old bull pointed to Paul's throat. "What's wrong with you? Cancer?"

Paul nodded. That was easiest.

"See anybody running away after the shot?"

Paul shook his head.

The bull boomed over his shoulder at the young cop, who was now ringed by men, women, children. "Keep 'em away from the carriage, goddamit! But don't let 'em leave!" He blasted Paul's ear, "You heard the shot. Where'd it come from?"

"Backfire."

"You thought it was *backfire*?"

Paul nodded.

"You a wiseguy?"

Paul shook his head.

"What do you do, wiseguy?"

"Drive hack."

"Why aren't you?"

"Day off."

"Come here on your day off?"

Be careful! He'll take me in. The Boss'll be angry. Why aren't they taking care of her? She looks hurt. She looks dead. I'm all mixed up. What did he say? His voice hurts...

"I asked you—"

"Yes. Sit here. On my day off."

Why did I tell him? Why is he staring at me?

Paul felt fear. The cop was old but big.

The cop pointed at the carriage. "Seen that carriage before?"

Paul shook his head.

"What company you hack for?"

"Indie."

The cop opened Paul's wallet, studied his driver's license, read the words aloud: "Paul Page. One Rose Road. Where is Rose Road?"

"Battery."

"Still reside there?"

Paul nodded.

"Rose Road…Rose Road…" He rumbled through years of street names in his head. "Old graveyard there?"

Paul nodded.

"Busted-down shacks near a busted-down warehouse?"

Paul nodded.

"You live in one of those shacks?"

Paul nodded.

The cop slapped the wallet shut, pushed it into Paul's chest. "Stay put on that bench. Homicide'll want to talk to you." He left to question the people his young partner had detained. Paul sat down slowly, his eyes on Ivory Face, still lying on the ground looking bloodied and lifeless just like the dead man who lay only steps away. Why weren't they doing anything about her? About the baby? How could a baby shoot that man?

Angry voices invaded his thoughts. The balloon peddler was screaming at the cops:

"I saw the baby shoot that gun!"

"Listen to him," a man called out. "He's a witness."

"You cops are a joke!" a woman shouted.

The old bull controlled himself. "Ma'am, there's no gun in the carriage."

"Look again!" a man shouted.

Heckling didn't bother him. But one of those bastards could report him for not following up on a citizen's eyewitness bullshit. Four months to retirement, he had to tiptoe. Angrily, ashamed of himself, he returned to the carriage, trailed by the young cop.

He knew the people were watching him closely so he made a big deal of the way he looked in the carriage, saw nothing, just blood on the torn blue blanket and under it the baby, wailing. He whirled on the peddler, seizing chest bones, lifting the sparrow off his feet.

"You spread word that baby fired the gun, you castrated sonofabitch, I'll book you in the shithouse."

Then, thinking a moment, he put the man down, turned back. The baby's shrill crying tore the cop's ears but oddly enough it wasn't the sound that bothered him. He looked in the carriage for the third time because he remembered that rip in the blue blanket. It was hard to see in the blood. But he remembered it, now studied it, kept leaning over, bending lower. He lifted the blood-splotched blanket. Why the hell hadn't he done this before?

Between the baby's blue booties was a tiny hole in the white comforter. Slowly lifting it, he met the muzzle looking up at him.

His partner was by his side. "I'll be a sonofabitch, you'll retire a sergeant!" The young cop reached down for the baby, and was jerked back hard and fast.

"The nut that rigged it could've planted a booby trap under the baby," the old cop said.

"Bullshit!"

"I seen 'em in the war in toilets, water faucets, under dishes an' corpses."

"Bullshit!"

"Okay, go on, then, pick up the baby."

The young cop's hands reached down, touched the crying baby and froze.

2

Word was spreading there was not just a gun but a bomb under the baby's ass. Barricades had been rushed in, hastily erected, barely keeping the crowd back. The Pickpocket Squad was busy. It was a field day for cannons lifting wallets, flipping open shoulder-straps in the press of bodies. One enterprising book-man, a U.S. Army veteran who usually sold off a folding card table by the entrance to the park, had a box of pocket Bibles, going quick at $10 a copy to help pray for the baby. A guitar player with stringy hair and a rainbow strap ad-libbed a song about *the baby who pulled the trigger, shot us all*. Singing slow, strumming, now on the twenty-third verse, inspiration failing him, upturned baseball cap by his feet showing only a handful of coins, as much copper as silver. Television and newspaper cameras swiveled at each hint of movement, hung down again disappointed when no explosion came.

One news photographer, on deadline and out of patience, ran toward the baby in the carriage. A mounted policeman galloped after him. The crowd roared. Leaping down from the horse, the policeman got the photographer in a half-nelson, took his Nikon away from him.

The balloon peddler worked small groups in the crowd, giving his eyewitness account over and over.

The old cop led Paul off the bench, which another cop was piling high with equipment, and past the barriers, waving front-line people back with his club. They stopped by a tall lamp planted at the curb, the paint along its long metal column peeling.

"This spot belongs to you, Paul. Don't move from it." Paul

watched him rejoin the young cop guarding the carriage. Behind Paul, the crowd was swelling. The rumor of gun and bomb under the crying baby was frightening, made people squirm. Even so, they had gathered like locusts to watch.

Paul didn't hate the people in the crowd, but he couldn't understand them. Watching for a baby to die, horribly. Maybe putting themselves in danger too. Why?

Paul turned away, looked over the heads of the cops, into the eyes of the police horse fifteen feet in front of him, a beautiful Blood Bay that made Paul's mind race back…

…to horses staring at him from that big book when his father was trying to get him to talk…and with great effort after four years he managed to repeat the kind of horse each one was… white Albino…yellowish Buckeye…brown Chestnut…golden Calico…

The Blood Bay staring at him was flanked by other mounted police horses forming a half-circle around the carriage. Foot cops stood behind the mounted cops. Behind them all, an ambulance waited, rear doors open. Ivory Face was in it, on a stretcher. But the ambulance didn't rush her to the hospital, so Paul figured she must be okay. They were waiting for the baby.

Paul thought about the man, the stranger, who had been put into a canvas bag and driven off. The word *jealous* came to mind, but this time only the word. He felt nothing. He knew what the word meant. He felt nothing.

There must be a reason that the stranger bothered him.

Why must everything have a reason?

Why was Ivory Face important to him? Every morning for two months when she pushed the carriage past him, she looked at him but he knew that she really didn't see him. She looked right through him as if he weren't there. He didn't exist to her. Like other people, she saw him but didn't see him.

When he was a child, a toddler, one of his teachers had called him a cipher, the word taunting him. Later, when he had learned to read, he looked up the word and it meant zero...nothing.

He remembered the first time he overheard his parents talking about him. He was about three years old. He could hear and see, but he was mute. They had tried to make a sound come from his throat. They couldn't. They couldn't even get a rasp out of him. When he slipped in the bathtub, hurt his finger, he cried tears but made no sound. His parents were worried he'd remain silent all his life. They would never put him in an institution where he'd be with children like him...but they were frightened for him, frightened about what kind of life he would have.

His thoughts went back to Ivory Face.

Why was he interested in her?

Why must everything have a reason?

Since seeing her for the first time, he'd had her face before him each time he closed his eyes. She was beautiful, but it was more than that. Or less than that. It wasn't about beauty. The look in her eyes: haunted. Hunted. Like there was something waiting for her, just over her shoulder or past the next corner, waiting for her and her baby. Something was causing her pain, was causing her fear. She was maybe twenty years old, twenty-one, but her eyes were so much older. He remembered his mother's eyes, at the end. *If I can ease one life the aching, Or cool one pain...*

Paul saw someone running at him. Not a photographer this time, a woman. She had broken through the barricade, slipped past the policeman, and was heading for the carriage, $10 Bible held high. One of the cops went to intercept her, keep her away from the scene, and she veered to the side, barreling into Paul shoulder-first. The impact drove him back, and he lost his balance. Then the cop was on her, wrestling her away. Seeing her struggle in the policeman's grip, a man on the other side of the barricade ducked under, shouting, waving a fist in the air. Others in the crowd took up the shout. Paul, on his ass in the dirt, looked up at the faces, previously tense, now angry. He thought: *They'd better do something soon.*

3

Ivory Face twisted sideways on the cot of the waiting ambulance, balanced her flyweight on a fragile elbow, pressed her delicately chiseled face against the window and watched cops keeping the crowd away from her.

Sitting beside her was Helen Zara.

"Feel well enough to answer questions now?"

Ivory Face slightly turned her head, distorting her face.

"Yes."

"What's his name?"

"Frankie Troy."

"Police record?"

"Wouldn't surprise me."

"Father of the baby?"

"Yes."

"What's Frankie's real name?"

"That's the name I married. I'm his widow. Michelle Troy. What about my baby?"

"Can't be moved till specialists get here."

"I've got to change his diapers, feed him. They can do their work without my baby."

"They can't."

"Why not?"

"The gun's under your baby."

Michelle's eyes turned glassy. Zara knew it was time to get the doctor back but she pulled out a silver flask, unscrewed the top, poured bourbon down Michelle's throat, and waited until air gurgled through Michelle's lips. Zara closed the flask.

"I'm all right, Lieutenant. Ask your questions."

"Who taught your baby to pull the monkey's tail when the music stopped playing?"

"Frankie."

"How many times did he walk the carriage with you?"

"Only once."

"Was he on your left or right?"

"On my right."

"The whole time?"

"Yes."

"Who installed the monkey and the music box?"

"Frankie."

"Anyone help him?"

"No."

"Did you see him install it?"

"Yes."

"When?"

"Two days ago."

"You mean that in two days he taught the baby to pull the monkey's tail to start the music?"

"My baby's smart."

"Where did he install it?"

"Under the stairway on the ground floor."

"Is that where you always keep the carriage?"

"Yes. We live in a walkup, fourth floor. My baby sleeps in a crib."

"The other tenants know the carriage was kept under the stairway?"

"Yes."

"Who else knew?"

"The superintendent."

"Who else?"

"Frankie."

"How long've you lived there?"

"Eight months."

"How did Frankie get along with the tenants?"

"He didn't know any of them. He barged in a couple days ago, found out where we lived."

"You were hiding from Frankie?"

"Damn right I was."

"Who told him where you lived?"

"Who cares? He used the monkey and music box to try to win me back."

"Did he threaten you if you didn't take him back?"

"He just begged and cried."

"When did you run out on him?"

"A year ago."

"Short marriage."

"Not short enough."

"Did he ever beat you?"

"No."

"Try to get you to push dope?"

"No."

"Ever pimp for you?"

"No."

"Why did you leave him?"

"People leave people."

"Why did *you*?"

"People don't like people."

"Why did you marry him?"

"I got pregnant."

"Are your parents alive?"

"No."

"No family?"

"Only the baby."

"Where did you marry Frankie?"

"On a boat."

"Where?"

"Crossing the Hudson."

"What boat?"

"Small."

"Rental?"

"Yes."

"What's the name of the boat?"

"No name."

"Catholic marriage?"

"Justice of the Peace."

"What's his name?"

"Don't know. Everyone was drunk."

"Were *you*?"

"All of us."

"Who else?"

"Guy who handled the boat. Willie something…"

"Has anyone threatened you recently?"

"Why me?"

"You could've been on Frankie's right, where the gun was pointed."

Remembering: "Oh, my God! I was! I was on his right! When we headed out. Then this woman dropped a bag of oranges. Frankie helped her pick them up."

"Why didn't he step back on your left side where he had been?"

"I moved to fix the blanket."

"So, has anyone threatened you?"

"You asked me."

"You didn't answer it."

"…A man phoned last night."

"What time?"

"About seven. Frankie was out. The man said Frankie owed him ten thousand dollars and Frankie'd be sorry if he didn't pay before eleven o'clock."

"Deadline was eleven o'clock last night?"

"Yes."

"What name did he give you?"

"He didn't."

"Did you ask him?"

"No."

"A man phoned and threatened your husband and you didn't ask the man his name?"

"That's Frankie's problem."

"You told Frankie about the threat?"

"Of course."

"What did he say?"

"He laughed. He knew the screwball. He said forget it."

"Did Frankie tell you the man's name?"

"Just called him a...black psycho."

"I mean his name."

"Frankie said that's what he called him—Black Psycho."

"Did Frankie tell you where this 'Black Psycho' lived?"

"That was Frankie's problem."

"Did the man sound drunk? High?"

"No."

"How old?"

"Hard to tell."

"Accent?"

"No."

"Profanity?"

"No."

"Stutter?"

"No."

"Cough?"

"No."

"Did he talk fast?"

"No."

"Slow?"

"Normal."

"Who were Frankie's black friends?"

"I don't know."

"Any friends of Frankie been in a mental ward?"

"I never met his friends."

"Why not?"

"Wouldn't like them."

"Because they're into narcotics?"

"Wouldn't like them."

"How long did you know Frankie before you married him?"

"One week."

"How did you meet him?"

"I got out of the subway. It was raining. He had an umbrella and walked me to where I lived."

"Where did you live then?"

"504 West 176th Street."

"How did Frankie make a dollar?"

"I never asked."

"Did you move in with Frankie?"

"Yes."

"Where?"

"Saint Charles Hotel, West 96th Street."

"Did you work when you met him?"

"Cashier. French rotisserie restaurant. 137th and Broadway."

"Still work there?"

"No. I'm at the Rex Western Grill on…"

"I know it. What daycare do you leave the baby with when you go to work?"

"Daycare? Can't afford daycare."

"Who looks after your baby when you work?"

"I do."

"At Rex Grill?"

"Yes."

"Where's the carriage kept?"

"A storeroom off the kitchen. The owner, his wife and the help all chip in. They all love my baby."

"Did Frankie give you the ten thousand?"

"You kidding?"

"It wasn't on his body."

"That's Frankie's problem."

"It's your problem now."

"Are you crazy? I have nothing to do with him or his money."

"It was a business bullet, Mrs. Troy. You get hit, Frankie pays. Frankie's hit, you pay."

Through the window Zara saw the Bomb Squad van pass. She stood up, bending over to clear the low roof of the ambulance. She spoke very quietly. "Mrs. Troy, they're going to check the carriage. The man who planted the gun could've planted some kind of a booby trap too. To do the maximum damage, and cover his tracks."

"Booby trap?"

"Your baby will be okay, Mrs. Troy. We'll see to it. And we can give you protection for the day, maybe the week. But we can't protect you forever. One day you'll be right back where you are now. There's no guarantee we'll find the man who did this. And if we don't, even a year from now, he'll look you up and he'll be very mad. Raise that money."

"I can't."

"Pay him or your baby'll die a baby."

4

Camera crews on the roofs of three network trucks were ready when Zara climbed out of the ambulance, strode past a white-clad doctor sneaking a smoke, then marched through the opening made by cops keeping the press and the crowd back.

Shoulder-mounted cameras weighed heavily on operators keeping their balance by their assistants' grips on their hips. News photographers and a platoon of reporters fell in behind the Pied Piper of the NYPD without firing a single question.

They knew Zara's trademark. When ready, she'd make only one statement. To some of the print buzzards, Zara was arrogant, to others she was eccentric, but to all she was news. And professionalism, brevity, honesty. But most of all news.

Zara knew how they saw her and embraced it. Journalists had made her a tabloid figure, a star, rather than the working cop she was. So be it. If it helped bring killers in, she'd tolerate the headlines, the photos in the *Post* and the *News*, the insinuations from some in the department that she sought the attention out. She didn't. A case was a case. A pro hit man or a domestic killer were the same to her. They killed. They must be put out of circulation.

She didn't believe in redemption when it came to taking a human life. To her that was breaking the law of life, not the law written somewhere on a piece of paper. She didn't believe in the why of murder, in any medical or psychological explanations for it. The hell with why. What, where, when, who. You kill, you're caught, the door slams behind you. You can spend the rest of your life in a cage, or you can do the decent thing and kill yourself. That was fine. She never begrudged a killer a second killing, as long as the second victim was himself. And if he needed to be helped along a little, she didn't mind that either. She had a dozen shootings to her name, every one of them righteous.

Of course it made her a target, too. For wanted fugitives, for criminals who hated that there was a cop they couldn't buy, couldn't finagle, couldn't blackmail. This was her city, and she walked its streets, didn't hide behind bulletproof glass or an office posting, strode with balls, but was always alert. Even now, tailed by the press, anyone masquerading as a cop or a reporter could open up the back of her skull with a bullet. She didn't let it bother her. Fear came with the badge. No one forced her. It was her choice.

She lived alone in a small East Harlem apartment in the heavily populated Spanish area that once was inhabited almost entirely by blacks. She slept on the ground floor with unbarred window always unlocked. In the summer, she left it open, let in some air. She breakfasted round the corner, hating to make coffee. She hated to cook. She'd grab a sandwich for lunch, but dined like a queen at Dinty's Chop House.

Her clothes cost a heavy dollar. Immaculate, she always smelled good.

A born bloodhound, though she had lost the scent of many fugitives too. Which is why she'd given Michelle Troy the advice she had, as much as it pained her to do it. Paying a murderer disgusted her, but it wasn't the widow's job to fight one. That was the police's job, and until they did it Mrs. Troy had to do what she had to do, to keep herself and her baby alive. Meanwhile, Zara would work the case, do her damnedest to nail the killer. She'd nailed 77 to date, killed twelve of them. It wasn't an art. It wasn't a science either. It was shoe leather and sweat, and sometimes luck, though you could help luck along. She was helped by informers. Some stoolies informed for vengeance. Pros were paid. She preferred pros.

Majority of them were ex-cons. Without a canary, she was in trouble. It was ball-breaking enough to find the spoor of a killer in New York City. Almost impossible without a tip. Every homicide cop had a roster of informers. She had one of the best. She never paid them grudgingly. They had their way of earning a living, she had hers. In murder, every Judas was an angel. She had always wondered what would have happened at Little Big Horn if there had been a stoolie in the Sioux. Probably Custer would have been made president.

She was approaching the police-blocked dirt path leading to the carriage. The press knew that in a moment they would lose her. This was their last chance to get a statement. So they dashed past her and walked backwards facing her, quickening their pace so she wouldn't steamroll over them before she vanished behind the final cop barrier.

She stopped. The cameras focused on Zara's black eyes under groomed black hair, not kinky at all at the moment since just two days earlier she'd had it hot-pressed straight. Face black marble. Heavy breasts covered but not hidden by buttoned, custom-tailored gray jacket. Holster bulge invisible. Handcuffs invisible. Shirt white. Tie black. Long, lean legs striding under matching gray skirt. Black shoes with spike heels that had doubled as a weapon in the hands of the 34-year-old, six-foot-three-inch legend that give the New York Police Department such élan. She lived up to the reporters' expectations and made her one statement:

"Here's what we know. There's been a murder. When the baby in that carriage pulled the tail of the toy monkey, it triggered a loaded gun concealed between the baby's feet. Frankie

Troy was shot dead. His widow, Michelle, is waiting in the ambulance for her baby. There is reason to believe there may be a bomb under the baby. Our job is to get the baby out safely and you're going to help us do it by staying the hell away. Come within three feet of that carriage and I've given instructions to shoot. I'm dead serious." No one doubted it.

She turned to go. Jaediker of the *Daily News* shouted:

"Any suspects, Lieutenant?"

"A threat was called in, by an unidentified male who may go by the street name 'Black Psycho.' "

"Black...?"

"Psycho, that's right, Mr. Jaediker. They come in all colors, even mine. Now move back."

The media and the cops parted for her as she strode forward, as single-minded as a torpedo. She saw the men in the crowd watching her, and knew there was something in their eyes other than respect. Sometimes it was lust, sometimes fear. Sometimes anger. Sometimes...

Zara imagined what it had been like for her ancestor Jero Zara, the first nigra cop assigned to protect Andrew Johnson in New York. Jero Zara was killed by a bullet intended for Johnson, who became President when Lincoln was assassinated. She imagined her grandfather, Tom Zara, the first nigger to command the pioneering Vice Squad in the Force. Tom Zara was shot in the back by the pioneering Murder, Inc.

She walked with her head up and her back straight.

From a distance came the crying, the baby in that carriage busting its lungs to live in the world of savagery it had been born into.

Like Zara had cried, a baby sitting on her father's knee, her mother standing beside them proudly, the three of them posing for the newspaper cameras the day her father, Ray Zara, became the first colored Captain of Detectives. He never liked the word colored, preferring Negro to the day he was hammered to death in a Harlem race riot.

The same savage world had awaited the baby sitting on Ray Zara's knee, now working as the first black female Homicide Detective First Class, battle-scarred, with five citations for bravery, and as contemptuous of pithy epithets as her daddy had been. Nigra, nigger, colored, now black. What would they next change the color of black to?

Her mind turned to Frankie Troy. The dead man rankled her.

If he had no record, she had nothing. If he had no friends, she had only the widow's word based on Frankie's word that a man called Black Psycho had threatened his life. She only had the widow's word about the ten thousand dollars Frankie supposedly owed.

If she could find out what business transactions Frankie Troy was involved in, maybe she'd have something to go on. But Michelle Troy looked to be no help there.

Was Black Psycho an actual psycho, a psych ward patient, a medicated schizophrenic? Or was it just a sobriquet, a nom de guerre? In gutter business or pavement conning, characters called each other psychos. Like Crazy Eddie wasn't really crazy. Just his prices were insane.

Her watch said 10:30. Kelleher should be finished checking Frankie Troy's prints. Zara was banking on those prints. She had to know all about Frankie Troy before she could go after his killer.

A sudden roar made her look up. A news helicopter was hovering above the carriage. They were filming three men wheeling a big machine down the ramp of the Bomb Squad van, moving it across grass to the side of the carriage. One officer waved the helicopter away but it remained. A second camera was on the crying baby.

Zara pulled out her gun, aimed it at the cameras. The chopper swept off like a hawk.

Would she have fired? Didn't matter. What mattered was, they believed she would.

Reputation. It cost something, but it was worth something too.

Paul watched Zara put her gun away. He'd seen her first only at a distance, a woman crossing No Man's Land. Not a single cop ran out to order her behind the cordon. Which meant she was a cop herself. When she got closer, he saw who she was. Black female detective, over six feet tall—there was only one. The Boss had told him about Zara, how she'd shot a pirate who killed a bagman and got away with his bag of cash. Zara tracked down the pirate, who drew first. She shot him between the eyes, read his rights to the corpse. In the hijacked bag was $12 million, which she turned over to her captain. The pirate was black. The Boss said that Zara was color blind when it came to homicide.

Paul looked over toward the ambulance, saw Ivory Face sitting up, watching the scene anxiously. He wanted to go over to her, find out if she was all right, tell her she didn't have to face this alone.

But when he made a move in her direction, the cop on the Blood Bay drove Paul back to his spot.

Zara watched the Bomb Squad ready the X-ray. If there was a bomb…if it exploded with that baby still on top of it…

What happened six years ago could happen again. Six years ago Tolly Coleman used the headline BLACK MAN BLOWS UP WHITE WOMAN WITH GRENADE to cause a riot. A massacre— fourteen blacks had been killed. The men who held the bats, the pipes, the bricks were punished, sentenced, but Coleman? Coleman's weapons were words. Zara failed to nail Tolly Coleman with multiple murder.

Of course Tolly Coleman was dead now. Four months later Tolly Coleman had raped a 15-year-old black girl in her basement. In court, found guilty, Tolly Coleman went berserk, seized a cop's gun, shot him, ran out into the street shooting people, and was shot dead by another cop in front of the traffic-jammed Criminal Courts Building.

But Tolly Coleman's organization, White America First, was still alive. The headline BLACK PSYCHO MURDERS WHITE BABY could bring another massacre.

But then, hell, so could BLACK PSYCHO USES WHITE BABY TO KILL ITS FATHER.

Zara had to talk to the Police Commissioner. He'd listen to her. A battalion of cops at the White America First headquarters would be enough to stop them from using this incident as a reason to butcher more blacks.

She would speak to the Commissioner right after the Bomb Squad did its job.

But the baby came first.

5

Caked blood stung the baby's face. Its howls could be heard all over Central Park. Zara squatted down beside the three men at the foot of the carriage.

She had seen baby skeletons in the remains of fires; hoisted from a rotted barge; under garbage; in stinking wooden boxes abandoned by mothers; in sewers, attics, excavation dumps.

Now—through the powerful X-ray machine—she saw, for the first time in her life, a tiny skeleton screaming for help. From the moving skull to the moving phalanges, she saw a living skeleton thrashing, wailing.

Charlie pointed. "The extension's a different make."

Zara ignored the dead wire holding up the toy monkey to focus on the extension spliced to it and continuing through tiny metal rings behind the upholstery of the carriage.

Charlie felt her body trembling against his.

"You okay, Lieutenant?"

"Are you?"

"No," Charlie said.

Zara's eyes followed the extension down the side, snaking under the comforter to end fastened to the trigger. The small gun was snugly wedged in a wooden box. The muzzle was between the tiny tarsal bones of the baby's kicking feet.

Charlie said, "A pro would've used more metal rings to make sure the extension wouldn't snag."

"But it didn't snag."

"No, it didn't."

"Is that shape under the pelvis the bomb?"

"No, that's part of the carriage."

"Under the femur?"

"No. It's under the spinal column."

She saw a small, round area of darkness on the X-ray. "You sure that's what it is?"

"Uh-huh. See that thinner wire that blends with the cartilage?"

"No."

"Lowest vertebra."

"Still can't see it."

"Near the disk?"

"Still can't see it, Charlie."

"Hidden behind the markings of the gun butt."

"Thin as a strand of hair?"

"That's extension number two tied to the trigger."

"*Two* wires on the trigger?"

"Uh-huh. When the wire pulled the trigger that fired the gun, the second extension simultaneously activated the agitator over here." He pointed.

"But then the bomb's a dud, Charlie. It didn't go off."

"It's reverse action. Weight keeps it from exploding."

"The baby's weight?"

"Uh-huh."

"You mean lift the baby—and it blows?"

"Uh-huh."

The three men rose, stretched their legs. Zara followed them to the van twenty feet away. Charlie gave her an auxiliary suit and the four donned their padded gear. They returned to the carriage. The crying of the baby grew louder, the repetitive ear-knifing squeal of a trapped and wounded cat.

Charlie moved to one side of the carriage, George beside him. Joe squatted across from them on the other side and gestured to Zara who squatted beside him. All wore protective gloves but Charlie.

Silence fell over the crowd as they watched. They didn't know what was happening, but they knew something was.

Zara watched Charlie lowering his hands. His nails were cut short. She saw Charlie's flesh vanish and then, through the baby's ribs, his finger bone-tips appear, creeping along the squirming skeleton toward the small round object under it.

This time she could make out part of the mechanism inside the object…a mechanism like the works inside a tiny watch.

"One inch right," Joe said.

Zara watched Charlie's bone-tips moving right in direct line with the object. Seeing them through the bomb, through the baby, made Zara hold her breath.

Charlie sneaked five finger bones, palm up, under the skeleton as he sneaked his other finger bones toward the object. Bone-tips touched it. The skeleton shifted partially off the object.

"Careful!"

Charlie's bone fingers in unison stopped the shifting.

"Back one," Joe said. "Left three quarters of an inch."

Zara watched finger bones move the squirming skeleton back above the object.

"On target," Joe said.

Finger bone-tips repeated the procedure, slowly shifting the skeleton with one hand, slipping the other hand toward the object. The skeleton of a fly landed on the tiny jaw bone, at the corner of the skull's mouth. Zara watched finger bone-tips coming at her, creeping over the object until it was completely covered.

Then she saw the bone fingers pressing down hard on the object.

"Now," Charlie said.

George lifted the baby. The skeleton fly took off. Flesh returned.

George hit the ground face down, covering the baby with his body. Zara hit the ground on the other side. Charlie raced with the object in his cupped hands to the van, Joe running beside him. Charlie thrust his hands into the van. Joe carefully closed the door until it reached Charlie's hands.

Charlie jerked empty hands out as Joe slammed the door shut. The blast shook the van. Earth trembled. The crowd shook.

Joe swung the door open. Smoke burst out from the van. Zara heard the siren. Through the swirling black and gray smoke she caught a flash of the ambulance coming toward her. Shedding suit and gloves swiftly, Zara took the baby from George, still howling, but free now, safe. She hugged him to her breast.

"Get that carriage to the lab!" Zara said.

Paul saw her running with the baby toward the ambulance, climbing in, saw Ivory Face reach for her baby as the doctor, inside with them, pulled the rear door shut. The crowd's silence broke, sound erupting again, some applause, some cheers, some shouts. But the balance shifted quickly, away from euphoria. Resentment swept the people, escalated as the police raised batons and tried to disperse the crowd. All the tension, pent up, had to go somewhere. One man stepped past the barricade, demanding something loudly of the policeman in front of him. Then another. Then all the barricades were going down.

6

One of the first swept up in the press of bodies, Paul crashed into the Blood Bay, which reared, throwing the cop. Hoofs missed Paul by inches.

Dodging them cost him his footing. Paul rolled and skidded and crashed into others buffeted like leaves in a cyclone.

Panic took over.

Paul ran, slipped, ducked behind a bench. Took an elbow to the eye. Through a haze he saw the ambulance carrying Ivory Face speed away, siren screaming. People were chasing after it on foot. Journalists, maybe. Maybe spectators. It was like trying to catch up with a bullet in flight.

Another elbow, and Paul went down. *In one corner of his brain he could see himself running in the rain at 12 and suffering his first attack, the first of the splitting headaches...or was he 14 then?...it was the headache that eventually led to his brainquake...*

...at 14 running in the rain he saw for the first time pink rain...

...at 15 running in the rain he found refuge in a bookshop from the storm...he had never seen so many books...

...he picked up a book and rain from his clothes dropped on it...it was called 100 FAVORITE POEMS...he didn't know what a poem was...

...he wiped the rain off and opened the book and one word stood out like a giant: SOLITUDE...the words were not like words in the books he read...there were only three or four words on a line...more words under it...sometimes only one or two words...he read the whole line...he read the whole poem...he

read words that danced for him and words that he understood
and words that understood him and were about him...words
about being alone and liking to be alone...

...and that night, at the table in the shack, he tried to write
his first poem, but it was hard to find words that meant what he
felt...and he devoured every new word he could...

...at 16 he rode in the rain with his father, known all up and
down the West Side as Barney the Bookie...a name Paul had
loved hearing as a boy, it was so musical...and they collected
small racing bets at different stores where the owner took bets
for Barney...

...then his father gave him $10 a week to walk a route around
the Battery and collect the bets that were given to him in envelopes...once when his father found scribbling on the back of an
envelope and was puzzled and read the scribbling aloud, "The
last horizon never goes away, it is there to stay day after day,"
Paul told him it was a poem he wrote, and his father was proud
until Paul told him he wanted to be a poet, and his father was
upset...because though Paul would never get a normal job for
many reasons, he couldn't feed himself writing poems...Paul
had to have a job that came with security, a paycheck while he
did it and a pension after, so he wouldn't die a bum looking for
handouts...and Barney only knew one person that would give
Paul a steady job like that...Paul could write his poems at night,
and have security for the rest of his life...

7

The baptism of Pegasus Storage and Moving Company in 1902 was held on a triangular dirt lot in New York City. Thousands came to hear President Theodore Roosevelt reminisce about Pete Pegasus, who rode with Teddy's Rough Riders in Cuba in 1898.

Decades later skyscraper snobs dubbed Pegasus "Flatiron Island" because of its snub-nosed prow and wide stern. The current ten-story structure housing offices and storage room, built in 1919, occupied the same triangular block.

The Lilliputian island in the turbulent sea of traffic was dwarfed by the world's tallest office buildings. At its south end was Police Headquarters. At its tip, the PEGASUS DELIVERY sign over the entrance with its trademark, a winged horse.

In the eye of the horse was a concealed camera.

In a small stone cell on the seventh floor a 60-year-old was sitting by the window watching traffic on a monitor when a blue pickup pulled to a stop. The lettering on its door read INTERBOROUGH TRANSIT. The man noted the time on a long yellow pad and watched the blue-clad driver open the rear door and drag out a big canvas mailsack bulging with parcels that he carried into the building.

The 60-year-old man turned to another monitor and saw the driver emerge from the elevator on the eighth floor and advance to the camera to insert his card in the wall slot. An iron door slid open. He stepped into a small office. The door slid shut.

The watcher returned his attention to the traffic outside.

※

Mr. Yoshimura was at his desk checking brown-paper-bound stacks of cash. In front of him on six monitors his crew was sorting bills in denominations of $20 and $50 and $100. Four musical chimes rang. He glanced up at the number 28 blinking red on the wall. He pushed a button. The blinking stopped. He pushed a second button. A wall bin opened up. The bin was between the windowless Receiving Room and the blue-clad driver in the small office. The driver's hands began dumping parcels from his canvas bag into the waist-high bin. The driver's face could not be seen.

On the other side of the bin, men tossed the parcels on a long metal table. Others cut them open, dumped cash on the table. Others fed the empty parcels into a mammoth shredder. Others fed the cash from the table into four automatic X-ray machines to detect counterfeit bills.

On each of the X-ray machines was the name of their former owner: UNITED STATES TREASURY.

A bell rang. Machine #3 ejected a flurry of $100 bills that fell into the slot for funny money. The bills were brought to Mr. Yoshimura, who banded and bagged them, stapled the bag to a yellow card, and neatly wrote "28" on it. When the X-ray machines finished their screening, the cash was dumped into a big basket that was put in the dumbwaiter. Mr. Yoshimura placed the bagged bills with their yellow card on top of the rest of the cash, pushed a button. The dumbwaiter started its ascent.

Bossing the Laundry Room on the ninth floor, Mr. Grigor watched the dumbwaiter ascend to a stop, plucked the phony bills from the yellow card, and brought them to his desk as a man dumped the basket out on a long table. While his crew separated the denominations and fed the bills into three counting and packaging machines (also stamped UNITED STATES TREASURY),

Mr. Grigor fanned the bills that had been marked 28 on the yellow card and examined them with his good eye.

Near him, Moe Scolari, placing stacks of cash on a long table, knocked over a stack. In domino fashion several stacks tumbled to the floor.

"Why so nervous, Moe?"

"I need another century, Mr. Grigor."

"You already owe me a hundred twenty-five."

Mr. Grigor glanced at his watch, pulled out a slip of blue paper from his shirt pocket, checked the coded drops and amount for the day. Moe picked up the fallen stacks and neatly arranged them on the table.

"I'm hurting, Mr. Grigor."

"I'm no bank." Turning to a bony man checking stacks on another table, Mr. Grigor said, "Eleven A.M. Drop 92. Five hundred thousand."

The bony man drew a small leather notebook from his upper vest pocket, and an old Waterman pen from the other pocket, unscrewed the top, neatly code-entered time, drop, amount. Dangling on his watchchain was a gold fob. His cufflinks were gold.

"How about you, Mr. Hendrix?" Moe said.

"A penny loaned is a penny flushed down the toilet." Hendrix closed the pen, shoved it back in vest pocket, began to place stacks of bound cash in a basket.

Mr. Grigor pulled out three twenties and a ten from his pocket. "Here's sixty, Moe," handing over the twenties. "Makes a hundred eighty-five you owe me."

"Thanks, Mr. Grigor."

"I'll buy lunch." Mr. Grigor waved the remaining bill. "This'll cover a couple hamburgers."

*

On the tenth floor the Boss ignored the TV news replay of the mob in Central Park. She was worried. Very, very worried. Paul's attacks kept her up nights. Brainquake, he called it. Seeing crazy things in pink. She suffered from bad headaches herself and weird nightmares, but nothing like Paul's sickness.

If it was a brain tumor, Dr. Adson would drill a hole in Paul's skull, implant a radioactive drip to attack the tumor and, fingers crossed, Paul would be okay. But she couldn't write it off that easily. It was Paul's skull. Paul was special.

She had violated a rule by going outside their own medical ring to contact Dr. Adson. If the organization's staff of doctors knew about Paul's brainquake, he'd be shot at once and so would she for not reporting it.

When she saw Dr. Adson on the cover of *Time* she had taken a chance and gone to him. She'd used a phony name. Tops in his field, she was sure the neurologist knew other doctors on his level that could help with her particular need.

And he did. He recommended several throat and ear specialists to examine her deaf-mute daughter. Dr. Adson had encouraged her to never give up hope that one day Samantha would speak and hear.

So she broke house rules. She told him about Paul, the taxi driver who ran errands for her when she was in the city, and who helped her take care of her daughter. Paul called his sickness a brainquake and that interested Dr. Adson, who scheduled an appointment. Any minute Paul would show up and tell her what Dr. Adson had said.

When she first learned of Paul's attacks, she panicked. What if he had one of his brainquakes while carrying a bag with millions of dollars? She should never have given him the job. But she had, for reasons both personal and professional. In some ways he was the perfect bagman. She hired only those existing at the far end of solitude; those with gaps between them and society. She patiently nursed those gaps with her bagmen. With Paul it was easy.

But with Paul, she also bent backwards.

The minute a bagman carried his bag into the battlefield he was vulnerable to pirates. She got used to writing off killed-in-action bagmen.

But if Paul were killed, she could never write him off. Not Paul. She had never promised his father, Barney the Bookie, that Paul would always be safe. But she had made that promise to herself because he was Barney's son.

Barney took bets from her when she was Rebecca Plummer, an 18-year-old hatcheck girl at Dinty's Chop House where the sporting and theatrical crowd dined. She studied turf sheets, placed $2 bets. When she owed him $10 he took her marker and that trust in her started their long relationship. When she increased bets and lost heavily, he still took her markers. And when he introduced her to the gentle-mannered Max Fillion—Max the Mouthpiece, lawyer for Pegasus Delivery—it changed her life.

The Boss owed Barney.

She would still be checking hats at Dinty's if not for him. He sold Max the idea of getting her a job at Pegasus. She knew little about Barney except that he and his wife refused to place their child in an institution. They taught the boy to read, write and talk a little. When Barney's wife died of cancer, their son was ten years old. Barney kept on teaching him. Raised him by himself. She loved Barney for it.

Barney, too, had inspired her to never give up hope that her daughter would hear and speak.

She remembered the first time Barney came to her about Paul. Every word of that moment was tattooed in her brain...

...She was lunching with her daughter at Dinty's Chop House, pointing out where she used to check hats and coats, when Barney walked up to their corner booth. He looked terrible. Pale. Sweating. And sick. She just couldn't tell him how awful he looked.

"This is my daughter, Samantha." The Boss' voice was low. "She's fifteen. Join us for lunch, Barney."

Slowly Barney sank into the chair, watching as the Boss explained to her daughter in sign language that this was a man who'd helped her, a special friend. She could see Barney was shaken. She had never told Barney she had a daughter, never mind that she was deaf and mute.

Barney kept staring at the blue-eyed, black-haired girl talking to her mother in sign language. Samantha was a dead ringer for the Boss. Both were beautiful. Samantha extended her hand. Still in shock, Barney shook it. Her hand was a feather, her skin satin.

"She said she's happy to meet the legendary Barney the Bookie."

Barney smiled at that, or tried to. It was a wan attempt. He was here for a reason. Desperation filled his face.

"I need help, Rebecca."

"How much, Barney?"-

"Not cash."

"What kind of help?"

"A job for my son."

"What kind of job?"

"Bagman."

The Boss looked in his eyes, which stared back, pleading. How did he know? When did he find out? From whom? What she bossed for the organization was a well-kept secret, even from men like Barney, who were in a corner of the business themselves. Only those involved in her operations knew. Unless Max had told him…? But Max never would. He was called "Mouthpiece," but what he knew best of all was how to keep his mouth shut.

And Pegasus was a legitimate cover. Barney could have asked for a job for his son in the truck pool, storage, transportation, business office, complaint department. All were legitimate. City, state, federally licensed. Taxes paid on the nose for some eighty years. No worker in the legit half knew what business was going on in the other half.

What Barney knew, that one word he had spoken, could cost him a bullet in the head. She looked away, down at her hands, at the Racing Form *beside her plate. Her silence meant she scratched Paul. She didn't want to see the look of failure in Barney's face.*

He said nothing. She kept looking at the Racing Form.

"Who do you like in the fifth?" She did a pretty good job keeping the tension out of her voice. Barney didn't answer. She steeled herself, glanced up at him. He was shaking like a malaria case, his voice was barely audible.

"Goldilocks," Barney said. "Kentucky winner."

"I like Lightning Bolt." She couldn't keep her voice steady. "Won the Swaps. What do you think, between them?"

His face looked dreadful. Looked dead. She knew there was no one else who would give a job to his son.

"I'm no Solomon, Rebecca. One horse or the other. You pick." Barney made a movement to leave.

She seized his hand. "Wait a minute, Barney. I want to place some bets. Samantha knows horses."

He watched her talk to Samantha, fingers sketching diagrams in the air. Samantha's hands didn't hesitate.

"Samantha's choice is Goldilocks, five hundred to win." The Boss waited.

Barney took out his pad with trembling hands, jotted down the bet. The Boss watched Samantha's fingers, which were still in motion .

"Three hundred on Big Red One to place," the Boss said.

Barney fumbled with his pencil. Paul would never get a job. Barney knew he shouldn't be here fucking around with goddam bets. He'd struck out with Rebecca. But he jotted down the bet.

Samantha's fingers continued their silent soliloquy.

"Two hundred on Tinikling to show." The Boss watched Barney jot it down and rise to his feet. Her heart froze. She read his face. She read Barney thinking that after he died, what would his son do on his own? She read in Barney's face his fear that the boy would become a bum, live on handouts, die a bum.

"What's your son's name?"

"Paul."

"Age?"

"Seventeen."

"Police record?"

"None."

"Vices?"

"None."

"Friends?"

"Loner."

"Girls?"

"None."

"Reflex?"

"Slow."

"Improving?"

"Yes."

"Face?"

"Cipher."

That night when she phoned Barney, his son said, in the rasp she would come to know like her own voice, that Barney wasn't booking bets anymore, and hung up. She paid for Barney's funeral in cash, leaving no name.

The sudden blast of the Colonel Bogey March and the blinking red light on her desk brought her back to work. A button stopped the music. She had chosen the tune because she liked it the minute she heard it in the movie *Bridge on the River Kwai*. Her Maltese, Knight, jumped on her cluttered desk. The bluish-gray fur of the cat matched the Boss' eyes. She called him Knight because the blue arrowheads pointing inward above his eyes looked like the cross of the Knights of Malta.

The Boss was 49, looked 35. The contours of her face were those of a young Garbo without a speck of makeup or any of the popular overhauling actresses or models were subject to. Tall, with high cheekbones and breasts modest but firm under a light blue blouse, she crossed her office shining like the star of a Paris collection. Legs perfect, slim. The kind that would give Paris couture a blood transfusion.

She reached the heavy walnut table against the bare wall, pushed a button under it. A wall panel slid open. The dumbwaiter ascended to a stop. She lifted the basket in it, glanced at the bag of phony bills stapled to the yellow card with the number 28 on it.

Under the table were many black and brown leather bags on the floor. One bag was sticking halfway out. Her dark blue shoe pushed it back and she carried the basket to her desk, dialed one of the many multicolored cordless phones.

"Ginko here, Boss."

"A phony ten grand came from 28."

"There's six drops it—"

"I know how many it has to go through. The fall guy is the one that sent it to me. You, Ginko."

"I got no machine, Boss!"

"You got one of the best forgers spotting for you, Ginko. When he struck out, you swung the bat. You've got twenty-four hours to come up with kosher bills. From your wallet."

She hung up, burned the bills three, four at a time in her large stone ashtray. It took a while. When she was done, she burned the yellow note. Then she opened the safe under her desk, took out a batch of clean bills, counted them, and substituted them in the stack.

Her black phone rang. A light on it blinked.

"Yes?"

"It's important, Rebecca. I'll be in your office in twenty minutes." Max hung up.

She froze. It was no coincidence. Max knew. And not about the phony bills, either. That wouldn't have made him come in person. It must be Paul. But how? How in the hell could he know? Could he have gotten to Dr. Adson somehow? If he knew, it meant Paul was already hit. Why phone her? To tell her to her face that he was an old friend but that she had to be hit, too?

Or to tell her to run, get lost, disappear?

No. Max wasn't that much of a friend. He had a wife and family to protect.

She phoned Dr. Adson, learned from his secretary that Paul never showed up. She hung up. Accident! He was in the hospital? Or killed in a car crash. He wasn't carrying a bag. She would be off the hook, in that case. A second later she hated herself. She was ashamed to feel safe if Paul was killed in an accident and didn't have a bag on him. If he had an accident, he was dead or unconscious in some hospital. He couldn't phone her if he was unconscious.

She dazedly counted the brown-paper-bound stacks of cash on her desk, made sure the total was $500,000, returned the basket to the dumbwaiter. Her trouble phone rang. She streaked to the red blinking light, grabbed the phone.

"Yes?"

"There's a *For Sale* sign on Zookie's window. Been there two days. Back door's boarded. Not a toy in the window."

"Hold on, Walter." She muted the red phone, dropped it on a pile of file folders on her desk, pushed papers aside, pushed Knight aside but the cat wouldn't move. She felt the bottle under the folders, lifted them. The red phone slipped, knocking over an empty perfume vial. She opened the small bottle, popped an aspirin, swallowed some water, picked up the red phone.

"Go on, Walter."

"Go on? I just told you."

"No toys in his window?"

"Nothing."

"Hold on, Walter." She put the red phone down, dialed the yellow.

"Apex Delivery."

"Jerry, did you get relay 412 this week?"

"Hold on, Boss."

She waited. She never figured Zookie had the guts to pull such a stupid thing. She picked up the empty perfume vial. On TV the replay was of Lieutenant Zara carrying a baby to an ambulance. How good the perfume smelled to Samantha when she was five years old. The Boss smiled, remembering how the child doused herself with it, emptying the vial.

"Zookie's Toy Shop?" Jerry said.

"Yes."

"Zookie said you knew about the 412 relay."

"*Zookie said?* Goddam it, Jerry, you know when a relay misses a schedule you're to phone me immediately."

She slammed the phone down, re-opened her desk safe, found a number in a little fat book, dialed it on the yellow phone.

"Hello?" A little girl's voice. Nervous.

"Is your daddy home?"

The Boss heard voices. An adult came to the phone, a woman.

"Zookie passed away three days ago." The woman's voice was shaky…even afraid.

The Boss hung up, dialed another number.

"Cornet Hardware."

"Danny," the Boss said, "take an extra drop in thirty minutes. Relay it 412. Thanks." She hung up, picked up the red phone, unmuted. "Walter. Cornet Hardware. Thirty minutes. Danny. Tall. Heavy. Fifty. Bald."

The Boss hung up. Goddam Zookie. Now she'd have to lean on his widow to get that fifty grand back. Thank God it wasn't a million or more. A yellow light blinked. On the alley monitor Farnsworth was waiting. She pushed a button. He went into the building. Why should she get angry at Zookie? People die. The widow, of course, would know nothing about the fifty grand. It would be a pity to lean on her. Or maybe the widow's taking a long shot. Maybe she's got it stashed and counting on nobody leaning on a widow who has a child.

The pink light blinked. On the monitor Farnsworth was waiting in a stone cell. She pushed the floor button. A steel door noiselessly slid open. Farnsworth entered her office carrying his brown bag, which he placed on her desk. The door slid shut. He opened the bag. The cat sniffed around it. The Boss placed stacks of cash in his bag, closed it.

"What wheels last week to the ballet school?"

"Taxi."

"Use your motorcycle." The Boss looked at her watch. "Olga will be in the cloakroom in twenty-five minutes. It's next to a big painting of Baryshnikov."

Farnsworth picked up his bag, crossed to the exit door on the opposite side of the office. The door slid open. He stepped into a small elevator. The door slid shut.

On her monitor, as always, she watched Farnsworth emerge from the elevator in the deserted, brightly illuminated basement and walk toward the camera so that she could see he was Farnsworth and no hijacker. The street monitor was in back of the building. She watched him pass the Pegasus motor pool. He crossed the street, passed motorcycle cops roaring into the motor pool of Police Headquarters, passed cops talking near one of the fleet of squad cars, passed several cops entering Headquarters, reached a small garage, its door opening by remote control. The monitor in the garage picked him up walking past his taxi, past a small van, placing his brown bag in a green wooden box strapped to his motorcycle luggage grill, donning goggles and helmet, riding out. On the street he disappeared in traffic. She watched if any vehicle pulled away from the curb to follow him. None did.

8

The Boss waited for Max.

She leaned back tensely in her big red swivel chair and stared at the door that he would be coming through to tell her face to face what he hadn't been able to tell her on the phone. The red leather chair was not an ordinary red. She had selected a particular orange-red—a color that fascinated her when she spotted it on the underside of the wings of a redwing thrush when she was going through a book of birds. The leather was dyed special to order, and it cost her barely anything because the shop selling the furniture was one of her drops.

Her eyes frozen on the door, her mind clogged with Paul's brainquake, she caught herself reliving her first meeting with Paul, three years after he began with the organization in a trainee job. She could plainly see the steel door sliding open...*and twenty-year-old Paul walked into her office...he glanced through her tenth-floor penthouse window at the skyscrapers towering over them.*

"Paul Page?"

"Where's the Boss?"

"I'm the Boss."

His cipher face showed no reaction to learning that the Boss was a woman. She invited him with a gesture to sit on the other orange-red leather chair by the side of her desk. She watched him almost shyly sink into it, deflating his lean body so as not to attract any attention. He clasped both kneecaps like a child and looked timid. Bagmen often did when they first reported to her.

But she knew that there was nothing timid about any of them, not the ones that made it to her office. Timid meant cowardly. A coward could never pass the three-year test he had passed.

There he sat. Barney's boy. Trained by nature to have that blank face he wore. Trained for three years by Hoppie to never exhibit stupid bravery, trained to use his head, trained it was healthier to out-drive, out-walk, out-smart a pirate and lose him, trained that the gun was the bagman's last resort.

Trained not to be a trigger-happy macho or trigger-happy cop or trigger-happy FBI man or trigger-happy CIA man.

She loathed the gun. It was manufactured to kill humans and animals. She had no control of the gun. Her bagmen loathed the gun. They were healthy in mind. That's what she and her bag-men really had in common. She was sure that Paul also loathed the gun—or Hoppie would have scratched him from the field.

She studied Paul's armor, the affect of the recluse, and tried to imagine his early withdrawal from life. She saw in him the seed of seclusion so many people dreamed of but couldn't attain because they weren't born sick in the head. Only twice had she put on a mentally retarded bagman. Three years of conditioning made them dependable robots in her kennel.

She observed his eyes staring at the exit door on the other side of the office.

"I have no secretary," she said. "That's the exit."

His face remained a cipher.

"What did Barney tell you about mailmen, Paul?"

At the mention of his father's name, his expression of nothing showed nothing.

"Did you pay the undertaker?" Paul said.

She detected the barest sound of scraping sandpaper when

he spoke. She figured that was the closest he would come to showing any kind of emotion.

"I owed Barney track losses."

He remained blank. No thanks. Nothing. And it didn't surprise her. She asked her question again:

"What did Barney tell you about mailmen?"

"They got pensions."

"Did he tell you they carry money in the bag?"

Paul shook his head.

"But you know."

Paul nodded.

"Did Hoppie ever tell you, over the past three years?"

Paul shook his head.

"You figured it out by yourself?"

Paul nodded.

"How?"

"The gun."

"You like the gun?"

He shook his head.

"You hate it?"

He nodded.

"Want a Vitamin C?"

He shook his head. She popped one in her mouth, drank water, and said, "At least I'll die happy."

She chuckled. No reaction from Paul.

She studied his blank face that was created for nobody to remember. Nice features, but impossible for any caricaturist to find a single quality to draw or emphasize. Eyes, nose, mouth, chin, contours normal like millions of people who have faces easily forgotten. Paul had not a single distinctive quality one could describe. He was twenty and looked like anyone. Nothing stood out.

Not too tall, not too short. T-shirt. Levis like millions of young men. Slim. Father virile, son a clump of clay. She was frustrated because parsing bagmen was like juggling smoke. To separate each part of what it took to make a bagman always baffled her. They all possessed the same psychological barrier of self-created isolation in the biggest crowd in the world.

What did it take to be the most trusted men in the most dangerous business in New York City? What gave them that incredible, dependable virtue of loyalty and trust? What made them so impervious to money? To all that cash they carried every day and every night?

Bank tellers steal. Bank directors embezzle. Cashiers steal. Bartenders steal. Politicians steal. Government officials embezzle. But when one of them was caught, he didn't face a bullet in the brain.

That bullet in the brain didn't keep a bagman honest.

Their honesty was something that she could never figure out, no matter how often she tried. A bagman made good money but never in the class of other jobs; never a fortune. Brokerage houses paid hundreds of millions of dollars in bonuses to their young executives before filing for bankruptcy. That was out-and-out stealing and many young men wanted to work in brokerage houses for that reason.

Bagmen carried hundreds of millions without opening the bag to borrow a few thousand. Rarely had a bagman that vanished with his bag got away with it. The ones that tried it were caught. Only when a pirate hijacked and killed a bagman was the bagman absolved. The pirate was eventually caught and killed. Whatever was left of the hijacked money was returned to her.

Looking at Paul she finally suspected how Barney had learned about the job, and about the qualifications for it. Some retired bagman who played the horses, placed bets with Barney, must've got drunk, run off at the mouth, told Barney that she was the Boss of all the bagmen in Manhattan. That son of yours, he must have said. What a bagman that boy would make.

She watched Paul's eyes gliding past the things on her desk, past the monitors, past the battery of multicolored phones, past her Maltese cat rubbing its nose against the big glass bowl illuminating goldfish in a desert landscape, and then his eyes stopped and remained rooted on the black and brown leather bags that were under the table against the wall.

"There are rules, Paul. Break one, you're dead."

His eyes glided back to hers.

"No girls. No wife. Not now, not ever. No friends. No ambition. No hobbies. No alcohol. No dope. No gambling. No debts. No talk when delivering the mail. No borrowing from the bag. No quitting. No selling your experiences after you retire. Never tell anyone you're a bagman."

He remained silent.

"You understand the rules?"

Paul nodded.

"You want to carry the bag?"

Paul nodded.

"Five hundred a week as a starter. Raises every six months. Bonuses. Sick benefits. Medical care. Hospital expenses. You'll have a small van, taxi and motorcycle. The taxi'll be your work umbrella. You'll open a savings account near where you live and deposit the average weekly take of a New York City taxi driver. Your home in the Battery is fine. That will be your only address. Our accountant will file your tax returns. You will never meet him. In another bank at the other end of the city you will open a safe deposit box under the name of Patrick McManus. In that box you will keep all the excess cash you earn as a bagman.

You'll inherit route 116 from a mailman who just retired. Hoppie will introduce you to the drops on route 116. Pick out a bag over there."

Paul picked an old black leather one. No combination. Cracks. The bag was as faceless as Paul.

9

Blinking crimson reflected on the Boss' face. The ringing of trouble snapped her back to the present. She seized the red phone. As she picked it up, the blinking stopped and she heard:

"Farnsworth! Hijacked!"

"Are you hurt?"

His motorcycle was twisted around a busted hydrant. Empty green wooden box drenched by geysers of water attacking window of public phone booth. Nowhere in sight was Farnsworth's bag. Blood covered, phone pressed to his mouth, barely breathing.

Spitting blood, he said, "He got the bag! I'm dead." And he was, dropping the phone a second after he spoke his final word.

The Boss controlled the panic exploding inside her like a grenade. She had to think calmly, act calmly, speak calmly as she glanced at Mr. Yoshimura and his crew on the monitor, dialed, watched him pick up the phone on the desk. He was in a very good mood.

"Yes, Boss?" was his cheerful greeting.

"There's a mole in Receiving."

His crew could not hear her voice. But Mr. Yoshimura heard it like the blast of an A-bomb. Having been reared by proud parents in Tokyo, he controlled his voice, but although sounding reserved, panic sneaked in with every word.

"Not in my department, Boss."

"A mailman's dead, a half-million gone!"

Mr. Yoshimura lost control. His voice shook with anger.

"*I vouch for every man here!*"

His men stopped working, glanced at each other.

"Who vouches for *you*, Mr. Yoshimura?"

"*You*, Boss! *You* hired me!"

"Tonight every man gets another lie-detector test. *I'll* ask the questions. You'll be the first one in the line!"

She hung up, turned to the Laundry monitor. With growing rage she dialed once. Mr. Grigor left the table and hurried to his desk, picking up the phone.

"Yes, Boss?"

"A pirate just got one of our men, Mr. Grigor. And he wasn't followed from the building."

"*There's no mole in my crew, Boss!*"

His men held their breath. Young Moe's hands froze on a stack of bills. Mr. Hendrix winced.

"We lost a bagman and a half-million!" said the Boss. "Tonight every man gets another lie-detector test."

"I run the cleanest laundry in Manhattan!"

"That's where you'll find dirt!"

On the TV replay, people were going wild running after the ambulance. The trouble phone rang again. Christ! Another hijack? She swept up the red phone at the speed of light.

"This is Zookie," a voice said, faster than the speed of light. "I told my wife to say I'm dead, I didn't relay the last drop. I spent the fifty grand on my kid. She's got cancer!"

"You think I'll buy it because your kid got cancer?"

"I'll work it out!"

"How?"

"I gotta stay alive."

"Why?"

"I gotta break my ass for a miracle to save my kid."

The alley door blinked. On the monitor Williams was waiting with his bag. She pushed the button. He entered the building.

"Got a receipt for that fifty grand, Zookie?"

"In my hand, Boss. I owed for a year. The doc said no full payment, no more treatments."

"Send it to me."

"Right away, Boss. Am I chopped?"

"Next twenty months you get zero from me—nothing. I don't care how you eat, don't care how you live. You pay the rest the day the twenty months are up, or you're not only chopped, you're dead."

"God bless—"

She hung up on him and furiously crossed to the dumb-waiter to shut off the chimes. Jesus Christ! Her whole life was one big boomerang. She took on Barney's son. Now it was Zookie's kid. She pushed the button. The panel opened. The dumbwaiter ascended to a stop. She didn't want to think what Zookie was going through. She picked up the basket and brought it to her desk, took out the stacks of cash. She normally paid him $2,000 a month for his toy-shop drop. Twenty months, that would be forty thousand. He'd have to raise the last ten on his own. He could do it. She'd cover it in the meantime. Nobody would lose.

Except his kid. Jesus Christ! What a boomerang for that bastard. His kid may leave the world before he made his last payment.

She watched Williams enter and put his bag on her desk and open it. Paul's age. Between them they had said about fifty words to her in the last ten years. She saw her fingers trembling as she picked up stacks and placed them on the desk. Forced herself to calm down.

"Still get your headaches, Williams?"

He nodded.

"Ever hear a flute?"

He shook his head.

"See any crazy colors?"

He shook his head. When she finished emptying the basket, she closed the bag. He put a slip of paper on the desk. She saw an address and phone number on it.

"My new address," Williams said.

"Trouble?"

Williams nodded.

"A sniffer?"

Williams nodded. "Black. Nosy."

"Same apartment building?"

Williams nodded.

"What wheels last week to the art gallery?"

"Taxi."

"Use the van. A pirate scored. Mailman dead."

Williams showed no reaction as he left. On monitors she watched him walk into a different small garage near Police HQ and she waited until he drove the van out of the garage and down the street and no vehicle followed the van. Though if there was a mole, what did it matter that no one followed? Looking at the name and address on the slip of paper, she made a phone call and ordered a check on the sniffer.

"I gotta break my ass for a miracle to save my kid," Zookie had said.

So did the Boss.

Her mother was born a deaf-mute. Her father was a numbers runner. She grew up using sign language to communicate with her mother. She learned that her father worked for a syndicate that employed hundreds of runners, men who picked up small bets from shop owners, clerks, taxi drivers, tobacco stores, cops, pimps, whores, firemen, and truckers—all gambling $2 and up on picking the last three figures of the day's trading at the Stock Exchange. The figures were published every day in the last edition of the newspapers.

She shared a small apartment in Washington Heights with her mother and father. Specialists were too expensive, demanding money in advance to treat her mother, to try to get her to hear or speak.

And you could live without hearing, without speaking. Cancer... She knew the hell Zookie was living in.

She was a hatcheck girl when her father keeled over from a heart attack. The next day her mother died from the shock. A week later the double funeral, paid by Barney, who drove her to the cemetery. Max the Mouthpiece got her the job with the legitimate half of Pegasus in the Dispatch Department for $300 a week.

What her mother could never do because of lack of money, the Boss was determined to do for the deaf-mute baby she adopted at the orphanage. She'd named the baby Samantha, after her mother. The three hundred dollars weekly went to a nurse who knew sign language, to rent and to food. Several promotions followed. The raises went to specialists. No matter how many times she was told Samantha would never hear or speak, Rebecca kept paying, kept insisting they keep trying. Upped to Assistant Dispatch Chief. Truckers who hauled pianos and furniture soon dropped their resentment toward the female over them. When she was put in charge of Dispatch, the truckers threw her a party. Word flew through the legitimate half of Pegasus that Rebecca knew how to treat her people. They felt at home with her. They trusted her.

Word of this trust reached Max who offered her a thousand a

week as assistant to the boss of bagmen in Manhattan. Max trusted her. If she turned it down the conversation had never taken place. Bagmen? The only conscience she had was her daughter's health. Rebecca accepted the job, spent every penny on new specialists. When her superior retired, Rebecca Plummer became boss of bagmen at $3,000 per week with a fat bonus every six months. She kept spending all her money on Samantha.

In a medical journal she read about Bill Wilson, a deaf-mute who partially licked it and was willing to help others. Bill was 26. He worked closely with Samantha, using his experience to help her. When Samantha was 23, she married Bill.

The Boss picked a bigger apartment that they all lived in. She knew that Samantha was in good hands. But she kept bringing in doctors. All her bonuses went right to the most expensive specialists. She bankrolled Bill and Samantha to Europe to contact specialists there and hunt for a miracle no matter how much it cost. The news was always bad but the Boss never gave up.

She never would.

The light blinked. On the monitor Max was waiting. She pushed the floor button. The door slid open. Max came in. He was pinching the bridge of his nose. He looked pained.

The Boss knew it was about Paul.

"I need an aspirin," Max said. "Bad headache all day."

She gave him a pill from her bottle. He swallowed it dry.

"I could've told you on the phone, Rebecca, but this news...I wanted to tell you to your face." He put a hand on her shoulder. "The throne okayed you handling all five boroughs. You'll of course keep Manhattan as your main office, but they'll all report to you. Triple salary. Double bonus every six months." The proud smile on his face turned to a grimace, like he was tasting something sour. "What the hell did you give me, Rebecca?"

She couldn't contain her relief. She hugged him.

"Vitamin C, Max!"

"Goddam it, Rebecca, you trying to poison me? All I asked for was a goddam aspirin."

10

It was dark when Paul was discharged from the emergency room. He flagged a taxi, was driven back to Central Park. His taxi was still there. He climbed behind the wheel, his head still whirling, bandaged face aching, bruised eye smarting. Paul drove slowly through the streets. No bones were broken. He was trying to fit the pieces together. He'd had an attack when the man was shot. Why didn't he have one when the bomb went off? When the people rioted?

Had it all even really happened? Was it all in his head? A mirage…

…*they were sitting in faded blue canvas folding chairs…he and his mother…outside the shack…and the sky was muddy… she was reading* Robinson Crusoe *aloud…word by word and spelling the words…and she saw him pointing at the sky…*

"Ship." *He forced the word out. He was seven. He had learned some words.*

His mother looked up at the skyscrapers.

"There's no ship. It's a mirage, Paul. Mirage. Say mirage."

"Mirage."

"M-i-r-a-g-e. M-i-r-a-g-e." *She printed it out on the pad.* "M-i-r-a-g-e. Spell it out with me, Paul." *He did again and again and kept repeating the word.*

She hugged him.

"Good. Write it, Paul."

He printed it slowly.

"Good, Paul. Mirage is something you see that is not really there. Do you understand?"

His face was blank.

"The ship in the sky is not real, Paul. On the water people see an island that is not there and they see ships that are not there and in the desert they see trees that are not there…they are not real. This book is real. I am real. Our home is real. The ship in the sky is not real. It is called a mirage, what you saw, not a ship, but a mirage. Now you tell me, Paul, what is a mirage?"

"Not real."

Ivory Face was real. What happened this morning was real. His bruises were real. The aching was real.

Why hadn't he spoken to Ivory Face before? Why did he lack the courage? His father once told him that he had courage. Paul remembered very clearly. It was after he put the pillow on his mother's face. *He didn't know that his father had been watching him. He didn't understand why his father didn't speak to him for weeks after that. And one day Barney asked him, "Did Ma ask you to cover her face with the pillow?" And Paul had nodded. "Why did she ask you, Paul?" said Barney. "To stop her pain, Pa." His father hugged him and cried and said Paul had more courage than anybody in the world.*

Where was that courage? What happened to it? Once, Barney had told him he had the wisdom of Solomon and the strength of Samson. He didn't know who they were, but it all had something to do with courage.

All he had to do was to say, "Hello, I am Paul. I would like to talk to you." That was all.

He had meant to ask his father many times what kind of courage he meant. The day he was picking up bets for him and told him he wanted to be a poet…that was the day he should have asked him, but that night his father died in his arms and the phone kept ringing and a woman asked for Barney and things happened so fast. The man who took care of the funeral told him it was all paid for. And Paul alone at the cemetery.

Soaked. The grave was covered with canvas to keep the rain out and a voice said, "Your father fixed a spot for you to be a mailman." It was Hoppie. He offered Paul $50 a week to learn how to be a mailman and Paul nodded.

His taxi was halfway to Pegasus. What was he going to tell the Boss about not keeping the appointment with Dr. Adson? The appointment was for him, not the Boss. He never lied to her. But now… He would tell her he was in the park because he liked the park.

There was no need to mention Ivory Face. Why should he? He didn't know her. He had never spoken to her. As he piloted his taxi through the streets he knew so well, he remembered Hoppie teaching him. For a whole year, every day, while he was getting $50 a week and living alone in the Battery shack, Hoppie drove him through every street and alley in New York City that Paul had to know if he got the job of mailman.

He should be with Ivory Face right now. He knew that she was lonely, had followed her a few times, saw where she worked, never saw her with anybody until that stranger, and now even he was gone…

In the first year under Hoppie's tutelage Paul learned landmarks he could spot blocks away, even at night.

Nights when he wasn't working, he tried to write poems, read books his mother had given him, studied words in the dictionary.

Hoppie taught him how to back up fast without lights in a dark alley, how to avoid blind dead ends, how to escape from a pirate by driving behind 24-sheet billboards on empty lots through camouflaged rubble.

Paul learned how to lose a pirate on wheels in the snow, the rain, on the waterfront, on roofs, in the subway, in elevators, markets, theatres, bus depots, train stations, airports, in churches, in a crowd, a rally, at ballgames and how to use streets under construction.

He learned how to use a gun to protect the mail the way the FBI used guns to protect the United States.

In the third year of training he learned how to carry the bag. Not too fast. Not too slow. How to use store window reflections to spot a pirate following him. He had to carry the bag the way Hoppie did. Like a businessman carrying a briefcase. He had to learn what to do if, making a delivery, he came across an accident near the drop.

It was forbidden to go to the same barber twice, shop at the same market, eat at the same place, buy his clothes at the same store.

He learned how to drive a hyped-up taxi, a small van, a motorcycle.

He learned to avoid traffic jams by taking shortcuts. He learned he must never drive fast unless fleeing from a pirate. He was taught how to use a Polaroid. Off work, he knew that he was under surveillance by Hoppie.

For three years, he had periodic brainquakes. They didn't show in his cipher face. Hoppie was unaware of the attacks. He had annual physical checkups by a company doctor, always passed, lucky he never had a brainquake in the doctor's office.

Hoppie did all the talking. That suited Paul. The final day at the end of the third year, Hoppie took him to meet the Boss for the first time. On the way, Hoppie braked.

"Goddam it, Paul, I forgot!"

Hoppie U-turned, almost sideswiping a passing truck.

"Jesus Christ, Paul, I'd've had my ass reamed if I didn't take you to Yonkers first. There's a place you got to see before you start carrying the bag."

"What place?"

"Your future, goddam it," laughed Hoppie, "is in Yonkers."

In the suburb of New York, they pulled up to a big isolated house. It was surrounded by trees. It was kept very clean. He knew what the word future meant. His father had explained it very clearly. He couldn't understand why this big house was his future.

Inside, Hoppie took him on a tour. Paul saw old men playing cards, chess, checkers, staring out windows. Many had canes to help them walk.

"For retired bagmen," Hoppie said. "When you're pensioned off, you can live here for nothing or you can live alone. Most bagmen, the older they get, the more they're hungry for a little company. Most of 'em here are over the hill with no memories. Those attendants there in white shirts are also retired bagmen who like helping the older ones."

Hoppie took him to the cemetery behind the house.

"Only for bagmen. Few guys in any goddam other business get this kind of security when they're old."

After Paul had had a good look, Hoppie led him back to the car.

At a fast clip, Hoppie drove Paul to the Pegasus Building. On the way, he asked Paul if he was scared to meet the Boss. Paul didn't understand what he meant. Why would he be scared?

"How about the job? You scared of pirates, of guys coming after you with goddam machine guns?"

Paul shook his head.

"Good," Hoppie said. "Good boy. Only one thing you should be scared of, and that's the people you work for."

"Why?"

Hoppie drove a while, silent at the wheel, then looked over at Paul beside him. "You treat them well, they treat you well. Better than well. Like you just seen. But that's a two-way street.

You treat them bad, you break the faith or do something you shouldn't've, you steal or rat or if you ever, ever talk to the fucking cops…there's no mercy. You need to understand that. No mercy."

Hoppie waited for Paul to nod, to say or do something to show the words were penetrating that thick skull of his, but he just watched, blank. "I keep my nose clean, Paul, so I got nothing to be scared of. But that don't mean I never been scared. Because I seen what they done to other guys. This one time…" He shivered, and the car swerved slightly as it ran through him. "This poor stoolie bastard. They put a hit out on him. The hitter caught up with him outside his home, busted the bastard's spine. Then he slammed him up against the wall and drove spikes through his hands and feet. Into the wall. Left him hanging there for his family to find. Fucking crucified him. Goddam poor stoolie."

Paul said nothing. But the image stayed with him.

For four years Paul carried the bag without incident, until one morning at eleven o'clock. His small cream-colored van was rolling at 35 mph. Traffic was normal.

He was 24 years old. Making a delivery to a man waiting for him in the toilet on the second floor of the Criminal Courts Building. The man was a judge who had a private can in his chambers on the third floor, but Paul didn't know this. He just knew where to go when. The judge had seen Paul every month for four years for the few seconds it took Paul to transfer an envelope containing $200,000 from his bag to the judge's briefcase. The judge never remembered Paul's face.

The delivery, one of the easiest on Paul's route, turned shaky when a pirate's blue sedan appeared on Paul's left. The pirate waved his gun for Paul to pull up at the curb. Paul gunned the hyped-up engine, leaving the pirate far behind. Paul knew the exact escape route and took it. It would take as little as 28 seconds to lose the blue car, as much as a full minute. It depended on how fast Paul zigzagged through the tied-up traffic in front of the Criminal Courts Building. He heard gunshots. Women were screaming. He braked hard into the stalled car in front of him. He could see the blue sedan in the rear-view mirror coming fast.

Paul seized his gun, heard the flute drowning out more gunshots and men yelling. The brainquake hit. It lasted in pink for seven seconds. Paul saw a crazy man firing into a crowd of people and then the man was shot dead by a cop. In his rear-view mirror Paul saw two cops lifting the dead pirate out of the blue sedan. Paul waited twenty minutes for the traffic to start again, parked his van in the regular spot, made the delivery to the judge in the men's room. From a corridor phone booth in the building, Paul phoned the Boss and reported what happened.

"Did you get a photo of the dead pirate?"

"He had no face, Boss."

He gave her the license number of the blue sedan instead.

In his sixth year as a bagman he discovered a new emotion.

He was headed to a night drop only a short walk from his shack. Fireworks were exploding in the sky. Battery Park was jammed. People were celebrating the hundredth birthday of the Statue of Liberty. Paul used an alley packed with cars, headed toward his drop's building. A big dog appeared, trotted beside him sniffing his bag.

There was a gunshot as people cheered the American flag bursting in red, white and blue lights. The dog yelped. Fell. Paul ducked behind the dead dog. Paul's eyes were glued on the darkness, watching for the second burst. It came. Paul fired three times.

Paul ran toward the pirate in the darkness, lit sporadically by flares exploding in the sky. He frisked the body for ID, found none, took his camera from his pocket and grabbed a shot of the young dead face.

Then Paul went on toward the building. He dreaded to go in—to go up. He feared heights. Always did on this drop. He went in, pushed the button. The silent ascent of the elevator sucked the wind out of him.

He got off at the fortieth floor, wondering when the pirate had spotted him around Battery Park. Had he been waiting for Paul? How did he know this shortcut?

The elevator opened and he went down the long corridor to the back door of the drop, where a man in a tuxedo was waiting for him.

The man led Paul into a huge penthouse and up a flight of stairs to an office that had no lights on inside. Through a big window Paul saw that a party was on, on the building's roof. The sky burst with more colors. He saw the illuminated Statue of Liberty and hundreds of boats. Waiters carried trays of champagne glasses. There were other men in tuxedos. Women in evening dresses. A hired band on the roof played the national anthem.

The guests were from different countries, many dressed in their national garb. White. Black. Oriental. Paul had no idea, then, that they were representatives of the international cartels of dope trafficking and money laundering.

Laser beams on the Statue of Liberty were blinding as the guests sang along with the *Star-Spangled Banner* while Paul transferred $15 million in cash from his bag into the open fat briefcase held by the drop on the desk.

The next morning the Boss was staring at the photo Paul had taken, and Paul was sick.

He had killed a boy. The new emotion made him queasy. He felt guilt for the first time in his life.

The Boss saw that emotion, not in his face but in the way he shook. She gave him a drink of water that he gulped down. It didn't help.

"You shouldn't feel bad about it, Paul. That thirteen-year-old bastard was an addict with a record. Two years ago he bashed his mother, busted her skull for a few bucks in her purse. They put him in a reformatory, but he broke out, and on the way out smashed in the head of a cop in a squad car with a brick. The gun he shot at you with? Was the cop's gun. Only reason he missed hitting you was probably because he needed a fix, his hands were shaking so he hit the dog instead. The little bastard didn't know what you were carrying, he was just looking for anyone he could get a few bucks off, and he would gladly have killed you for those few bucks. You're guilty of nothing, Paul. You killed an animal, in self-defense."

It took Paul years to overcome that guilt.

In ten years Paul had become a seasoned bagman. Sometimes the Boss would briefly invade his cocoon with talk. It was okay. He liked her. She was warm. She never tampered with his cocoon after working hours. They never talked about Barney.

For ten years Paul had read a book every four days, and he kept writing poems. For ten years he stood above the fray of the business that paid him. He was not a player. He was just a mailman. He never cared where the money came from or to whom he delivered it or if he carried five thousand or five million or fifty million in cash.

He'd never again felt guilt about the job.

U.S. mailmen carried dirty money and they slept well. Workers in munitions plants made war money and they slept well. Politicians, bankers, and businessmen made dirty money and they slept well. Judges, lawyers, cops, doctors, dentists made dirty money and they slept well.

Paul slept well every night in his Battery shack, despite the noise of rutting cats whining for relief in the decayed graveyard behind the shack.

But for the last two months Paul hadn't been able to sleep because of Ivory Face.

11

The Boss was placing stacks in his bag. "I know what happened, Paul. You thought he'd open your brain with a buzz saw so you sat down in Central Park to work up your courage and got caught in that riot." She glanced up at his bandaged bruises and torn clothes. "You're very lucky. Thirty people were seriously injured, they're not out of the hospital yet. You're tougher than they are." She put a gentle hand on his arm. "I alerted Johnson you'll be late. Still feel you can make the drop?"

Paul nodded.

"I phoned Dr. Adson when you didn't show up, made an appointment same time tomorrow."

Paul nodded. She closed the bag. Paul picked it up.

"What did you drive to Johnson last week?"

"Motorcycle."

"Use your taxi." The Boss waited a moment. "Did you get a whiff of poppy in his darkroom last week?"

Paul shook his head.

"A pirate's loose, Paul. A bagman's dead."

Paul left.

The moon was over Manhattan. Paul drove slowly, hoping that Ivory Face wouldn't move to another place. He'd have trouble finding her. He didn't think she'd go pushing the carriage in the park again for a long time—if ever.

He glanced at the gun on his seat. Then at the rear-view mirror. He turned on the radio, got the news.

"*...spokesperson reports the police are investigating partial fingerprints found on the baby carriage and the concealed gun...*"

Headlights were tailing him, keeping the same distance. Paul maintained the same speed, turned the next corner.

Paul saw the headlights behind him turning the corner, maintaining the same distance.

"...*In a statement, Lieutenant Zara indicated that Michelle Troy was being offered police protection....*"

Paul increased his speed. So did the car, maintaining the same distance.

Michelle Troy.

So Ivory Face now had a name.

Paul's taxi whipped into a familiar alley barricaded with wooden sawhorses topped with red reflectors. He smashed through them. Didn't bother weaving to avoid a bullet—Paul knew the pirate wouldn't chance hitting the gas tank and losing the bag in flames. The pirate's car kept the same distance.

"...*Dr. Todd McCarthy of the Medical Examiner's Office said the baby suffered no internal injuries...*"

The taxi jackhammered over exposed sewer pipes. Paul battled to keep control. The pirate car stayed on him, closing the distance between them. The taxi erupted from the alley and almost crashed into the water truck moving slowly up the street. The pavement was wet. The taxi slid sideways, brushing gas pumps at a corner gas station.

Paul saw the pirate car skid into a pump.

The taxi shook as the explosion spewed shards of glass. Paul pulled into a side street, stopped as he heard the flute playing. The last of the newsman's words were drowned out by the brainquake.

When the second pump exploded it was in pink. Paul saw Ivory Face running toward him, naked, and throwing the crying baby into his headlights.

His head resting on the steering wheel. Smoke drifted past

Paul. The smoke was no longer pink. Through the pain in his head he heard sirens. Real sirens. Not a mirage.

It took Paul ten minutes to get to the drop, bypassing streets police and fire trucks were using. Paul finally approached Johnson's shop. The window was dark except for a buzzing neon sign selling PASSPORT PHOTOS and two little spotlights aimed at a blowup of a baby and one of a wedding couple.

Parking in the alley behind the aging gray pickup that bore the words JOHNSON'S PHOTO STUDIO, Paul got out with his bag, glanced down the long, deserted area. Sirens still blaring, but in the distance. A cat sniffing trash cans behind the butcher shop next door to Johnson's.

Through the barred back-door window, in a thin streak of light coming from the open door of the backroom's small fridge, he saw Johnson sprawled on the floor. One hand was still in the fridge. His arm kept the door from closing.

Removing a loose brick from the wall, Paul took out the key, unlocked the door, went in, closed the door, pulled the blind down, checked the body. Johnson was still alive. Paul swiftly pulled out the tray of ice cubes, pulled down Johnson's trousers and shorts, packed ice cubes on Johnson's balls, pulled out a bottle of milk, poured it down Johnson's throat. Johnson coughed, gagged.

Paul spotted the pipe on the floor, smashed it with his foot, flushed the ball of gummy opium down the toilet. Johnson opened his bleary eyes, watched Paul transfer the bundles of cash into a big cardboard box labeled PHOTOGRAPHIC PAPER. Paul put the cover back on the box, phoned the Boss.

"Mail delivered. Pirate, but he crashed."

"You okay?"

"Yes."

"Pirate dead?"

"Yes.

"Get a photo of him?"

"Cremated."

"His wheels, too?"

"Yes."

"Is Johnson back on opium?"

"Drinking milk."

"Don't forget Dr. Adson in the morning. Get some sleep. Good night, Paul."

Paul put the phone down, closed his bag.

"I owe you again, Paul," Johnson mumbled.

Paul left. Johnson packed more ice cubes on his balls.

12

Paul's headlights swept past a big cat caterwauling in the grave-yard. His beams flooded the clapboard shed as he drove in, switched off the motor. He sat and thought about his attack.

His father's dying words, "Red explosion," came back to him, and an icicle slowly ran through him. In this last brainquake, the pink smoke did look a little red.

Paul never had the chance to ask his father how red that explosion was. It could've been light red or blood red.

"The race was fixed against us, Paul," Barney once said when he learned of Paul's pink brainquakes. "Nobody can climb into our brain and repair the damage."

The caterwauling got louder. It hurt inside his head, but he knew it wasn't the noise. It was that red in pink, screaming that his sickness was getting worse. He climbed out of the taxi with his empty bag and loaded gun and slowly headed toward the shack.

Paul walked past the four sentries that guarded the shack, remembered the way Barney had told him about them when he was small...

A pile of shattered stone. *"Meet Backfire, Paul. One of the guards. That rubble was under cannons that blew up their own gun crews in the American Revolution."*

A pile of rotted beams over a deep pit.

"Rathole is the second guard, Paul. In that pit the first gangs of New York used to hide."

Paul turned toward the half-collapsed warehouse beside the shack.

"*Hijack is the third guard, Paul. Your grandfather used to stock his hijacked bootlegged whiskey in that warehouse.*"

Paul's eyes shifted to the remains of the graveyard.

"*Skullyard is the fourth guard, Paul. Used to be a very popular cemetery only people with dough could afford. It died when Thomas Jefferson got to be President.*"

Paul had learned to find his way home by those guards. He felt safe surrounded by them.

Safe from the thousands of window lights of skyscrapers where night workers were cleaning up thousands of offices and vacuuming thousands of carpets and waxing thousands of corridors in the tallest giants in the world. They weren't tall enough to stop the moonlight from hitting the lawn chair on the little square of dirt behind the shack. He sat down by the small table. On it, a half-filled bottle of orange soda was attacked by flies and mosquitoes. Next to the bottle was Paul's pad and pencil.

He remembered one day when he was nine his father sitting him down in the chair and telling him that although they owned the lot and shack, inherited from his grandpa, now some people were talking about buying it to put up another one of those giant buildings. His father knew nobody in City Hall to stop them from forcing him to sell. Their shack stood in the way of big business' progress.

Paul remembered the sickness that filled him. His father knew the shack was Paul's castaway hut, the lot his island, the weeds his trees, the skyscrapers his clouds. His mother was already sick by then. Where would they move?

In the end, the builders didn't build. The seventies came, and the city's brush with bankruptcy, and his mother died, and then his father, and here he was. Nobody had ever come to bother them again about buying the lot.

Paul carried his bag and gun into the shack, placed them on

the table in the small living room, went into the bathroom, turned on the light. In the mirror, he stared at his bandaged face, his torn clothes, and wondered if he'd ever see Michelle Troy again. His fingers fumbled as he undressed. Exhausted, he was asleep in a minute.

13

"So you drive a cab, Paul? Jesus." Dr. Adson held his cigar above the X-ray of a brain on his desk. "If I pushed a hack, I'd blow my stack in a week."

Paul was waiting for the long ash to drop on the X-ray.

"You picked a good word for your sickness," Dr. Adson went on. "Brainquake's a pretty fair description for your attacks. Like an earthquake, only in there." He tapped his own skull.

The ash dropped on the X-ray. Dr. Adson blew the ash away, shook the X-ray. "I'll study this, probably need to take some more. How old are you?"

"Thirty."

"How long've you been driving a taxi?"

"Ten years."

"When did you have your first attack?"

"I was fourteen."

"Heard a flute, you say, saw everything in pink?"

Paul shook his head. "Not yet. Just headaches."

"Then over the years you heard the sound of the flute and began seeing things in pink?"

Paul nodded.

"Were you born a mute?"

Paul nodded.

"Ever institutionalized?"

"No."

"Who taught you to talk?"

"My parents."

"They deserve the Nobel Prize. Most parents drop kids in

institutions. Out of shame, or they just don't have the energy to deal with it. Are your parents alive?"

"No."

"Did you mother have a brain disease?"

"No."

"What did she die of?"

"Cancer."

"How old were you?"

"Ten."

Something in his voice. Dr. Adson said,

"Did you see her die?"

"Yes."

He jotted a note.

"What did your father die of?"

"Brainquake."

"I want to see his X-rays."

"He didn't trust doctors."

"Terrific." Dr. Adson shook his head. "Could've done you a favor if he had. Though who knows, plenty that goes on in there you can't see on an X-ray. The brain's a tricky rascal. Nerve cells and fibers that are a feast for jackals. That's what I call the little bastards an X-ray won't catch."

He slid the X-ray and his notes into a manila folder.

"It'll take weeks of treatment, more X-rays, more questions before I make up my mind about surgery. And if I do go into your brain, that's no guarantee I'll find that jackal. You understand?"

Paul nodded.

"Did your father see his brain split open like a quake hit it?"

Paul nodded.

"And did he hear the flute playing before the quake hit?"

"No."

"What did he hear?"

"Galloping."

"What kind of galloping?"

"Horses."

"What did he do for a living?"

"Bookie."

"How old was he when he died?"

"Forty-nine."

"How do you know he died of a brainquake?"

"He died in my arms."

"How old were you?"

"Seventeen."

"Did he say anything before he died?"

"Red explosion."

14

The noon sky was being darkened by thunderclouds. In her small walkup, Michelle changed the water and carefully placed six long-stemmed red roses in the vase by the window. The nightmare still clung to her. *If she hadn't fainted when Frankie was shot dead…if she had picked up her baby from the carriage…*

Thunder brought rain. She glanced at her baby sleeping in the crib, sucking tenderly on some tiny toy, then from the fourth-floor window looked down at moving umbrellas hammered by rain and, thank God, saw no police cars waiting in the street. They'd offered; she'd declined. She had convinced Lieutenant Zara that cops hanging around the street to protect her would draw voyeurs and alert the press, make her life a circus and leave her less safe, not more. Lieutenant Zara had accepted her reason for not wanting protection, though she warned her not to let her guard down. If this Black Psycho was still out for money or for blood…

A taxi stopped in front of the building, and she tensed, one hand clenching around the cord of her Venetian blinds. But a moment later, the driver stepped out with a familiar package in hand: a long-stemmed, cellophane-wrapped rose. She smiled as he climbed the short set of steps to her building.

The delivery came as a relief, a small sign that maybe the last twenty-four hours hadn't changed everything. Every day, for how long now? A new rose. A new blue envelope, too, with a new poem in it—but no name, nothing to identify the sender. This was the first time she'd actually caught sight of the person leaving them. She plucked a dollar from her purse, went to the door, and listened to the footsteps of the taxi driver clapping up to the second floor, then the third.

When she heard the driver's footsteps reach her floor and then stop, she pulled the door open, catching Paul bending down to carefully place the rose on the floor. Paul showed no surprise at being caught. He showed no emotion at all, just straightened up with the rose in hand. She looked at his cipher face and wondered who'd sent him, day after day, with the anonymous gift.

Paul couldn't believe that she was within touching distance, smiling at him. Under his blank exterior, his heart was suddenly racing.

She noticed his bruised face as he held out the rose. She took it, saw the blue envelope under the cellophane.

"Thank you." Her gentle voice matched her face. Her eyes matched her blue robe. "Are you the one who's been leaving these every morning?"

Paul nodded. Inside he was ashamed of himself. This was his chance to talk to her. He was a coward no matter what his father had said. He saw her hold out the dollar but didn't take it.

"Oh," Michelle said, pulling back the hand with the money in it, "I'm sorry. He took care of tips, too?"

Paul managed a short nod.

She was more curious than ever. "Who is he?"

Paul was bursting to tell her, but shook his head instead.

For weeks Michelle had suspected someone in the building, either a nut or some guy on the make. But paying a taxi driver every morning to deliver a rose—that ruled out a neighbor, and besides, it was a lot of trouble to go to. And expense. Who would do it? She'd never found any card with the florist's name. The poems were always handwritten on plain blue cards.

"Can't you tell me anything? What does he look like?"

Before he could answer, a sound behind her made her

whirl—the sound of her baby gasping. Through the bars of the crib, she could see his tiny face turning blue. The toy he'd been sucking on was gone. "Oh my god!"

She ran to the crib, leaving the front door open. Didn't even hear Paul race in behind her. She lifted her baby out but didn't know how to help him. He was struggling to breathe, choking to death.

Paul lifted the baby out of her hands, carried him to the table, cleared the baby's airway with a finger, then bent to perform mouth-to-mouth.

Horrified, Michelle watched him inhale, then exhale air into her baby's mouth. Inhale. Exhale. Inhale. Exhale. Her baby was dead!

But air filled the baby's lungs. It cried. The crying got louder. Healthier. Michelle picked up the baby, held it close, walked back and forth, thumping the baby on the back. She was crying too, now. Twice in two days! Two times she'd almost lost her son, her baby, her only one. If it hadn't been for…

She turned to thank Paul.

He was gone.

She hurried to the window. Rain made it impossible for her to read the plate number of the taxi. But she saw him come out of her building and drive off.

That night it was still raining. The Boss was optimistic.

"Jackal, huh? Well, if anybody can grab that jackal by the balls, it's Dr. Adson."

She placed a wrapped stack of cash in Paul's bag, covered it with a white sheet of cardboard, placed another similar package on top of it, covered that with another piece of cardboard, and placed a third package on top of that. Then a third sheet of cardboard.

"Triple drop, Paul." She closed his bulging bag.

Wearing a raincoat with big deep inside pockets for gun and camera, Paul stood at the window watching the skyscraper lights blinking in the rain. In one of the deep pockets he fingered a tiny plastic lamb.

"Top deck, Champ's," the Boss said. "Middle deck, the bank. Bottom deck, Menkin."

She gave him two keys on a ring. She held one up.

"What's this one for, Paul?"

"*Captain Blood.*"

"Stay overnight in Jersey. Grand View Motel. Don't check in." The Boss held up the second key. "Room four is reserved for you. Eight in the morning, Atlantic City will make a drop in room four. Use the van."

Rain hammered the van as it pulled up in front of Champ's Gym. He sprung a big panel door under the glove compartment, pulled out his bag, shut the panel, darted through the rain into Champ's, and climbed the long, steep, narrow stairway, ignoring sign after sign urging him to GET IN SHAPE! and STAY FIT!

He entered the gym. Men punching bags, lifting weights. He knocked at the office and the door was opened by a 70-year-old with a face that showed every one of the five dozen bouts he'd fought. Paul entered. The champ closed the door from the inside.

The fighters plastered on the walls were the only witness to the top deck of cash being dropped into a big laundry bag. Paul left with his bag one-third lighter. The champ locked the door, filled the laundry bag with dirty towels, snapped a lock chain round the top, opened a side door. In an outer room, a man was going through an old physical culture magazine published by Bernarr Macfadden. In the corner were a stack of health magazines dating back sixty years. The man, whose cauliflowered ears and busted nose matched the champ's, stood and put on his slicker. On its back was stamped MANHATTAN LAUNDRY. He swung the laundry bag over his shoulder and left through the back door.

The rainstorm was building up. Paul drove through traffic, watching the wipers. Their sound was like the sound he made inhaling and exhaling into the baby's mouth. Hoppie had taught Paul how to save the life of a drop in the middle of a drop. It took a long time to replace a dead drop.

On the van's phone, Paul called the bank. The contact would be back in the office in two hours. To kill time, Paul drove to where Michelle lived, parked nearby, watched the light in her window, pictured her with the baby.

A fist seized his heart and twisted. Not a single squad car in the street. No cops to protect her. Whatever the newsman had said on the radio didn't matter. She was alone. The man who killed her baby's father could walk in and throw another bomb into her apartment.

Paul had a gun. He could protect her. He could stand watch all night. But what about the bank drop? What could he tell the Boss?

Maybe Lieutenant Zara was with her right now, he thought— that was why there were no cops outside. He could go ahead with the drops, she'd be safe…

In his mind, he again saw Michelle's eyes sparkling when she asked about his roses—she wanted to know who sent them, what he looked like. They'd made her happy. *He* had made her happy. He suddenly felt filled with confidence, enough to tell her right now who sent those roses and who wrote those poems.

Paul imagined himself jumping out of the van, running across the street and up the staircase. He would tell her. They would talk…

His confidence melted. He could see her face if he told her

he was her secret admirer. Yes. A taxi driver. With bruises and bandages and a voice like sandpaper.

He would tell her, and she would laugh.

Paul drove for blocks in the rain. When he phoned the bank, the drop was waiting. He parked at the rear of the bank. The office was big. The banker watched Paul stuff the second deck of cash into a big golf bag. Paul left.

The banker counted the money, all two million dollars of it. In the morning he would deposit it in the Manhattan Cancer Foundation to be laundered through three other banks under other dummy names.

Paul pulled up in front of the big window of the Hudson Café on the waterfront. He phoned the Boss to tell her he had made two deliveries, was going to eat at the Hudson Café before going to New Jersey. He ran through the rain and sat at a table near the window. He could see his van. He ordered veal cutlets, hashed potatoes, coffee. The television news was on. Someone was introducing Cornelius Hampshire who was being awarded the American Humanitarian Medal by the President of the United States for his contribution to the War on Drugs. He stood next to George Bush, both men beaming, hands clasped. Paul turned back to the window.

He sipped his black coffee. It was lukewarm and bitter.

The veal cutlets were hard.

On the TV, Hampshire was speaking: "...*on the East Coast we're seeing cocaine from the West Indies and Malaya. Many of the places that produce this poison are smuggling it to Germany, Britain and the Netherlands. We must join with our international allies to fight the scourge...*"

Paul ordered apple pie and another coffee, then left both untasted. He paid his bill and made his way back past the van to the pier.

✻

Bombarded by thunder, lightning and seasickness, Paul wres-
tled with the wheel in the pitching cabin of *Captain Blood*, a
36-foot motorboat crossing the Hudson River, bucking wind,
waves and slashing rain. He kept his eyes on the compass. He'd
never be able to see the Jersey shore from this far. The sky was
black.

He was a bit over halfway across when a light beam hit the
cabin. His right window was destroyed by machine gun bullets.
Dropping to the floor, he fired three times through the window,
shattering the searchlight on the pirate's boat.

Captain Blood came equipped with a pair of infrared binocs,
the sort used by the Police Harbor Patrol. Looking through them,
he saw the pirate boat bobbing in the water. No more shots
were fired at him. Paul waited a full five minutes. Maybe he'd
gotten lucky and hit more than just the light. If the pirate was
dead, Paul had to get a picture of him for the Boss.

He pushed closer to the pirate boat.

Lightning revealed the pirate bumping against his own hull.
Paul veered to avoid smashing the body. He throttled to idle,
emerged into the rain, leaned against the rail, bent down as
waves slammed the body to him, seized it. With both hands,
he pulled it aboard, dragged it into the cabin, searched it for
an ID, found none. He took a flash photo of the pirate's face,
dragged the body out, dumped it overboard, roared off.

He was off course according to the compass, but through the
infrared binocs he spotted what looked like the shore. His heart
was trip-hammering, he was exhausted, ready to collapse. He
couldn't. He had to find a tree. Any tree. He spotted one, headed
to it. He piloted the boat in until ground stopped him. He
jumped out with his bag, tied *Captain Blood* to the tree.

For an hour he walked through forest. He didn't know where

he was or how far from the drop. Lightning bolts illuminated a huge billboard that said GARDEN STATE. Good. At least he was in the right state.

He fought the rain until he found a wide field and crossed it and came upon a dirt road. Again in the glare of lightning bolts he saw the steeple of a church. He had found his landmark.

Matt Menkin's smiling face was on a mammoth wall poster: DUMPED WASTE POISONS OUR KIDS. Below the poster, Menkin was watching the wet, exhausted Paul transfer the final stack of cash from his bag into a brown suitcase on a long table piled with campaign flyers and telephones. Finished, Paul closed the bag and, half-conscious, walked back out through the big deserted campaign headquarters, passing posters that said VOTE MENKIN, SAVE A KID'S LIFE…MENKIN FOR GOVERNOR… MENKIN WILL SAVE NEW JERSEY.

Paul found the Grand View Motel, unlocked the door to room four, collapsed on the bed. Persistent buzzing opened his eyes. Still in his raincoat, his empty bag on the floor, he got to his feet, glanced at his watch. 8:30. He opened the door.

She came in like a shot. So did the sunlight. The rain had stopped. He started to close the door.

"Don't shut it. Leave it open an inch." She dropped the shoulder bag she was carrying on the bed, checked her gun with silencer, then began to remove rubber-banded bundles of cash from the bag. Paul opened his on the bed beside hers. She began to transfer the cash. "A pirate's on my ass. Spent half an hour trying to lose him. Couldn't." They heard a car approaching, stopping, footsteps on stone walk. She aimed her gun at the door just an instant before it was kicked open. The man in the doorway had a semiautomatic half raised, his finger on the trigger. She fired two muffled shots, dragged the body into the room, shut the door, locked it, frisked the body for ID, found one, tossed it to Paul and resumed transferring cash from one bag to the other. Paul was startled by her casualness, her efficiency.

"My camera's fucked up," she said. "Take one for me."

Paul dug out his Polaroid, aimed it at the dead pirate's face and thought it was strange. The man looked like the pirate he shot in the river. The resemblance confused him. He began to sweat, heard the flute.

The brainquake came in pink. Michelle's baby was alone in the baby carriage on the river. The baby was holding a gun and there was a shot—

His camera flash stopped the brainquake. Gone was the color pink. He took a second picture, gave it to her. She opened the door.

"Where's your wheels?" she asked.

"Boat."

She drove him to the river bank. He spotted *Captain Blood* a few hundred yards away, tied to the tree. Twenty minutes later he was crossing the Hudson, his mind bursting with: *What made the pink vanish when you took the flash photo of the dead pirate?* He tried to piece together the connection. He would ask Dr. Adson. He would not tell him about what really happened, of course, just that when he took a picture of something, a flash picture, the quake stopped. He thought it was a good sign. Dr. Adson would know.

He tied up *Captain Blood* near the river café, and drove his van slowly, carefully through traffic. He wondered how many bagwomen there were. Did they have the same rules as bagmen?

He parked the van in one of the private little garages not far from the Pegasus truck pool. He got out with his bag, passed his taxi and motorcycle, walked out of the garage. Doors closed by remote control. Down the alley to the Pegasus side door, where he pushed a button.

He knew the Boss was looking at him on the monitor. There was a click. He opened the door, stepped into the small entrance. The alley door shut behind him. He got into the elevator, pushed the sole button on the opposite wall, got out on the tenth floor, stepped into a small office, pushed the green wall button. The steel door slid open.

The Boss was pleased. He had scored 100% in the triple play. He showed her the two photos. One showed the river pirate. The other was the pirate in the Jersey motel. They could have been brothers.

He took out the Atlantic City cash and placed all the bundles on her desk. The Boss was still studying the two photos.

"I'll phone you later in the afternoon for the next drop, Paul."

Paul left with his empty bag.

The Boss glanced at the Laundry crew on the monitor, dialed. Hendrix picked up the phone.

"Yes, Boss?"

"Where's Mr. Grigor?"

"Day off, Boss. He's at his beach house."

The Boss hung up, phoned Max.

15

Eyes shut, meerschaum in mouth, Mr. Grigor in bright blue trunks enjoyed the warm sand under his back. No day to be at work. Especially not with all the hijackings raising everyone's blood pressure. Let the Boss hold his people's feet to the fire if she wanted to—wouldn't do any good, and he just as soon preferred not to be there for it.

His tilted ground umbrella protected him from the sight of the three young girls down the beach tossing an inflatable ball around. He preferred to ignore them, and be ignored by them. Not that he'd never been tempted, in his younger days. But he loved his wife, his family, and didn't need temptation at this point in his life. Not that sort, anyway.

He enjoyed the feeling of the sun beating down on his face. It made him look and feel younger.

He sighed. Tomorrow, back to the Laundry. Lie detector tests! They were obsolete—like the Boss. She was smart, sure, but he was smarter. It had taken him sixteen years but he had outsmarted her. He felt no guilt about betraying her. She was a sucker for having chosen him, for having trusted him. Over the previous two years he had devised a foolproof plan for how to launder his own heist, how to filter it through cunning outlets. It all had to be done very gradually so that when he was old enough to retire, and that would be years from now, he could bask in the sun for the rest of his days, with security for his family and no trace of sudden wealth.

He had meticulously planned the string of hijacks. By now

they were over, the last of the money safely stashed, and no one the wiser...

The corner of a Polaroid photo tapped against the bowl of his pipe. His eyes opened in anger that changed to shock. Held up, side by side in front of his eyes, were the two photos of the dead pirates.

"You thought we couldn't trace the Griff brothers back to you?" The voice behind the photos was soft.

Father Flanagan, on his knees, tossed the photos on the sand, pushed the pipe deep into Mr. Grigor's mouth to the bowl, twisted Mr. Grigor's head around and slammed his face into the sand. Mr. Grigor's body struggled, his feet kicked sand into the air, but the steel hands of the priest kept the suffocation process going smoothly.

Humming very softly, Father Flanagan caught a flash of the lovely movements of an 18-year-old beneath the edge of the umbrella. Her legs, then her hands as she bent to pick up the ball. Mr. Grigor stopped struggling and kicking.

The priest felt the pulse on Mr. Grigor's neck behind the ear. Twisting Mr. Grigor's sand-smudged head around, the priest couldn't understand why his victim had arranged the umbrella to block off his view of those girls. If it had been him... But then, if Mr. Grigor hadn't blocked the view he'd have had to find someplace else to carry out his assignment, so in that sense it was just as well. Producing a handkerchief, which he shook out, he brushed off all the sand from Mr. Grigor's face. He gently closed the eyes, brushed off more sand. Then he brushed off sand from the pipe, pulled it out until it was in a more natural-looking position in the dead man's mouth. Still humming, he slowly looked behind the umbrella. The girls were tossing the ball, laughing. He rose to his feet and walked off.

He didn't really like making the hit on a beach.

Suffocation was amateurish. Degrading. He missed his hammer, his spikes, a good solid wall. But this hit was an emergency, and when, in an emergency, an opportunity this good presented itself, one did what one had to.

Father Flanagan disliked emergency hits. They always altered his modus operandi.

But Mr. Grigor was a major hit, and it had been clear when the instructions came down that it had to be completed the same day.

He reached the parking lot, climbed into his car.

Well, it was completed now.

Father Flanagan was just one of the names he used. Others included Father Rafferty and Father O'Rourke. Forty-five, handsome, medium height, physically fit. In his profession, the priest's uniform was a godsend. More than once he had been asked by cops to say a prayer over the man he had just hit. No outfit made you more invisible, more clearly beyond suspicion, than a clerical collar. Only those he hit knew seconds before meeting God—or Satan—that their killer was a priest.

He had never hit a wrong victim or an innocent bystander. He was professional to the bone. The only notion the police had was that his hits were killings by a religious fanatic using the same method over and over: crucifying the target on the wall, driving spikes through palms and feet. It couldn't help but send investigators off in the wrong direction.

Only one person in the entire organization knew what Father Flanagan looked like. That was Cornelius Hampshire. Father Flanagan chuckled softly to himself. Maybe there was a costume even better than that of a priest—being America's second-most-honored philanthropist, mascot of crusading causes, darling of political circles, that tended to put you beyond suspicion as well. Father Flanagan worked exclusively for Cornelius Hampshire. Ten years ago, Hampshire had hired him to remove a business competitor. Hampshire didn't seem shocked when he read the newspaper clipping Father Flanagan handed him a few days later. Hampshire never asked why he had chosen crucifixion for the hit. Hampshire minded his own business. Father Flanagan liked it that way.

The removal of the crucified competitor made it possible for Hampshire to form the powerful amalgam of four dozen entities, onshore and off, that was Galaxy Inc., the parent of Pegasus.

Father Flanagan was assigned only to major hits. A major hit meant an internal one—a target who knew a name, nickname, AKA, a code, a scrambled fax number. Any piece of knowledge that would give the police, the FBI, the CIA, a Congressional committee a hook, a way in. Any of those pieces could detonate a small bomb that would trigger a cascade of dominos. Explosion after explosion would climb the ladder until it reached the highest domino, in the clouds were Hampshire ruled.

Hampshire paid the priest $200,000 a hit.

Father Flanagan wasn't greedy. Money enough rolled in to satisfy him. And he was worth every dollar to Hampshire. The priest didn't drink or do dope. He never gambled. He lived a simple life. He was on the move quite a lot, not only in the United States, but in Europe and Asia…wherever the target fled.

His only vice was blessed sex. He had a perpetual erection for young beautiful girls. But he only acted on it when he knew it was safe, and rarely slept with the same one twice.

After his first hit for Hampshire, when they had met face-to-face, Father Flanagan never saw Hampshire again. All their business was done on the phone. Hampshire was the only one who had the priest's number. The phone was in a small apartment the priest didn't live in. His link with Hampshire was the answering machine on the phone. Father Flanagan would find a message to call. No name left. He would phone Hampshire at a certain number, get instructions, hang up.

Father Flanagan's cash buildup was kept in a bank's safety deposit box. He had no bank account, paid everything in cash, or with money orders purchased at a succession of post offices.

Given the business Hampshire trafficked in, he could afford a hundred pro hit men, but he trusted none of them until he met Father Flanagan. When the priest was on a job, Hampshire slept like a baby.

Father Flanagan was aware of Hampshire's trust in him and would never do anything to squander it. Trust was precious, worth more than money. In the end, a man's reputation, a man's name and what it stood for, was all a man had.

Father Flanagan was raised in a New York City orphanage from the time he was a nameless baby, abandoned there in a cardboard box. Years later he learned there were all kinds of orphanages. His was the worst throwback to Dickens' Victorian orphanages. From the time he could walk, he was punished round the clock. When he was six, he began to realize that the sick men and women assigned to care for him enjoyed beating him. He hadn't yet learned the word, but he had learned what a sadist was.

At fourteen, he escaped from the orphanage, became a street hustler, was repeatedly raped, turned to petty thievery, was never caught. At eighteen, and hungry, he enlisted as a rifleman in Vietnam, was honorably discharged with a bullet in his kneecap, and was briefly guided by a priest while the war was still going on.

It brought back memories for Father Flanagan, and not welcome ones. He was haunted by the hollowness of priests, ministers and rabbis praying over his dead comrades after fire-fights in Nam. It was all one big vacuum to him. He had never seen a prayer bring a dying soldier back to life. It made him sick to think of all those poor dead bastards being prayed over. So many of them.

Back stateside, while futilely seeking employment, he struck gold when he accidentally ran into a buddy of his from infantry squad who had become a hit man. His buddy said it was a good racket, like in the war. Only you got real loot when you killed somebody.

His buddy had a $10,000 contract to blow a narcotics importer. But his buddy's shoulder wound was hurting again, and cocaine didn't help. He was afraid he'd fuck up the job. He offered to split the fee if the priest made the hit.

In cold blood? No way.

Like knocking off Vietcong in cold blood, his buddy pointed out. Uncle Sam called the shots and for what? What the hell was it all about? What was it for?

Now it was for $5,000. Take it or leave it.

His buddy said it wouldn't be hard to find a guy who wanted to make a quick $5,000.

So he agreed. It was the day Nixon ordered full bombing of North Vietnam, and the idea of dressing as a priest made sense to him. It was also his twisted sense of humor that appealed to him.

He became a hit man. A hit man survived on performance. A record had to be built up. A name. Those who did the hiring had a list. To get on that list was Flanagan's obsession.

When he made the list, he was sent for by Hampshire of Galaxy Inc. It was then that he got the idea. As long as he impersonated a priest, why not go hell for broke and crucify the target? It appealed to him. He didn't think it was insane.

Who gave a damn how you killed a target? The result was

what mattered. But he had stumbled on a homicidal trademark that was original.

Some people in the news business, writing about his hits, called him a psycho. But that was just to sell newspapers.

He never thought of himself as a psycho, since he was sane enough to know that psychos never analyzed their acts. And didn't he analyze everything he did? Didn't he?

16

The helicopter approached the yacht anchored off Manhattan, gently set down on the deck constructed for it. The pilot hopped out. Wearing a baseball cap, leather windbreaker over tan polo shirt, levis and cowboy boots, he glanced at the skyscrapers and could see on top of one of them the enormous sign GALAXY INC. He looked at it with pride, as well he might. The pilot was Cornelius Hampshire.

His steel czar grandfather had financed a couple of revolutions. His father had floated Allied loans in the United States during World War II. And now, at 75, their heir sat atop an empire they couldn't have imagined. He was the most powerful man throughout the civilized and uncivilized world of crime.

In the conference room below the aft deck, four lieutenants were waiting for him around a circular mahogany table. On it, besides drinks and coffee, was one book: the Congressional Directory.

There was no one else in the room. The lieutenants made their own drinks.

A phone sat by each chair. Wall clocks showed world time. Screens with figures gliding by showed the world's latest trades, currency rates, interest rates.

On a television screen mounted in the center of one wall, Senator Orlando was giving a speech emphasizing the importance of supporting Hampshire's battle against narcotics. It was a recording, and Orlando froze in the middle of his sentence as Cornelius pressed the Pause button on a remote control. He set the control down.

One of the lieutenants, a graying man in his fifties with worry lines deeply etched in his forehead, said, "Just decoded from Miley, U.S. ground jets wiped out Field 59 and downed our plane flying semi-refined coca base to the lab for processing."

"Save Field 68," Hampshire said. "Have Peters deliver anti-aircraft guns to it. Round up every mercenary specializing in ack-ack."

His eyes were on Senator Orlando, mouth agape, pointing index finger poised in mid-gesture. "Where do things stand with our friend there?"

Another lieutenant spoke up: "Orlando can't be bought."

"We've found nothing on him?"

"No, sir."

"Nothing on his wife?"

"Nothing."

"You've got to be able to get *something* on the bastard."

"If we did, he'd give it to the press and resign. He's that kind."

"He's holding up our deal with Atlantic."

The third lieutenant: "He's killed our deal with Atlantic."

Hampshire digested the news, accepted it, moved on. No point getting angry. It was only money.

But they'd find a way to make Orlando pay for it.

He turned to the last lieutenant: "What's the latest on that L.A. piracy last week?"

"Grapevine points at the bagman."

"No bagman engineers his own death."

"Piracy last night on the Hudson and in Jersey were aborted. Both hijackers dead. Brothers."

"I know," Hampshire said. "There was a mole in the Manhattan laundry."

"And…?"

"There isn't anymore. What about Menkin?"

The first lieutenant: "Menkin confirmed."

"Bring me up on Jorjo."

"The bribe didn't work. Buenos Aires has him in investigative custody."

"Goddam it."

"Jorjo's a sphinx."

"Under fire a sphinx will name names. Have Jorjo hit immediately."

"They have him tucked away pretty securely."

"His mistress?"

"Tucked away."

"What have we got?"

"I have a friend there who could round up a fire team."

"Do it." Back to the second lieutenant: "What about the turnover?"

"Status quo, sir."

"Luxembourg and Australia?"

"They've agreed to join the pack."

"How many is that?"

"Eight."

"Good. Michael, what's going on with Citra?"

"She's being executed Friday."

"Get our liaison to buy her freedom. Give him a million."

"He's being executed with her."

"Goddam it! She's the best distributor in Malaya."

"She was."

"What about Russia?"

"The ban on farms growing poppies shot opium prices sky high."

"Addicts'll pay the difference. Take advantage of the revolt of the ruble. And, oh yes, on the baseball scandal? Kill any bastard selling drugs to ballplayers. I love that game. Don't fuck around with baseball. Ever."

"Yes, sir."

"Citra. Break her out. Understand? I don't care how, but you break her out before Friday and find her a spot in Burma. Or in Thailand. How's McCall doing?"

"Still hooked on his own heroin."

"Send his ashes to some anti-smoking organization. What about that Fed mole in Chicago?"

The first lieutenant: "Turned out to be Arnie Campbell."

The second lieutenant choked on his drink.

"Drown him," Hampshire said.

The second lieutenant: "*He's my wife's cousin!*"

"I know," Hampshire said.

"She won't like him swallowing half of Lake Michigan."

"Neither will he. What progress on Jose Alvarado?"

The first again, worry lines deepening: "The Left's kidnapping candidates, the Right's assassinating them. Jose doesn't know what side to run for."

Hampshire said, "Scratch him. That country's too complicated. It'll be another Panama or Nicaragua. Is Lopez still hiding?"

"Manhunt for him's the biggest ever in the country. I recommend we drop him."

"On the contrary," Hampshire said. "Back the guerrillas, back the far right, back the death squads, back the government forces, back the rival narcotics gangs. Keep the war going…and Lopez'll keep operating cocaine on the move while they blow each other up."

Hampshire headed for the door.

"Oh—I had a drink with Randolph Railey last night before he went back to Philadelphia," he said. The reaction to the name was palpable. The other four men were all ears. "In a few days,

Railey's buyouts will be announced as going bankrupt. National Trust took a beating. His two investments in banks are having heart attacks. He's been spending his own personal funds to keep up his payrolls. His back's against the wall and I've got a clutch on his balls. He's busted. So I made a deal with him last night.

"Beginning this week, a bagman will deliver ten million to Railey every week on the nose for two years. Total of a billion. For that we'll own him, down to the last stitch in his Fruit of the Looms. Everything he's got. Just let Orlando try to stop us then."

The third of the lieutenants, the youngest, was the only one who said anything.

"But sir, he's under investigation. The Senate Committee will strip Railey bare-ass in public."

"Not when it's packed with our own men," Hampshire said.

"It won't work, sir. God knows I want it to work, but it won't work. It can't."

"Why not?"

"You know who's the whip of the committee investigating Railey's corporate structure?"

"Dan Witherspoon."

"Exactly! And Witherspoon's even more untouchable than Orlando. He'll peel off layer after layer of those corporate shells until he reaches us. I know what I'm talking about. I've known Witherspoon for ten years."

"You know who's known him twenty? Randolph Railey. And unless *you* had your cock in his mouth last night, I think Railey knows him just a little bit better than you. Gentlemen," Hampshire said, "we are adjourned."

"Like to…like to talk to you."

Paul held out the cellophane-wrapped rose.

Michelle stared. It was the taxi driver. The one who'd been delivering the flowers. The one who'd saved her baby's life. She stepped aside and let him in.

He entered somewhat nervously, she thought. She shut the door, carefully pulled off the cellophane, and still holding the rose, she opened the small blue envelope stapled to the cellophane, took out the blue card and read the poem.

> *Like the sponge of a bulrush,*
> *tipped with a dying flower,*
> *Ivory Face brought life to cattail brown,*
> *Ivory Face didn't let it down.*

"It's beautiful…don't understand it, but it's…" She saw no reaction in his face and quickly added, "Lots of poems I like I don't understand." Still no reaction. "Can't you tell me anything about the person who wrote it?"

"…I did."

"You?"

He nodded.

The silence that followed didn't seem to make him uneasy at all, even when it dragged on. Michelle wasn't exactly sure how she felt, but uneasy was definitely part of it. Was he telling the truth? If he did write the poems…if he was her anonymous admirer… But who *was* he? How did he even know her, to start coming by in the first place? "Did you know my husband? Frankie?"

He shook his head.

He couldn't be the one who wrote it. This man? He couldn't be.

"What's a bulrush?" Michelle tested him.

"Sponge."

"Sponge?"

He nodded.

"What type of sponge?"

"Swamp."

She looked back down at the card.

"Ivory Face?"

"You."

She turned away, set the card down. Felt rather than saw him still standing there beside her. "Would you like some coffee?" she said quietly.

When she didn't get a response, she looked back and saw him nodding.

She put the pot on, then placed the rose in the vase, alongside the others. She saw him looking at the baby in the crib.

"Thank you. For…"

Paul nodded.

She brought the pot to the table and poured two cups.

"Please, sit down."

Paul did.

She sat across from him. He kept his eyes on her very steadily. She couldn't read what was behind his eyes, but she made herself meet them.

"How do you know me?" Michelle sipped her coffee.

"The park."

"You saw me in the park? You mean the other day?"

"Two months ago."

"And just decided to, what…follow me home?"

"Didn't want to never see you again."

"Why didn't you just say something? In the park?"

Paul looked down, shrugged. His expression never changed, but something in his eyes looked embarrassed, even ashamed.

"You can't talk well? There's something wrong with your voice?"

Another shrug, a small nod.

"It's okay—it's okay," Michelle said. "You didn't do anything bad, it's just…the whole thing's a little strange."

Sandpaper on stone: "Sorry."

"No, no, it's…it's okay."

She pushed the other coffee cup toward him. Eventually he picked it up, took a tiny sip, set it down.

He looked like a brute, the worst sort of man, and with that expressionless face he could easily be one. But—

If he'd meant to hurt her, he could have. Instead, he'd saved her son's life. Given her half a flower shop's worth of roses. Written a book's worth of poems. Clearly his intentions were something closer to the opposite.

Which in her prior life would've meant exactly nothing to her. But that was another life. Before Frankie got killed and her baby almost blown up, before she found herself alone, with the eyes of the police on her. Beggars can't be choosers, and the attentions even of a man like this, if he wanted to help, were nothing to take lightly. There was so much she needed. And he seemed to want to provide.

And he was capable. When near-tragedy struck, it was in-credible the way he knew what to do, and how fast he did it, to save her baby from choking to death. How very fast.

"You want to know me even though they call me a gun widow?"

Paul nodded.

"A gun widow means a gangster's widow. That doesn't bother you?"

Paul shook his head.

He was not bad-looking, she thought, if in a totally forgettable way. There was no other way she could describe him. Except for his eyes. There was something in his eyes that was sadly beautiful. She wondered if it was always there, or only now, while he was here with her.

And that thing in his eyes—it wasn't lust. Attraction certainly; she knew she was beautiful, was used to the looks men got around her, could distinguish among them. Most men gave her a defensive feeling. She sensed with animal instinct when a man looked at her and wanted to lay her. This man's look said he wanted something different. It was like he wanted to protect her.

"Were you there when the bomb went off? Is that where you got those bruises?"

He nodded, then shot to his feet when a knock came at the door.

So fast.

He raised one finger, dropped his other hand into the deep pocket of his coat.

Then a voice, a woman's, said, "NYPD. You there, Mrs. Troy?"

She walked to the door and opened it.

Lieutenant Zara was standing there.

18

"We left your carriage under the stairway, Mrs. Troy." Zara's eyes swept to Paul, then back to Michelle. "Forensics decided to hang onto the monkey and the music box."

"Burn them."

"I don't blame you. Still don't want our protection?"

"If that psycho sees cops around me, he'll think I *do* have the money."

"He'll phone again. What'll you tell him?"

"The truth."

"He won't buy it."

"Then I'll tell him in person."

"You're not serious."

"You know I am."

"Aren't you afraid to face him?"

"Terrified…but if I run, he'll find me. If I don't run, maybe he'll believe me."

Zara turned to Paul. "You one of Frankie's friends?"

"He certainly is not!"

"You're Paul Page?" Zara said.

Paul nodded.

"How long've you known Michelle?"

Michelle blurted, "How do you know his name?"

"On his hack license. I saw him get out of his taxi and come in here carrying a rose."

"Anything criminal about that?" Michelle snapped.

"Same sort that was taped to your carriage hood."

"So?"

Zara turned to Paul again. "How long've you known Mrs. Troy, Mr. Page?"

"Couple days."

"How did you meet?"

"Why are you cross-examining him?" Michelle's voice rose.

"How did you meet her?"

"Delivering flowers."

"Who sent the flowers?"

"Me."

"Why?"

"Friendship."

Zara eyed him. "How close is this friendship?" she said.

"Not like you're thinking," Michelle said. "He saved my baby's life. My baby couldn't breathe; his face turned blue. Mr. Page gave him mouth-to-mouth."

Zara returned her gaze to Michelle. "I found one of Frankie's friends, Mrs. Troy. He's in prison. For fifty bucks and a carton of cigarettes, he gave me a rundown on your husband. He was a two-bit hoodlum, a pusher. A real sweetheart, pushed crack to kids."

"Now you're beginning to understand why I ran out on him."

"I am."

"And the Black Psycho?"

"The distributor he owed money to was black. Haven't gotten any confirmation on the street name. But it's a lead. A small one."

"I know it's hard. You've got so little to go on. I hope you don't throw in the towel on the case…"

"I never throw in the towel." Zara turned back to Paul. "I remember your name now. Officer O'Hanlon mentioned it. Said you were the closest witness to the shooting."

"Big old cop?"

"Not young." She stirred her memory, came up with a detail

from the report. "Do you really live down by that old graveyard, in one of those abandoned shacks?"

"Not abandoned."

"Where did you learn resuscitation?"

"Taxi driver. You have to know."

She looked from one of them to the other. "Mrs. Troy can use a friend," she said. "Just be careful, both of you. And Mrs. Troy... call me if you change your mind." With that, Zara walked out.

Michelle got up, paced twice around the room. Zara's presence still hung there, like she was still watching them. "I'm going to take the baby to the park," Michelle said.

"*Now?*"

"Why not? He hasn't had his walk in days."

"Can I go with you?"

"Oh, Paul...thank you...but you must have places you need to be..."

"Can I walk with you?"

"Of course."

For the first time, she saw a spark in his eyes. Then they went blank again, but that didn't change the fact that she'd seen it. Somewhere in him there was emotion, the capacity for joy. She felt quite good that she had broken the barrier, and surprised that she felt good about it. Who was he? A stranger, practically. But also her self-styled guardian angel. And who was she to turn that down? Yes, there was something wrong with him; clearly there was. But whatever was wrong with him, it had to be some kind of harmless defect. Some kind of delay in his thinking. Certainly not in his acting. And what did she need most right now, a man who would think or one who would act?

These thoughts overlapped each other as she prepared her baby for the carriage ride.

❖

They pushed the baby carriage in Central Park, but Michelle kept away from the path she'd been on the day of the gunshot and the bomb. She had taped the newest red rose to the hood.

"Why did you call me Ivory Face?"

"You have one."

"Ivory is hard."

"Ivory is beautiful."

The baby began to cry. They sat on a bench. From the blue bag in the carriage pocket, Michelle pulled out a box. Paul watched her change the baby's diaper. She placed the old diaper in a bag, dropped it in a trash can and was rejoining Paul on the bench when two men approached, stopped, stared at them. One looked older, one younger, both with black hair and long jaws, dark features. Paul was reminded of the two pirates. Brothers, the Boss had told him.

Michelle ignored their staring at her.

"Aren't you…?" one of them said.

"No." She glared at them, and after a time the two men left.

"They recognized me."

Paul took out a folded page of the *Daily News* from his wallet. He'd slid it in beside his money, his driver's license and the slot for his pencil. She saw a photo of herself in the ambulance, taken through the open rear doors. She couldn't recognize herself, the picture was so grainy.

"Would you recognize me from that picture?"

Paul shook his head.

Michelle read the caption, pointed at two words the writer had chosen to describe Frankie. "Did you read that?"

Paul nodded.

"*Wife of mafia figure Frankie Troy.* You heard what Lieutenant Zara called him. A two-bit hoodlum. She should know.

Would you still want to be my friend if he had been a mafia figure?"

Paul nodded.

"You know why I married him?"

"Baby."

"You read it in the paper."

Paul nodded.

"You read a lot?"

"Every day."

"Habit you picked up in school?"

"Never went to school."

"Who taught you to read?"

"Parents."

"And to write?"

Paul nodded. "And to talk."

"Are they alive?"

Paul shook his head.

"You live alone?"

Paul nodded.

"Any friends?"

Paul shook his head.

"You *like* living alone?"

Paul thought about that for a moment, then nodded, and then said, "When I saw you…"

She waited.

"Had different feeling."

"About living alone?"

Paul shook his head.

"What kind of different feeling, Paul?"

"Don't know."

"You don't know what kind of different feeling you had?"

"Don't know."

"Did you ever have that different kind of feeling before?"

Paul shook his head.

Michelle smiled. "Maybe it was love at first sight."

"Maybe."

"You think you love me?" Then, before he could answer: "Never mind, Paul. Forget I asked that. I don't mean to make you uncomfortable."

"Hungry?"

The question came from left field and she smiled.

"Starving." She laughed. "Right now I would kill for a steak."

"Cold chicken?"

"I love cold chicken."

She caught that spark again in his eyes. The spark lasted about three seconds. She was making progress.

"Got some at my place."

"Where you live? The shack?"

He nodded.

"Paul, I'd love to have some cold chicken in your shack."

Michelle sat in the back of the taxi, the baby in her arms, the blue bag on the seat beside her. She kept looking at Paul's photo on the license. He looked younger, but his face was still blank.

"When was this picture taken?"

"Ten years ago."

"Ever read Oscar Wilde?"

"Not up to W yet."

"*Picture of Dorian Gray*?"

Paul shook his head. She caught his answer in the rear-view mirror.

"It's about a man who kept his young face as he grew old." Michelle smiled. "It's a horror story."

"Horror?"

"Well, he was a mean, selfish sonofabitch. But every evil emotion in him only showed up in the painting. His face stayed beautiful."

"Like Jekyll and Hyde."

She'd never read it, but remembered something from a movie. "Sort of. Every person has good thoughts and evil thoughts."

She watched his face in the mirror. It remained blank. He was concentrating on driving carefully, with a baby in the car.

Again she looked at his picture. He looked like a priest, she thought. He behaved like one. She was suddenly conscious of the wall of celibacy between them. She wasn't used to it. Conscious of a new experience having a man as a friend and only as a friend.

He pulled up near a liquor store. Took a deep breath. "Like some wine?" Thinking, can't give her orange soda.

"I'd love some."

He bought a bottle of wine and a corkscrew, the first of either he'd ever held. Handed the brown paper sack to her through the window, climbed in behind the wheel again, and drove off toward the Battery.

19

She felt his eyes on her, watching for her reaction as he helped her out with the baby and took the blue bag and her shoulder-strap purse and the paper bag from the liquor store.

Michelle studied the clapboard shack on its little patch of dirt and concrete, living in the shadow of its giant neighbors, close to the ground, lost, forgotten. Its survival in the towering forest of skyscrapers was inspiring. It was the perfect place for a character like Paul to hide himself from New York City's barbarians. She couldn't imagine anyone else but Paul living in this shack.

She smiled at him. "How did you find it?"

"Born in it."

She glanced at the weeds, the puddle of rainwater, the one yellow flower growing between cracks in the asphalt.

"I don't see any graveyard," said Michelle.

He led her to the rubble, pointed at what was left of a gravestone. She could just make out the dates, *1675–1750*.

Paul brought her to the door, opened it without a key.

"This is still New York City, Paul. Anybody could just walk in and steal everything."

"Nobody comes."

They entered the three-room shack. Neat, almost bare, like his face and his life. He was living in his own world. The shack and Paul were one.

"There was no name on that alley we turned off," said Michelle.

"Rain washed it off."

"Yesterday's rainstorm?"

He shook his head. "Night my father was born here."

Paul helped her prop the baby on a pillow in the chair, tied it with his bathrobe belt so as not to fall off, went into the tiny kitchen to prepare the food.

Michelle passed an antique table in the middle of the room, looked into the curtained-off bedroom area. Spartan. A bed. A small lamp table beside it. An alarm clock near the phone. On the floor scattered sheets of paper and an old dictionary.

Back in the main area, Paul cleared some space on the table, moving pads, more sheets of paper. In a corner, a bookshelf held volumes of poetry, some battered novels, a cookbook. And another big dictionary. On the walls were many color photos of horses, including one of a jockey sitting high in the saddle holding one handle of a silver cup and a man standing next to the horse holding the other.

"You like horses, don't you?" Michelle said.

"Yes."

"You bet on them?"

"No."

"Who's the man standing by the horse that won the cup?"

"My father."

"Did he own it?"

"He was a bookie."

"Do you have a picture of your mother?"

Paul brought the chicken and the wine bottle to the table, took out his wallet, and plucked a photo from it. He handed it to her. She looked at the small, old photo. His mother was smiling and very beautiful.

"When did she die?"

"I was ten," said Paul.

She returned the photo. He put it back and pocketed the wallet. He pulled out the chair for her. Opened the bottle, poured wine for her in a water glass, and water for himself from a water pitcher.

She lifted her wine in toast. He lifted his water.

"No alcohol?"

"Never."

"Thank you, Paul. For everything."

"White or leg?"

"White, please."

He cut off several slices for her, twisted the leg off for himself. They enjoyed the cold chicken. The baby had milk from its bottle. Paul went into the kitchen, found some baby food in the blue bag, warmed it up and brought it out in the smallest bowl he had.

He pushed the baby's chair closer to Michelle, watched her feed the baby with a spoon, wiping off the dribblings from its chin.

"How long has your family owned this lot?" said Michelle.

"Since my Grandpa. He was a bootlegger."

"And daddy was a bookie. What did your mother do, run guns?"

"Seamstress."

She nodded. "How did you get interested in poetry?"

He got up, went to the shelf, returned with a very old book, turned to the poem, pointed at one word in a stanza. Solitude.

"How old were you when you first saw that poem?"

"Fifteen."

"Who's your favorite poet?"

"Emily Dickinson."

"What did she write?"

"*If I can stop one heart from breaking,*" he recited, slowly, and she waited until he was done.

"That's beautiful, Paul."

He nodded.

"And you write poetry too. To woo women. You're a taxi-driving Cyrano."

No reaction.

"You never saw *Cyrano de Bergerac*? They made a movie."

Paul shook his head.

"It's about this guy, Cyrano, who's in love with a girl called Roxanne. But she's in love with his friend. When they go to war, the friend gets killed, but Cyrano keeps writing letters to her from his friend so she won't find out he's dead. He doesn't have the courage to tell her that he wrote the letters and that he loves her."

Paul thought about it.

"He's a soldier?"

"The best in France."

"Why doesn't he have courage?"

"He has a giant nose. He's very sensitive about how ugly he looks and what people say about him and how they laugh at him behind his back. Of course, they never tell him to his face that his nose is too big and too ugly—he'd challenge them to a duel if they did, and they know they'd lose. He's that good with a sword." She drank the last of her wine. "What was your reason, Paul? Why didn't you tell me the first time we met that *you* wrote those poems?"

Paul became flustered. He poured more wine for her but his fingers trembled. Wine spilled on the table.

He heard the flute and silently shouted, *Not now!*

The brainquake hit. *In pink he saw the Boss putting a gun into the baby's mouth. Paul seized the wine bottle, jumped to his feet. Glasses and dishes fell to the floor. He threw the bottle at the Boss, narrowly missing the baby.*

The quake stopped. Gone was the flute. Gone was the color pink.

Michelle shouted, "Are you crazy?" She snatched up her baby, who was screaming.

Paul stared at the broken bottle on the floor.

"The Boss had a gun in the baby's mouth…"

"What are you talking about? What boss? You just threw a fucking wine bottle at my baby!"

"Was protecting him—"

"You're insane!"

His hands hung limp. Face dripping with sweat.

Michelle grabbed her blue bag, slung her purse over her shoulder, ran out with the baby. Paul followed her, caught up to her by the alley.

"I'm not crazy. I swear. It's just…my brainquake. I see things…"

"You threw that bottle at my baby, you bastard!"

Paul tried to stop her. She cracked him hard across the face.

"I'm being treated for it," Paul said, his voice entreating. It was the most emotion she'd ever heard in his voice. "Dr. Adson. Brain surgeon. Says he can help."

She stopped, stared at him, still furious, still cradling her baby's fragile skull with one hand. And yet—this was the man who'd saved his life. He wouldn't deliberately hurt him, that made no sense. But a madman doesn't need to make sense.

"You're a goddam maniac. You should be locked up! I don't understand how the city lets you drive a cab—give me one good reason I shouldn't report you, get your license taken away!"

"Not really a cab driver," Paul said.

"*What?*"

"Michelle…"

"Explain, goddam it."

He felt himself twisting again, his heart wrung in an iron grip. To make her understand was suddenly the most important thing in his life.

"License is phony. They gave it to me. People I work for."

"What are you talking about?"

"Not a cabbie, I'm a mailman. A bagman—"

"Oh, Jesus."

"You know what that is?" He could see in her eyes that she did. She'd stepped back, several steps.

"No way," she said. "Fuck you. You're just a lunatic. I don't believe you."

"It's true."

"Then you're worse than Frankie was!"

He shook his head. "I'm no criminal."

"The hell you're not!"

"I do deliveries, that's all."

"And throw bottles at babies!"

"It's in my blood," Paul rasped. "My father had the same jackal in his brain. Dr. Adson said it's hered...hereditary. Help me."

"I don't care what you are, and I don't care why you are that way. I can't have you near my son. You get cured, we can talk. Not until then."

She strode off. He watched her until she disappeared on the path leading to the alley.

20

At 6:30 P.M., while Paul was delivering heroin profits to a drop at a Long Island estate and Cornelius Hampshire was delivering a speech to the media about the importance of stopping the heroin trade, Lieutenant Zara got what seemed like the first break in the case. It came from a dead dog and an informer, a black teenager who called herself Red and was usually dependable. The dog, Ringo, working with police, had sniffed out a $3 million cargo of dope on the dock. Drug smugglers put out a $25,000 contract on the dog. Red led Zara through hundreds of wrecked cars in the auto graveyard to where a man sat hunched on the hood of a Caddy convertible, gazing at a dead dog laid out on the busted steering wheel. Red darted away before he could see her. Watching Lieutenant Zara approach, the man lifted the dead dog up like a produce sack. Blood had dried around its gut hole.

"This is Ringo. Give me my twenty-five thousand."

This man certainly looked like he could be a psycho. And he was black. But that wasn't enough. Zara had to make sure he was the one she wanted.

"Not till I know when you rigged the gun and the bomb."

"Gun…bomb…"

"Gun. Bomb."

The man smiled. "The exact time?"

"As close to it as you can remember."

"When I blew a kiss."

"You blew a kiss to the carriage? To the victim…?"

"To Lincoln Clinic."

Psych ward. Protective custody. "How long were you there?"

"Six months."

He hurled the dog at Zara. She jumped out of the way.

"They let me go this morning," the man said, "because I'm not sick anymore."

Also at 6:30 P.M.: the two men who had stared at Michelle in the park were in their apartment on West 47th Street. They were, in fact, brothers. They were also gutter grifters. Muggers. Got by doing whatever would turn a buck.

Eddie, 27, was tall, well-dressed, the better-looking example of their parents' genetic blend. On him the black hair and black eyes and heavy jaw had a certain charm. On Al—29, stocky, slouching—they just looked dirty and deep-set and unshaven. Eddie wore a suit, even when it was hot out, even when he didn't have someplace to be. At least a suit jacket. Al wore whatever the hell his closet had in it.

The door buzzed.

Eddie opened it. Michelle strode in, handed the baby to him, then lunged like a jaguar at Al, punching, kicking, going for his face with nails extended. Eddie put the baby in the corner of the couch, pulled Michelle off Al, slammed her down beside the baby. The baby began to cry.

"He could've blown up our son!" Michelle shouted.

Al whimpered through blood. "It was timed to blow when the cops checked the carriage for prints!"

"The paper said it was a reverse-action bomb, you goddam moron!"

"Who knows about reverse action? I paid twenty-five bucks for it. The guy was hot. He told me what to push and took off!"

Al limped into the bathroom, came out with a wet towel, rubbed his face, continuing to whimper. "You wanted the cops to look for a psycho. I did my job. They're looking for a psycho."

"Why did you say a black psycho, Michelle?" Eddie asked.

"The cop was black. It came out of my mouth!"

"All right, all right. Let's drop it."

"If I hadn't been on Frankie's left side, the bullet would've got *me*!" She let that sink in for Eddie.

Al yelled, "I *told* you to stay on your left all the time, you bitch!"

Eddie smacked his brother. "If that bomb had killed our baby, Al, I'd've sawed off your goddam head."

Eddie poured three bourbons, passed out the drinks silently.

"Anyway, it worked," said Eddie. He was the only one who drank. "Cops think a psycho did it. Forget the fuck-up. Michelle's alive. The baby's alive. Forget it."

"Eddie," Michelle said very quietly, "you know I was cornered. Why I had to get rid of Frankie. If he found out you knocked me up, he'd've killed both of us. You know that."

"Course I know that."

"But from now on, Eddie, I don't want to see your brother anywhere near me *or* the baby, or I split *with* the baby. Do you understand me?" She said this last facing Al, though she was still talking to Eddie.

"We need Al to help pull it off."

"No, Eddie. He goes or I do."

"Ed—!" This from Al. Eddie patted the air in front of him, trying to keep things from boiling over.

"Why don't you go in the other room?"

"Ed!"

"Just for a minute. Michelle and I need to talk a bit."

"A minute's not going to do it," Michelle said.

"You gonna let her talk to me like that?"

"Just go."

"Just *you* don't forget," Al said, punctuating his remark with a jabbing forefinger, "one phone call from me to the cops, bitch, and you go away for twenty to life."

"Eddie?"

"Better believe, I'm *this* close to doing it." Holding his fingers a millimeter apart, right under her nose. "You'll fucking rot in jail, while Eddie and I sit on a beach in old Me-hee-ko."

"*Eddie!*"

"Go. Al? Go."

Al went. Fuming, but he went.

"I'm not joking. About him."

"Calm down."

"I don't trust him. I never have, but now…"

"You know he can hear you."

"Let him!"

"Michelle…"

"He's a loose cannon! He's dangerous, could get us both—"

Eddie put a hand on her arm. When she looked in his eyes, he shook his head minutely. His voice dropped to a whisper, not even a whisper, his lips just forming the outlines of the words: "I'll handle it." Out loud, changing the subject: "Who was the guy?"

"What guy?"

"With you, on the bench."

She took a deep breath, let it out. The bench. Oh. "That's Paul. He's…he saw what happened, offered to help out. You know, samaritan."

"Great. All we need. A good citizen."

"Not so good," Michelle said. "Told me he's a bagman."

"A bagman?" Eddie's expression turned sour.

"What?"

"A bagman doesn't tell strangers what he does."

"He's sick in the head," said Michelle.

❋

Paul drove back to the shack after his last drop, found a long-stemmed red rose wrapped in cellophane at his door. In the shack under the light his shaky fingers had trouble pulling out the small white card.

> *Who am I to judge you?*
> *9 A.M., your bench in the park.*
> *Ivory Face*

21

They kissed.

People passed. Mothers pushed carriages. Kids were playing. It seemed like an eternity. From the moment he ran through the park and spotted her on the bench near the bend in the path, he was sure it was a mirage. Then he sat down by her, and they instinctively kissed without touching each other.

When they stopped kissing on the lips, she kissed him on his eyes and nose and cheeks. She saw tears in his eyes. But the spark was in them too.

"You shouldn't have told me, Paul."

He knew what she meant, didn't want to hear it, but she persisted.

"I'll never let anyone know," Michelle said. "But what if they found out?"

"The Boss is good. She's my friend."

"She?"

He nodded.

"How good a friend?"

"She sent me to the doctor."

"She knows you're sick?"

"Wants to help me."

"Still. You can't tell her about me."

Paul opened his mouth but didn't say anything.

"If you tell her, they'll kill both of us. I don't want my baby brought to an orphanage by a cop."

"I won't tell her."

"It will be dangerous for you to see me again."

"I have to."

"I know," Michelle said.

At that instant, Al and Eddie came around the bend. They walked over to the bench, stood in front of Paul and Michelle.

"I told you guys already," said Michelle, "I'm not—"

"But you are, Mrs. Troy," said Eddie. "You most certainly are. You are the widow of the late Frankie Troy, God rest his soul, and who else are we supposed to talk to about the money Frankie owed us?"

Paul stood.

"You can sit down again, big boy," Eddie said, letting his suit jacket fall open and the gun at his hip show. "Unless you'd enjoy a 45-caliber enema."

Michelle put a hand on Paul's side, holding him back. To Eddie she said, "If you don't stop harassing me, I'm sure that officer will be glad to discuss it with you…"

Al and Eddie looked in the direction she was nodding, saw the approaching cop. Eddie backed off, buttoned his jacket. "Get the money, Mrs. Troy."

They walked off.

Paul started after them, but Michelle pulled him back to the bench.

"Forget it…they're just con men, leeches…it's because my picture was in the paper, they figure I'll be an easy mark. They claim Frankie owed them and how would I know he didn't." She kissed his hands covering hers.

"I don't know," Paul said finally. "Maybe Frankie did owe money. They sounded serious."

"Trust me, Paul."

"I do," he said. "But I don't want you to be alone when they come again."

"So come over."

"Tonight?"

"Whenever you want to."

"Dinner?"

"Bring some food. I'll cook it."

Paul glanced at his watch. "Dr. Adson."

She squeezed his hand for luck, they kissed and he left.

Al and Eddie followed him to his parked taxi, watched him get behind the wheel and drive off.

22

"Given any thought to finding a new job?" said Dr. Adson.

Paul shook his head.

"Got to get your nerves settled and stop your brain from pressure it doesn't need. Driving a cab in this city's no way to do that."

Just to be saying something, Paul said, "I'll look."

"I know a man running the cemetery north of Van Cortland Park. Plenty of quiet out there."

Paul shook his head.

"Not for you? All right. Another friend of mine works in the Public Library, at 42nd and Fifth. Microfilm department. Quiet. No stress. No customers barking at you. I can ask him. If it's no dice, I'll ask around."

Paul nodded. He knew Dr. Adson was trying to be helpful. But it wasn't his job that caused his brainquake, any more than being a bookie had caused his father's.

He looked across the desk at a row of X-rays of his brain resting on an illuminated stand.

"A few questions I didn't ask the last time, just for the record. Okay?"

Paul nodded.

"At any time do you suffer poor balance?"

"Sometimes. Heights."

"You feel unsteady in high places?"

Paul nodded.

"Elevators?"

Nodded.

"What about muscle stiffness?"

"No."

"Tremor? The shakes?"

"In elevators."

"Short-term memory problems?"

"No."

"Speech problems you were born with, so let's put that aside. You don't have Parkinson's or Alzheimer's. I found some signs of degenerative brain disorder." Dr. Adson leaned across the desk and, with the dead end of his cigar, tapped an X-ray on the stand. "But you don't have a tumor."

He leaned back in his chair.

"I've got to find the jackal, see what it looks like when it's attacking the good cells."

Dr. Adson swept a big blow-up photo from under the sea of X-rays and held it up. Paul stared at his own live brain, in color.

"Any more attacks?"

"One. Bad."

"Oh?"

"I saw someone I know put a gun in a baby's mouth. Threw a bottle at her. The bottle broke."

"That ended the attack?"

Paul nodded. "Broken bottle was on the floor."

"You actually threw the bottle while in your brainquake? Didn't just imagine it?"

"Yes."

Dr. Adson stood up, struck a match, held the flame over the end of his dead cigar, then put the cigar in his mouth, puffing slowly, pacing across to the big window facing skyscrapers, keeping his back to Paul. Smoke curled up.

"Last summer a woman I'd treated was lying in her bed, dreaming she burned down a sailboat, and she woke up standing on a dock to find that a sailboat was burning. She told the police it started in a dream." Dr. Adson turned. "It can happen. Tragedies can happen. Luckily certain cells in your brain make you step out of your hallucinations. As yours did, apparently. But not soon enough if that bottle got thrown."

"Can you help me?"

"Eventually, I hope. Right now I'm stymied."

"You giving up?"

"No, Paul," Dr. Adson said. "Being stymied and giving up are not the same."

23

Lights in the window of the butcher shop made Paul stop his van. He pulled out his bag. He went into the butcher shop, bought lamb chops, bought wine in the liquor store a few doors away, climbed back behind the wheel, put gun and bag back into the compartment, drove toward his last drop of the day.

It was getting dark. Like a legless man develops powerful arm muscles, Paul had developed a powerful sense of direction. He took pride in always using different streets, alleys, shortcuts for every drop. And this drop was special to him. He could find his way there blindfolded.

It was a pet shop and the woman there ran her own miniature zoo. It was the only drop that made Paul want to stay longer, to look at the fish, puppies, kittens, rabbits. He only ever spent ten seconds. But he savored those ten seconds. He especially liked one big bowl of goldfish, like the one the Boss had on her desk.

The woman there would start talking every time he came in. She talked a lot in those ten seconds. Paul didn't mind the woman talking that much. He liked anyone who took care of so many pets.

He stopped the van, looked around. He was near the George Washington Bridge. He should be across town near the East River. What was he doing so far uptown on the other side of Manhattan?

Never had he lost his sense of direction. Never. That's what made him one of the Boss' best bagmen. The Boss told him that many times because she knew it made him feel proud.

His head began to throb. The ache increased. He waited to hear the flute. He didn't hear it. He waited. Any second the brainquake would hit. He waited. The throbbing in his head continued. It was a different kind. Like a drop of water falling in the sink, a drop at a time.

Dr. Adson had asked him about short-term memory. Maybe the throbbing was that. Maybe it was the first sign that he had one of the diseases Dr. Adson talked about. But that couldn't be. Dr. Adson said it wasn't either of those diseases.

It was the jackal. The jackal was just attacking him in a different way now. It was slowly beginning to eat up the healthy cells in his brain. He fought the helplessness inside him. He touched his face. He was not sweating.

Then inside, the chill began to go away. He knew how he got lost. He was going to see Michelle tonight. That was why he got the lamb chops.

His need for Michelle was strong enough to make him forget how to get to that pet shop. Without speeding, he turned back. Every block he passed, his memory was getting sharper. By the time he reached the pet shop, he was excited about what had happened.

The chill meant Michelle blocked out everything in his brain.

In the back of the pet shop, the woman took a new fishbowl out of a big cardboard box. The bowl was very heavy. Paul helped her put it down gently in the corner. She never stopped talking as he transferred packages of cash from his bag into the cardboard box.

He parked his van in the small garage near Police Headquarters, carried the wine and lamb chops to his taxi. The seat of the taxi was more comfortable, and it made no difference to the Boss what vehicle he used to drive to his shack after a day's work.

As he shaved in the shack's tiny bathroom, he looked in the

mirror. He stopped shaving. He looked into his eyes for a long time. The more conscious he was of how blank they were, the more uncomfortable he became.

She accepted his cipher face. But for how long? One day she would get tired of looking at his dead eyes.

He was aware that people had all kinds of expressions. Their faces told him when they were happy or sad or angry. The muscles of their faces were healthy. His were not.

Maybe he was born without them. He could never know if anything in his eyes changed when Michelle made him happy unless he was looking into his eyes when she made him happy.

He thought of Michelle now, of her smiling at him, of her kissing him, and laughed inside. Laughed loud.

But in the mirror his eyes remained blank.

He put the razor down and pulled back the corners of his mouth to form a smile. The mouth and the lather made him look funny. He needed a way to see if there was a change in his eyes when something unusual happened. With lather still on his face, he got his gun. He held it close to his head, muzzle pointed at the bathroom ceiling, and fired one shot as he stared at his eyes.

The gunshot jerked his body, but his eyes remained blank.

Under the shower he thought about asking Dr. Adson. He was a brain doctor, but maybe he knew some other doctor who specialized in face muscles. It shouldn't be hard to X-ray his face muscles and fix them to react like they did in everybody else's face.

Or maybe when Dr. Adson cut out the jackal, maybe everything else would work. His face muscles. His way of talking.

The sound he made when he talked. He heard Michelle and the Boss and Dr. Adson. He heard what sounds they made. Even when the woman in the pet shop talked so much. He heard her words very clearly.

As he dried himself, he experimented.

"How are you, Michelle?" he said aloud, hearing each word like faintly scratching sandpaper.

He said "How" over and over again, trying to lose the scratching sound. He said "are" over and over again. The scratching only grew more pronounced.

When he repeated words to his mother and father, they never said anything about the scratching. They only concentrated on the words. At that time the sound must have been stronger. How they must have suffered hearing those sounds.

24

10 P.M. in his steamroom was Hampshire's hour for meditation. He was satisfied with life. His throne was the lowest wooden bench as sweat poured through his pores.

As a boy of wealth, he bought a very expensive brown calf-skin parchment once only to learn it was just colored paper that looked aged. He laughed about it now but had been humiliated then.

These words became his bible: *There's a sucker born every minute.* Barnum was right to never give a sucker an even break. The sucker was usually the one that was out to outsuck you.

His first act in business was to successfully outsmart the carnival operator in a shell game. He was nine years old.

He rose from the wooden bench, threw more water on the coals.

Throughout his career he had remained faithful to his father's last words to him: *"Crime pays."*

They weren't the old man's last words, just his last words to his son. He'd lived another decade. But they'd never spoken again.

Like most land and steel barons, his father was a crook to remember. Inheriting millions from him, Hampshire made them make more millions. There was no fun in making honest millions.

The breed he admired, to which he was happy to belong, was the men who pulled the strings. Like Boss Tweed of Tammany Hall who swindled the treasury of New York City out of millions. What a great President he would have made. Skim off the top, leave some for the people.

When Hampshire made his first illegal million, he felt clean. When he went full steam from nationwide to international crime, it made him feel cleaner. The more suckers, the better he felt. Without suckers, he'd starve for life.

Money meant nothing if you weren't living.

10 P.M. the Boss had dinner with Max at Dinty's Chop House. The Boss told Max about Samantha's progress, the latest specialists she was seeing. Max was happy for both of them.

Suddenly the Boss blurted it out from left field.

"Zookie's been on my mind."

"Toy shop?"

She nodded. "He pocketed a fifty thousand dollar drop to keep his kid alive. She's got cancer."

Max sliced off another piece of steak, chewed it thoughtfully. "You should have called me."

"Then he'd be dead now."

"That's right, Rebecca." Another bite, a swallow of water. "You should've, but I guess I'm glad you didn't. Zookie's been with us a long time."

"That's what I wanted to hear you say."

"You cover the hole in that drop?"

"Of course. Put fifty thousand of my own money in to balance the books."

"You fire him?"

"How am I supposed to get my money back if I do that? Got to take it out of his pay."

"You trust him?"

"It's Zookie."

"You're taking a hell of a chance," Max said.

"It's only money."

"Not for him."

✦

10 P.M. Zara was in a vacuum. Not a single informer on her list could come up with even a minuscule clue. She even went outside her list to bribe, cajole, threaten stoolies on other cops' shitlist. She was desperate. The gutter grapevine took advantage.

Pay first, Lieutenant, then I'll follow my hunch was the song sung by scum undependables milking her obsession with the case. Like a sheriff gathering a posse, she deputized workers on the streets, in mental clinics, in crack dens and homeless shelters. She bribed madams, pimps, whores known to service screwballs of every kind. It was ten o'clock and she was waiting for the phone to ring. Some canary would come through. Someone would have talked. Someone always did.

10 P.M. a red sedan pulled up in front of Michelle's apartment building. Paul's taxi was parked across the street. Al Cody got out and waited. Five minutes later, his brother Eddie pulled up in his green coupe and got out. They went into the apartment building, saw the baby carriage parked under the stairway, quietly climbed to the fourth floor.

At Michelle's door they listened. Eddie silently turned the knob. The door opened. He looked at Al just as surprised. They went in.

Al closed the door without a sound. In the soft blue light coming from the kitchenette they saw red roses near the window, remains of lamb chops on two plates, bottled water near a half-filled glass, a wine bottle near an empty wine glass, pot of coffee, two cups.

They passed the baby sleeping in the crib near the bedroom door, which was half-open. They stole into the bedroom. In the half-light they saw Paul's jacket neatly hanging on the back of a chair. His trousers folded over it. On the trousers were Paul's shirt and shorts.

Naked in bed, Paul and Michelle were asleep. His arm was around her. Al took out his camera. Eddie took out his gun and cracked Paul across the face with his other hand. Paul opened his eyes as he sat up. Flash of camera bulb startled Paul but his face remained blank as Al took his picture.

"That's for collection insurance, Mr. Hard-On," Eddie said. "Your wallet."

"My pocket." Paul's voice shook.

Al was by Michelle's side, one hand over her mouth. Her eyes popped out in terror.

"Get it, Speedy Gonzales," Eddie said.

Michelle bit Al's hand. He jerked it away. She screamed. Eddie leaned over. A slap across her face silenced the scream.

"One more sound out of you, you chiseling cunt, I'll throw your baby out the window without opening it up first."

Paul lifted the wallet out of his pocket. Eddie snatched it and, after some difficulty digging around one-handed, found the driver's license.

"Now we know where you hang up your used rubbers," Eddie said. "What do you do to turn a buck?"

"Drive taxi."

"The one down in front?"

Paul nodded. Eddie slapped, then back-slapped, his face.

"Didn't hear you, Mr. Cocksman."

"Yes. Hack in front."

"What's the meter reading of the widow in the sack?"

"You know I don't like dirty talk, Al," Eddie said without turning to his brother. "Let's stick to business."

He tossed the wallet in Paul's face, then eyed Michelle. "Black Psycho's holed up somewhere. Can't find him, so we'll talk business without him."

"We're not welchers. We'll give him his cut," Al said.

"We woke you up gently, Mrs. Troy. Didn't bust your nose, didn't even wake up the baby. You got two hours to dig up the ten grand owed us. We know from Frankie he gave you the whole twenty. All we want is our half. We'll drop in at midnight. If you don't have the money, Madonna and baby'll stop breathing."

They left. Plunging into pants, jamming his feet into his shoes, Paul grabbed his gun from his jacket pocket, ran out, pounded down the four flights, streaked out the street door to see them driving off, one car behind the other.

From her window, Michelle saw Paul dive behind his taxi wheel and crank the ignition. Nothing. He got out, popped the hood, found the wires they'd torn loose. Reattached them. But they were long gone.

He went back up to Michelle, still shaking, holding his gun. She gave him a glass of water. He gulped it down. It helped. He got control of himself, stopped shaking. He looked at his watch and phoned the Boss, heard the muted sound of the phone ringing. She was always there till eleven, or if she wasn't she forwarded her calls.

"Hello," the Boss said.

"Paul. Trouble."

"Can you come here?"

"Yes."

He put the phone down and said, "She'll come through."

He placed his gun on the table.

"Use this to scare them off till I get back with the money."

Paul ran out.

10:20 P.M. the Boss was boiling with anger.

"Did you sleep with her?"

"Yes."

"In the sack, hard-ons talk."

"She thinks I'm a taxi driver."

"Hard-ons trust any pussy."

"It isn't like that."

"Hard-ons name names."

She crossed the room, picked up an empty bag, returned, opened the bag, began to place packages of cash in it. But not cash for him, not cash to save Michelle's life.

He scribbled on a scrap of paper where she lived. "You've got to lend me the ten grand. I'll pay it back. Work it off. I promise."

It was a strain for him to get so many words out.

"If you pay, she's hooked. Next week the same threat for another ten grand. It'll go on till they bleed you dry. Forget them. I was going to phone you in the morning, but might as well make this drop now. It's in Philadelphia. Leave now, you beat the traffic."

"Send someone to take care of them. They're coming back. Have someone waiting outside. One phone call from you, they're gone."

"Hits are not in my department."

"You're the Boss!"

"Every boss has got a boss."

"I'm going to throw up."

"Use my can. Vomit her out of your system. Anybody who married Frankie Troy's got to be a whore."

"She's got a baby."

"Lots of whores are mothers."

"She's not a whore."

"If you see her again, I stop covering for you. Understand?"

There was a voice inside her crying, *Why are you being so hard on him when you were so understanding with Zookie?* But she knew the answer. First of all, Zookie needed the money for his sick daughter. But more than that, Zookie could take care of himself. Wouldn't let some manipulative little twat twist him around her little finger. Paul…

She saw Barney's eyes silently begging her to take care of his son, protect him.

Her voice softened. "You'll live, she'll live. They'll bleed her for whatever cash she has, but they won't kill her. Hell, she probably has the whole twenty under the bed, was just seeing if she could get you to eat it instead." The Boss gave him a key. "Gray roadster parked in front. Hyped to 120 mph." She wrote a number on a slip of paper. "Memorize this phone number, then tear it up. Pick up that *Time* magazine."

Paul did.

"The face on that cover is Mr. Railey. Burn his face and his name in your head. When you get to Philadelphia, call that number. Railey will answer the phone. He'll tell you when and where to meet him. Deliver the mail only to Railey. Understand?"

Paul nodded. She closed the bag, gave it to him.

"I'll contact Railey, tell him you're on the way."

11 P.M. Paul turned off the highway into the gas station, parked near the phone booth, opened the bag, opened each envelope, counted the money, closed the bag, stared at nothing. Beads of sweat. His face a cipher. He put the bag on the floorboard, got out of the roadster, walked seven steps into the phone booth, dialed, his eyes on the roadster.

"Hello," the Boss said.

"I opened the bag."

"Deliver the mail, Paul."

"They've got to be hit at midnight. In the street. Not in her apartment. When news says they're dead, I make the Railey drop."

"Paul—*please* make the delivery."

"No hit…you're out ten million."

He hung up, dialed Michelle.

"Paul! Where are you?"

"Highway."

"I can't face them alone!"

"I phoned the Boss. She doesn't want to lose the ten million I've got in my bag. Those brothers'll die at midnight. But don't wait there for them—you should get out now. Meet me in back. Leaving now to pick you up."

It was the longest speech of his life.

11:00 P.M. the Boss was still sitting like a marble statue, staring at the red phone. The cat jumped on her lap. The Boss picked up the phone, dialed, knowing she was killing Paul.

"Hello." Max's voice seemed so far away.

The Boss hung up. She couldn't kill Barney's son.

11:40 P.M. Michelle was waiting in the shadows by the rear entrance to her building. The baby in her arms was asleep. The blue bag dangled from Michelle's wrist. She shifted her shoulder-strap purse away from the baby's face, heard the honking.

The gray roadster whipped round the corner, stopped in front of her. Paul hopped out, helped her and the baby into the passenger seat. For ten minutes Paul kept his eyes glued to the road and the speed down to 40 mph, stopping at all red lights. Then Michelle spoke.

"Right after you phoned, one of them came back. Al. He didn't want to wait for Eddie. He got rough."

She felt Paul turning his head to look at her. She turned to face him. In the light of a passing streetlamp he saw her bruised face, the blood running down from her mouth.

"He pushed me around, said if I didn't lay him before Eddie got there, he'd beat up on the baby."

"What did you do?"

"I shot him. Dead."

"You left the body *there*?"

"What else could I do?"

"Cops'll be after you!"

He made an abrupt U-turn into approaching headlights. She instinctively pressed the baby closer as she slammed against the door. Paul steered between two trucks, raced back to her apartment, missed blinding lights charging at him, lunged past more trucks.

Michelle saw headlights filling the window, shut her eyes, swallowed diesel stench, kept her eyes shut.

Paul kept weaving out of the path of approaching headlights, darting in, darting out. Behind them, above the din of trucks, they heard a siren. In his rear-view mirror, he spotted the police car's blinking blue light coming at him like a comet.

Paul swerved between two trucks as the police car's deafening siren screamed past him. The screaming got weaker. Michelle opened her eyes. Paul reached the cross street, turned into it against oncoming traffic, stopped short, dousing his lights automatically.

Halfway down the block, they saw blinking lights of police cars and ambulance in front of Michelle's apartment building. Paul made another U-turn, drove off. His red lights came on, then turned the corner.

25

The tunnel between Al's lower teeth at closest focus was a cutaneous crypt. His tongue drooped down a corner of his mouth through red lava. Fingernail scratches were red trenches in a Sahara wadi. The ceiling bulb reflecting in his frozen eyes was elliptical Daliism. Taken by the police photographer for his personal collection, the photos would eventually win acclaim when he published them in an art book selling for fifty dollars a copy.

He returned to the mundane official coverage of Al sprawled on the floor littered with red roses and pieces of broken vase. It was boring but the picture editor had a hard-on for that stuff. Picture editors had no taste. They had no imagination, nor artistry. Rarely would one of them understand the many things a corpse reflected other than a body on the floor, in a tub, in the street. They were antiquated. Like Norman Rockwell today.

To catch the impact of sudden death, it took art. Only an artist could make that impact memorable, breathe life into death. Take this body. It was so goddam corny the photographer wanted to gag. Not the slightest spark of anything original to it. He could write the whole story of it himself, in words of one syllable. The man, the girl. The want. She's shy. He takes. She shoots. He's dead. She runs. One day he would have his book, and it would haunt everyone who saw it, because all kinds of violent death caught a different picture of beauty, of nature that homicide created. This shit here? Was why newspapers were used for lining litterboxes.

The flashbulbs didn't make Eddie blink. He ignored the man

taking pictures of Al. He ignored another man dusting everything for prints. Even the overturned chair. Eddie was watching Zara's high-heeled shoes advancing, avoiding the broken glassware and dishes and cups and the remnants of lamb chops.

Zara stopped in front of Eddie. A few feet away from her, the coroner's physician was writing his report of just another murder in his tiny notebook.

Zara said, "You came in, you found Al dead on the floor like that. Is that what you said?"

"Yeah, just like that," Eddie mumbled.

"You called the police right away."

"No. I told you I examined him." Eddie held his hands up. The fingers had streaks of blood on them. "He was stone dead."

"So you called the police."

"Yeah."

"You touched nothing else here."

"Nothing. What're you grilling *me* for? I wouldn't kill my own brother."

"Brothers do. Cain and Abel."

A cop brought Zara a plastic bag. She initialed the card attached to it, glanced at her watch, entered the time on the card. Eddie stared at Paul's gun in the plastic bag. It left with the cop.

"What was Al doing here?"

"Trying to collect ten grand she owed us."

"So she shot him."

"Yeah."

"If she shot him, don't you think she'd've made sure his body wouldn't be found here?"

"Who knows what was in her head? All I know, her gun was on the floor and she was gone with her baby. This is her joint. What's the big grilling about? Instead of asking me questions, you should be out hunting down that bitch. That's your job, Lieutenant."

Zara moved away to make room as the technicians swept through. Eddie saw the two men carrying the big canvas sack put it on the floor next to Eddie and pull down the zipper the length of his brother's body.

"How did she come to owe you ten grand?"

"We were partners with Frankie Troy in a deal."

"What kind of deal?"

"Poker." Eddie watched them put Al into the canvas sack, shove one of his feet in deeper, and zip the sack closed. "We staked Frankie a few grand in a floating game."

"Where was the game?"

Eddie watched his brother carried out in the sack.

"Frankie never said. He won twenty, he owed us ten. We couldn't find the bastard."

The others left. Only one cop remained.

"How do you know he won?"

"Phoned he'd pay."

"How long've you known his widow?"

"We didn't even know he was hitched until we nailed him in a cafeteria. Coupla days ago. Maybe three days ago."

"Why didn't you get the money then?"

"He was climbing the wall like he needed a fix. He gave her the twenty grand to get her back in bed. She ran off with their baby."

"How did you get her address from him?"

"We leaned on him a little."

"How little?"

"Al grabbed his balls."

"So Frankie also gave you this phone number."

"That's right, and I called her."

"No muscle talk?"

"Business call. She had our money. We wanted it."

"How does Black Psycho fit in?"

"Al and me figured the Psycho arranged the game, paid the hotel, called the players."

"You and Al did time for robbery."

"We were innocent."

"Where'd you get the money to stake Frankie?"

"Saved up."

"How?"

"Why d'you need to know?"

"I need to."

"Peddling phony watches in Central Park."

"We'll let that go. Did you ever contact the widow face to face?"

"Yeah, last night we dropped in to remind her."

"What time last night?"

"About ten."

"Was she alone?"

"In the sack with a guy named Paul Page."

"She introduced you to him when they were in the sack."

"I got his name from his driver's license. He said he was a hack jockey. We smelled his stink right away."

"What kind of stink?"

"He got her to stash the money. Frankie's dead. The jockey got himself a muffin weighing twenty grand."

"Did you threaten her?"

"No threat. We told her we'd come back in a day or two for our money and we left."

"A day or two, then you come back the same night."

"Less time for her to ditch the money."

"Why didn't she shoot you, too?"

"I told you! Al got here first."

"To push her around a little before you showed up?"

"Hell, no. I got tied up in traffic."

"Eddie, you got free board and bed in the psych ward for five weeks last year."

"I was using. I'm clean now."

"Maybe you got back on it. Maybe rock's got you roller skating on the ceiling fast enough to rig that gun in the carriage."

"She rigged it! She wanted Frankie dead so she could keep all the twenty grand."

"Don't be an idiot, Eddie. She was next to Frankie. A hair apart. Your bullet could've hit either one. You figured the survivor would be scared shitless and pay off."

"Bullshit, Lieutenant!"

"You're sweating."

"You'd sweat if a badge tried to nail a phony on you."

"You rigged the bomb, Eddie. You made up this Black Psycho."

"Why the hell would I do that?"

"To make us comb New York for him."

Eddie jumped up.

"Maybe Al pushed her around a little and she raked his face a little, but that bitch was alone with my brother and he never carried a gun. She shot him point blank in the face, and then she lost her shit and dropped the gun and grabbed her baby and ran off with twenty grand. She's a killer and you know it! And if you badges don't nail her *I'll* nail her, and you can haul me off her bloody corpse and I'll be happy to face the judge!"

26

Late news volume had been lowered. Window shade had been pulled down. Lowered voices were reporting news. In the faint light coming from behind the open bathroom door, the baby was sleeping in the middle of the motel room's double bed. On the baby's left, the blue diaper bag. On the wall, a sketch of a 17th-century farm captioned PETER STUYVESANT'S FARM (THE BOWERY).

Sitting on the baby's right, Michelle propped her head against a pillow. Her right ear was cocked to the quiet voice coming from the radio on the bed table a foot away. It was reporting Middle East events.

Sitting on the bed's edge, Paul's eyes were on the TV reporter quietly delivering a recap of European news. At Paul's feet was his bag. Behind the TV a larger sketch of a peg-legged man captioned PETER STUYVESANT, GOVERNOR OF NEW NETHERLANDS 1647–1664.

The radio voice stopped. A second later:

"*More complications for wife of shooting victim Frankie Troy shortly before midnight last night.*"

Paul darted to the radio, dropping to both knees. They clasped hands.

"*A white male, Albert Cody, 29, was found dead of a gunshot wound to the head in Michelle Troy's Manhattan apartment. The victim was found by his brother, Edward Cody, who notified the police. Michelle Troy is being sought by the police for questioning. Lieutenant Zara of Homicide refused to confirm or deny that the murder of Albert Cody was linked to the baby carriage shooting of Frankie Troy earlier this week. Cody's brother had this to say when questioned by our reporter."*

Eddie's voice burst from the speaker: *"I'll find the person who did this and make her pay for it…"*

The broadcast continued with other news.

Sweat trickled down Michelle's face, tracing narrow tracks along the caked blood covering her bruises. Paul went into the bathroom, returned with a wet towel to find her dialing the phone. Gently he stopped her. They spoke in whispers.

"I've got to call Zara," Michelle said.

He gently wiped her smeared face. "You're safe here."

"I'll be safer with Zara."

"Not while Eddie's looking for you."

"Why didn't your boss' men kill him?"

"Too many cops around, probably."

"You sure they'll kill him."

"Yes."

"When?"

"When he's alone."

"We'll hear it on the news?"

"Yes."

"Then you'll take me to Zara?"

"Yes."

"I'll tell her you gave me the gun because they said they would kill the baby, too."

"Yes."

"I'll tell her the truth. I killed Al because he was going to hurt my baby."

"Yes."

"Then my baby and me'll be free."

"Yes."

"And you?"

"Make my drop."

"Why?"

"I'm no thief."

"You're right. You made a deal with your boss."

"Yes."

"Won't she have you killed anyway? For blackmailing her?"

Paul closed his eyes, didn't answer.

Dawn fought through the distant treetops of Van Cortland Park. A nervous man and a hooker emerged from room two of the motel. He lifted the garage door. They drove out, passing the yellow neon: PETER STUYVESANT MOTEL, and the red neon under it: VACANCY.

Another car approached the signs, turned down the driveway to the office. Two kids jumped out, followed by their parents. The mother was carrying a crying baby. The father went into the office, emerged with the key, gave it to his wife. The kids followed her. The father opened the garage of number eight and drove in.

Room nine was on the corner. Its garage door closed. Window shade down. In room nine, Paul and Michelle were asleep. She was still half-sitting in bed, head slumped on pillow, the baby asleep beside her. Paul was still sitting on the floor, his head cradled on one arm across the bed. Soft music was on the radio. A whispered commercial was on TV.

Michelle was the first to stir when she faintly heard her baby crying. The crying got louder. It awakened her. It also awakened Paul. They both discovered her baby was still sound asleep. The crying came from the next room.

Paul turned the volume up on the TV. She did the same on the radio. Paul pulled the shade aside an inch. Sunlight struck his eye. Michelle kissed her baby awake, changed his diaper, gave him a bottle, which he sucked eagerly.

Paul's exhausted eyes began to close as he sat back on the floor. They shot open again when he heard:

"This photo of Paul Page was given to the police."

He and Michelle stared at Paul's face filling the TV screen.

"Police say they have found prints on the murder weapon belonging to both Page and Michelle Troy. Both are considered suspects in the shooting. Arrest warrants have been issued, and the police are urging them to come in for questioning."

They were statues. Then one moved. Michelle lifted the baby, held it close.

"My poor, poor baby!"

Paul tried to calm her down. She buried her head against him. The baby in her arms began whimpering. Paul kissed the baby, kissed Michelle, kept stroking their faces.

Michelle's body was shaking. "What'll happen to my baby? Oh, God, Paul, they'll put him in an orphanage! *An orphanage! An orphanage!*"

"They won't find us."

She pushed away from him, clinging onto her baby.

"There's cops everywhere! There's your boss' people everywhere! There's Eddie everywhere!"

"We'll hide."

"Where? Where? *Where?*"

"I don't know."

"Have to get out of the country."

"Where?"

"I have an old friend in Paris…grew up with him…"

"Paris, France?"

"Yes."

"You trust him?"

"With my life. With my baby's life." Then she couldn't stop the horror filling her face. "But how can we get there? Ships, planes, everything will have cops watching. Do you even have a passport?"

"No," Paul said. "But I know a man who can help us."

"Oh, God, Paul. Even if we can get there, it takes money to hide. *Money. Money!*"

"I have money."

"It takes a lot of money."

Paul lifted his bag from the floor, opened it. She stared at the brown-paper-bound stacks of cash.

"Ten million is a lot of money."

27

Sunlight flooded through Johnson's bedroom window. On the bedstand, a clock, phone, opium pipe. On a shelf by the wall, a plaster bust of Homer he'd found thrown out in an alley near Greenwich Avenue. The base was broken, so he had propped it up with a couple of old paperbacks: a copy of the *Iliad*, one of Stendhal, and some old potboiler with its cover missing.

The ringing phone couldn't invade his world as he slept above his photo shop. It was a world where opium dulled constant pain, stopped his coughing, gently smashed anxiety. He was having his special dream. He and his friend Homer were in white flowing togas, reclining on a massive moving white cloud, smoking their pipes, discussing opium's incredible virtues.

"It's a tragedy," Homer said. "So few people know that it's the drug of blessed sleep. I have contempt for cocaine in any form."

"Or morphine."

"Or any kind of shit."

"Or heroin."

"Detestable, Johnson. Made from crude opium, it dulls the brain. A cheap clone. Have you ever been in an opium den?"

"No, Homer. Have you?"

"No. What is that distant sound coming from below?"

"Just the phone ringing."

"The what?"

"Never mind."

"You know, some people prefer opium mixed with camphor."

"Or with hashish."

"And they smoke it like a cigarette. How disgusting."

"That paregoric taste."

"Disgusting."

"Ever tried Dover's Powder?"

"Cheap, cheap clone. They didn't want to call it opium."

"I knew a guy who thought that powder would cure his clap. Idiot!"

"Then there's that barbaric needle…"

"Uncivilized."

There was a pleasant silence as they smoked.

"That ringing is very annoying," Homer said. "It interferes with the rhythm of enjoyment."

The ringing became very loud and persistent. Johnson's hand probed through the cloud, trying to find the phone. Johnson fell off the cloud. Homer kept smoking. Falling through space, Johnson picked up the phone.

It was Paul's voice.

Johnson sat up in his bed. Paul was in trouble.

"Where are you?"

Paul told him.

Johnson swung out of bed. "Stay in that motel room till eight tonight. What wheels have you got?"

"Roadster."

"Plant it behind the billboard in that junk lot two blocks west of my shop. Cover it with busted cartons. Be at my alley door at 9:30."

Johnson put the phone down slowly but was thinking fast. A good smoke would help calm him down. But a pipe should be enjoyed. Not rushed. Under the shower his mind was thundering faster. He dressed swiftly, hurried down to his back-room studio, pulled up the trapdoor, turned on the light, flew down seven steps into his basement, cracked open what looked like a stone door, pulled the string. A bulb swinging from the ceiling revealed his workshop. He checked his supply of wigs, beards, dyes. The passport typewriter's ribbon was new. He took out rectangular and circular official stamps, then checked the amount of wig gook he had left in the jar.

He hurried upstairs to his cash register, pocketed all the cash, drove his pickup through early morning traffic, filled the tank at the gas station, bought a secondhand suitcase and a big, secondhand backpack he stuffed into the suitcase.

Then he went on a shopping spree.

Satisfied he had enough clothes, he bought more transparent tape, staples, scratch pads. Put everything in the suitcase except the staples and scratch pads, which he put aside in the small plastic bag they came in at the store.

He drove off. It would be some time before he'd see Paul again after tonight. Perhaps never. Ten years ago Paul had made his first drop with Johnson—one of his first drops, period—and that very first time he had found Johnson in trouble, lying half-dead on the floor. Paul knew the rules about finding a drop on dope, but he didn't report Johnson to the Boss.

Paul had covered for him many times over those ten years. Johnson had told him he needed the drop fee to buy more and more opium. Paul had never said a word.

Johnson didn't fear death. But he hated it. It would mean the end of enjoying the pipe. Paul had given him years of life, years of enjoyment. He owed him.

He parked his van in front of a diner, sat at the counter, ordered ham and eggs and black coffee and knew that soon his day of reckoning would come. Without Paul around, it would come sooner. Stepping out of his skin, he stood away from himself and looked at himself and saw what a failure he had become because of the pipe he loved so much.

Born on the Bowery, he got his first high on glue when he was nine, putting together a small model plane his bartender father had given him on his birthday. His father died in the saloon fire, his mother of leukemia a year later, and his own ambition, which he had forgotten, also died. So he became a cannon, got arrested, and wound up in a cell with Harlem Davenport, a passport forger who used to work in a photo shop that was a front for all sorts of illegal activities.

They became friends. When both were released, Harlem opened his own photo studio uptown, gave Johnson a job, taught him passport forgery and got him hooked on the pipe.

When Harlem closed the deal to use his shop as a bagman's drop, he found a more lucrative photo shop in Detroit, used the up-front fee to make a downpayment, and left the New York shop to Johnson to run. It was Johnson's responsibility to keep the shop doing business and to collect his $500 a week from Pegasus for keeping their bags circulating.

A man sat down next to Johnson in the diner and ordered cereal with milk, read his paper. Johnson saw Paul's picture on the front page. GUN WIDOW AND TAXI DRIVER SOUGHT FOR MURDER was the headline.

When Johnson approached his shop, Officer Benson was looking at the photos in the window. Johnson swung into the alley, parked his van, got out carrying only the small plastic bag.

"Morning, Officer."

"Morning, Johnson."

Johnson unlocked the door. The cop followed him in, closing the door. Johnson walked behind his counter, took out the scratch pads and box of staples from the plastic bag. Behind the counter was a stack of leather photo albums in different colors for sale. Next to the albums, a file box with customer names. Next to it, a box with yellow envelopes holding pictures ready to be picked up.

Officer Benson picked up a can that had a slit on its top for coins, studied the sticker: DAMON RUNYON CANCER FUND. The can was old. The sticker was old. Officer Benson shook it. Coins rattled. He dropped a quarter through the slot.

Office Benson said, "I never thought this kind of shit would hit the fan." He unfolded a newspaper, planted it on the counter. Page one, with Paul's three-column photo. The same headline as the paper in the diner. "What the hell do you think made him snap?"

"Why're you asking me?"

"You knew him."

"Not well. Hardly said two words to me, any time he came in."

"Thought he was a decent sort. Turns out he's just a thief with a hard-on. Couldn't resist all that cash he carried every day. He's made it rough on all of us."

"It's going to be rougher on him."

Officer Benson dropped another quarter through the slot. "We're all up shit creek if a kosher cop nails him before the Boss does."

Johnson hoped Paul got to Omaha Beach safely. Hoped even more that it didn't show in his face.

Officer Benson ripped off the top sheet of the scratch pad. He wrote down a number. "A hotline's been set up. You hear anything about that thief, phone this number."

He gave the sheet to Johnson.

"Memorize it. Burn it. The price tag on him is five hundred grand."

Five hundred. Jesus.

Johnson couldn't help himself from asking, "And if he's got the loaded bag on him?"

"An additional million."

28

In the bright full moon, the Boss was driven along the water-front. A slim man was waiting for them near a small motor launch. Max stopped the car. They looked at each other. Both knew what the result would be. But she had insisted. The longer she could postpone the hunt for Paul, the more time he would have.

When she told Max her idea, he knew he was sitting next to a dead woman. So he asked her what she wanted him to do with her body. Bury or cremate it?

He couldn't blame her for what she did. She owed Barney a lot. Max wouldn't have done that for anybody's son. Not even for his brother's son. Or would he have?

It was the first time in Max's life he was about to be an accessory to suicide. He didn't have to tell her how he felt. His face was a corpse. He hadn't and never would talk about Samantha's existence to his superior. He promised if he ever did meet Samantha, he would take her to Rebecca's phony grave with a phony gravestone in a legitimate cemetery and explain how her mother had died in an auto crash.

It was time.

"Thanks, Max."

"Goodbye, Rebecca."

She got out. Max drove off. She strode to the slim man. He helped her into the launch, then jumped in himself.

On the deck of the yacht, three men watched the launch approaching in the moonlight. With Hampshire were two of his lieutenants. He told them to leave him. They left.

Alone, he saw her coming closer. He could have asked Father Flanagan to handle her, but curiosity about what she'd done stayed his hand. Max, always the go-between, had filled him in with only the particulars Rebecca had shared.

Hampshire helped her aboard. The launch turned around, headed back to the lights of Manhattan.

"You came to make a personal pitch," Hampshire said. "Make it."

The Boss couldn't hide the surprise in her eyes.

"I owe a lot to his father. Paul was like my son. He fucked up— but he didn't do it to hurt us. Or to help himself, or to get rich. He fell in love."

"You're making the pitch to give him time."

"It's my only chance to help him."

"You struck out before you came to bat. I knew who Paul was early this morning."

The Boss reeled.

"When an indie cab driver's wanted by the cops, Security checks the names of every bagman in the five boroughs. He and the widow'll probably make their move tonight to get out of the country."

"Max knew nothing about the widow."

"I know."

Hampshire put his hands on the rail, looked at the skyscraper lights.

"You were dead the minute the bagman broke the rules. You didn't phone Max. But you didn't run off, you came head-on, hoping having the guts to face me would be of some help to Paul. It was a wasted gesture. Ten million isn't important. Opening the bag for himself is. Pictures of that thief have been faxed to every office we have, and put in the hands of informers all over the world. If the police get him carrying ten million dollars, they'll know it's bag money, and they'll resort to old-fashioned methods to make him talk, and he'll talk, and he'll name names. He'll name Pegasus and the FBI will move in and then he'll name Mr. Railey and Mr. Railey is jello and he'll name me—all this because of a bagman with a bankrupt brain."

All the Boss could say was: "He's sick."

"Who isn't?"

He raised two fingers toward the cabin.

A few minutes later the two lieutenants finished binding the Boss with rope and iron weights. She never tried to struggle. She showed fear in her face but didn't fight to live. The two lieutenants threw her overboard. The last face she saw was Hampshire's. It was a cipher face.

Through the moonlight, fish investigated the distorted eyes and distorted open mouth of Rebecca Plummer being pulled down into darkness.

29

Facing the camera for his passport photo, Paul was unrecogniz-able. Bronze makeup masked the tape tugging down his left cheekbone, changing the contour of his eyelid. Long-haired dark wig with ponytail. Dark brown beard. Earring, necklace. Battered brown leather jacket.

His picture was taken.

The baby was asleep in the chair.

Paul removed the gear, scrubbed off the makeup, removed wig, beard, tape, and donned his clothes.

Michelle checked her makeup, line of her mouth made slightly fuller, shiny black wig, gypsy earrings, gypsy necklace, gypsy blouse under old blue men's jacket.

Her picture was taken.

She removed wig, makeup, jewelry, slipped back into her clothes. On his passport typewriter, Johnson had entered their new names and U.S. birthdates, making Paul one year older and Michelle two years younger.

Paul placed both wigs in a cardboard box, the jewelry in a small leather pouch, shoved them in with the makeup box and clothes in the bulging suitcase.

Johnson pasted their photos in their passports.

Paul signed Henry Smith on his. Michelle signed Gaby Smith on hers. Johnson stamped the date, then ENTRIES/ENTREES, POLICE NATIONALE, CHARLES DE GAULLE, FRANCE in both pass-ports and looked at his watch.

"Time to go," Johnson said. "Got the two hundred grand ready, Paul?"

Paul nodded.

"Twenty thousand for the car?"

Paul nodded. Then he opened his black bag. "Take some."

Johnson stared at all that cash, pulled just the top $100 bill from one stack.

"That all?" Paul said.

"Enough for ice cubes."

Johnson's pickup passed Van Cortland Park, veered through a heavily wooded area, pulled up under a clump of trees. They got out, heard engines warming up.

Paul had the suitcase. Michelle held the baby and the blue diaper bag.

"Minute I get back I'll get rid of that roadster." Johnson pointed. "You're going behind those trees. Hangar near a dirt runway. Go to their office. You'll see two men, Woody has a beard, Cappy doesn't. Give Cappy the two hundred grand and say only two words to him: Brobant farm."

Silhouetted against the full moon, Cappy's small two-engine plane headed toward Newfoundland. The steady drone had put the baby to sleep in Michelle's arms. To make it more comfortable for her, Paul sat across the aisle by the window.

Michelle wasn't disturbed. She'd had no chance to be alone to phone Eddie, but there was time. Paul was looking out the window. He turned toward her. His face was blank. She smiled back. Not a word had been exchanged between them. They were as silent as Cappy, at the throttle of the six-seater, staring out into blackness.

Michelle's eyes roamed to the suitcase on the floor behind Paul. In it was their future. Hers. Eddie's. The baby's. It was a future that could only be created by angels, and each of them had a private angel. Thus far she didn't even have a sliver of guilt about her plan. Paul had told her about the tinge of red in the pink brainquake. He had told her how his father's brainquake exploded in red just before he died. He said he wanted to write a poem about how the slow change from pink to red meant death.

She wondered how long it had taken for his father to see the gradual change of pink turn to red. At the right moment, she would ask Paul if his father had told him. She felt so relieved that Frankie and Al were dead.

She missed Eddie. She remembered how hesitant he was when he had to bruise her face to make it look like Al had assaulted her. Eddie couldn't. They were fighting time. She had called Al and asked him to come over early, telling him she was sorry she had attacked him, she wanted to apologize, make it up to him, wanted to see him alone.

That was why they were fighting time—he was coming. It was Eddie's plan. But Eddie couldn't do it. She lost her temper, got him mad enough to slap her, hit her, make her mouth bleed.

Clipping her on the cheek was accidental. He apologized, kissed her. Got her blood all over his mouth. He washed it off quickly and left.

When she phoned him that Paul's boss was going to have him and Al hit on the street, he said the time had come. One of them had to take the fall so the other two could get away. It wasn't going to be him and it wasn't going to be her. That left Al. His own brother! He hesitated for the slightest fraction of an instant, remembering some day when they were both in diapers or playing in the yard. But it passed. Al was dangerous, to all of them. Al dead was safer than Al alive. So, sayonara. Goodbye Me-hee-ko, hello France.

When Al came in alone, she attacked him with such animal

fury he got all mixed up. She saw the confusion on his face as he warded off her blows. And then she shot him. Even dying, his eyes popped animal astonishment.

The drone of the engines made her close her eyes. Paul tapped her on her shoulder, lifted the baby, returned to his seat. Michelle fell asleep.

Paul loved to hold the sleeping baby. He watched reflections of the plane's blinking lights and waited for his fear, but it didn't come. Not even when they took off. Not even when he was higher than the highest skyscraper did that fear of height seize him. Maybe if he saw the ground from this altitude in the daytime his fear would return, but in the darkness it was just like being on the ground.

His head began to ache in a different way and he knew what it was. He had kept the thought away as long as he could. He thought about the Boss and wondered if she'd been killed because she covered for him. Maybe she was still alive. She should be. No. She had to be dead.

But a flash of hope shot through him.

The Boss was smart.

She was smart enough to come up with the ten million and have another bagman deliver it to Railey in Philadelphia. Who would get mad at her if she found a way to replace the money?

He wished Johnson had taken more—a grand, ten grand. Of course, he knew Johnson would spend the hundred he did take on opium. Paul couldn't understand why people sniffed or shot the needle or smoked poison when they knew it was killing them.

Holding the baby snugly, Paul dozed off. The jolt on the ground startled him and Michelle but not the baby. The plane had stopped somewhere to refuel. The pilot told him it was Iceland. Then the plane took off again.

At dawn Paul held his breath, waiting for the fear to slam him. It didn't. His face hesitantly pressing against the window, he looked down, passing over thousands of gravestones. All the gravestones were the same. Beyond them he saw the English Channel. Then nothing but land under him, almost close enough to touch. The plane landed on another dirt road like the one near Van Cortland Park and came to a stop where trees flanked the road.

They taxied up to a Normandy house, part stone, part wood. Out of it, a grim-faced woman emerged. An old shawl was over her shoulders. A dark apron was over her long dress. She wore sandals.

They got out of the plane without a word from Cappy, who had jumped out and gone into the house. The woman gestured to follow her. They did, Paul lugging their gear, Michelle holding the baby. The woman led them around to the back of the wooden side of the house. An old blue sedan was there.

"Twenty thousand," the woman said. "American."

Paul paid her. She gave him the key, vanished around the house. Paul put the suitcase in the trunk, helped Michelle and baby into the front seat and climbed behind the wheel. After a few tries, the engine came to life, sputtering.

Waiting for it to warm up, Paul looked around at the desolate area's small rocks, dirt mounds, few trees and great deal of brush.

"We're in Normandy," Michelle said. "It's in France."

"Near Paris?"

"Not far. That road runs along the beach. We'll find a sign."

They bumped along the narrow rutted road. Some houses dotted the rolling hills on their left. The English Channel on their right. They approached a massive boulder. Paul stopped behind it because it shielded them from the houses. He got out, spotted a dump heap twenty feet below in the brush hollow.

He opened the trunk, pulled out the suitcase. She put the baby on the floor of the sedan. Paul pulled out the makeup kit and the box with beard and wigs.

Both ignored German graffiti on the shell-pocked boulder. The swastika was faded.

Guided by his passport photo, Michelle made up his face, arranged his wig, rubbed the adhesive on his beard, fitted it on his cheeks. She put on her own makeup and wig as Paul set aside the clothes they were to change into, placed their sneakers on the pile, dumped out their extra changes, pulled out his black bag and the big folded backpack.

He put his bag into the backpack, dumped the extra clothes on top, then stuffed in the diapers, bags of baby food cans.

They stripped in front of the faded swastika, put on the clothes Johnson had gotten them. He put the clothes they shed into the trunk of the sedan, slammed the trunk shut.

Michelle took the baby and stepped away from the sedan. She watched Paul drive over the empty suitcase, going back and forth until it was a mess. He carried the mess down the slope to the dump, jammed the remains between rusty scrap iron and tin cans, bottles, all kids of refuse.

They drove on until he spotted another dump. He dumped their old clothes and shoes in this one. Now there was nothing to link the bagman and widow with this couple of American travelers.

Except the baby.

*

Omaha Beach was bristling with tourists. Some sort of folk music festival was going on. Some of the women had children or babies slung on their backs. Beards and faded clothes. Paul breathed easier: they'd fit right in. Guitars were playing as the blue sedan poked its way past several big buses parked off the road.

Jammed traffic waiting to uncoil forced Paul to stop. Hawkers with postcards, maps, brochures, small American and French flags moved through the sea of cars and crowds of people.

Michelle spotted a booth that said CHANGE among the many stands selling souvenirs, sandwiches, cold drinks. She pushed her way through and returned to the car with francs, as well as a *jambon-et-beurre* baguette and a liter of some sort of flavored water. They'd also warmed the baby's bottle for her.

A guide with a flag in hand was loudly telling a group about the invasion, pointing out landmarks on the beach. Paul and Michelle bit into their sandwich and the baby enjoyed the bottle. The traffic jam moved by inches.

"Americans?"

Half-poking his head in the driver's-side window, the uniformed French policeman held a hand out. Behind him, a plainclothes detective was waiting.

Paul nodded.

"Your passports, please."

Michelle gave Paul hers. He handed both through the window. The French officer and the plainclothes detective studied the passports, their eyes glancing up at Paul and Michelle. The passports were returned. The French officer and the plainclothes detective went on to the people in the car behind the blue sedan. They had a baby, too.

Paul and Michelle took another bite. Their hands shook. Guitar music was joined by a sax.

"How did they know?" Paul finally said.

"New York cops must've put the word out. Probably working with Interpol."

"What's that?"

"International Police. They work with almost every country in the world to look for fugitives. Their headquarters is in France. Lyon."

Blankly, Paul looked at her.

"You think I picked the wrong place to hide, don't you?" Michelle said.

Paul nodded.

"It's the best place, Paul. We got lucky—look at all these people here. With babies, too." Michelle smiled. No longer shaking. In complete control. "But even if this festival hadn't been here, it would still have been the best place for us. Because I know people here. We can disappear here."

Paul nodded.

"We're going to make it, Paul."

31

Woody's beard soaked in blood. Flat on his back in the New York hangar, blessedly unconscious until Father Flanagan's kid-gloved hand hammered the spike through his palm into the wide wooden table. Woody howled.

"Stop that."

Woody couldn't. The second spike was driven through his other palm into the table. Woody swallowed blood, choked on it.

"Johnson at the photo studio sent a man, a woman and a baby to Cappy to fly their asses out of the country, right?"

"*Right!*" Woody screamed.

"Quieter, please."

Swallowing more blood, Woody's scream faded to a whimper.

"How much did they pay Cappy?"

"*Two hundred grand…*"

"Where'd he fly them?"

The words were barely intelligible, spoken through a spill of blood. "*Brobant farm.*"

"There. That's better. And where is this Brobant farm?"

"*Omaha Beach.*"

"Where were they headed after Omaha Beach?"

"*Don't know…*"

Father Flanagan held the third spike an inch above Woody's eye, which was bulging from its socket.

"*Don't know!*"

"Make your peace with God."

Father Flanagan shifted the spike, teased Woody's bloody

lips apart with one thumb, and into his mouth it was jammed. The shrieking was harrowing. Metallic sound of hammer driving spike into the table brought blessed silence.

Vigorously slapping her face with cold water didn't help much. In the ladies' john, Zara stared at bloodshot eyes, twitching face muscles. A wreck. A big zero.

Captain Sherman sent for her.

"Woody and Cappy ring a bell, Lieutenant?"

Zara nodded. "Got their license revoked for smuggling religious statues from Europe. Among other things."

"License renewed couple months ago, Lieutenant. Flights limited to Jersey and Pennsylvania, though how much you want to bet they don't stop at those borders?"

"You want me to hassle them for license violations? I'm kind of busy."

"No, nothing like that. Some kids playing ball near Cappy's old hangar, one of them slammed a homer into it. This is what the outfielder found."

Captain Sherman held up a photo.

She took it, looked at the spikes driven through Woody's palms, the third through his bearded mouth into the table.

"Jesus. Woody must have gotten on the wrong side of the mob." She handed the photo back. "But I've got my hands full with another case, Captain."

"You so sure of that?"

Took Zara a second. "You think Spikes is after the cab driver and the widow? That'd take a mob ties at a higher level than little Frankie Troy."

"Word on the street is, a bag's gone missing."

"And?"

"So's your cab driver and your widow."

"How much in the bag?"

"No one's naming a number. But the way they're talking, it's got to have six zeros in it. At least."

"Why didn't I hear about this?"

"Must've asked the wrong people."

"I asked everyone."

"Asked the wrong questions, then."

"You think it's Page and the widow."

He tapped the photo hard. "I think it's our chance to get this son of a bitch at last."

Zara was already halfway out the door.

For five hours she waited alone in the hangar. In the corner were Woody's jeep and Cappy's motorcycle. She heard the plane touching down with squealing tires. A second later it taxied into the hangar, came to a jerking stop. Cappy got out, staring at the unmarked police car, saw no sign of Woody. Big as life was his old nemesis sitting on the scarred wooden table, legs crossed, staring at him.

"Hello, Cappy. Swallowing any more condoms filled with heroin?"

"Hauling me in for another X-ray, Lieutenant?"

"Nope."

"Seen Woody?"

Zara tapped the table.

Cappy approached uneasily, stared at the dried blood she was tapping.

"Woody's?"

"Every drop."

Zara produced the photo, dropped it face-up on the dried blood. Cappy gaped at his former partner crucified on the table. Zara dropped another photo on top of the first. Cappy stared at a young naked woman crucified on the wall of her hotel room. A third: a man, crucified against the side wall of his house. Cappy needed a drink. Zara handed him her silver flask. He drank as she spoke.

"Spikes left his calling card again, Cappy. Wants to distract us with it, hopes we label him a psycho and go chasing wild geese. But the man works for organized crime, always has. And right now there's only one pair of fugitives they want badly enough to call him in." She slapped the *Daily News* down on top of the photos. Paul and Michelle stared out from the paper like hunted animals. "The mafia wants them. I want Spikes."

Whiskey burned going down. He coughed. She went on.

"Guess Woody wouldn't talk. You're next on the cross."

"Me? I don't know anything! I don't know who these people are…" Pointing at the newspaper.

"Well, that's a shame, for you and me both. It's been nice knowing you." She got up, headed for the open hangar door.

"Wait! Wait…" Woody cleared his throat. "Can the police protect me?"

"Oh, now you think some attention from the police would be a good thing, do you?"

"Better than being nailed to a fucking table," Woody muttered.

Zara came back, tapped a long index finger on the newspaper photo. "You seen them?"

Cappy nodded. "And their baby."

"Cooperate and we'll save your ass, Cappy."

"I dumped 'em at Brobant farm near Omaha Beach."

"You talking about France?"

A nod.

"Price tag?"

"Couple hundred Gs."

"Say where they were headed after Omaha Beach?"

"I'd shout it if I knew. Swear to god."

Zara drove him in, turned him over to Captain Sherman. She found an urgent message to phone a Dr. Adson. She called him, learned he was treating the taxi driver.

"Who sent him to you, Dr. Adson?"

"Another patient of mine. I recommended specialists to treat her daughter, who suffers from a rare form of aphasia. I gather Paul ran errands for the mother. She asked me to help him. He suffers from an unusual brain condition as well."

"What kind, Dr. Adson?"

"There's no name in the record for it. He called it his 'brain-quake.'"

"What's that?"

"Seizures, auditory and visual hallucinations, violent impulses. Never seen anything quite like it."

"Dr. Adson, did he ever talk about what he did for a living?"

"Sure. I encouraged him to find something lower-stress."

"Than…?"

"Driving a cab. What did you mean?"

If the mob knew he'd treated Paul for a brain disorder, they'd kill him. "That's what I meant, Doctor. Driving a cab. We'll call you if we need anything else."

32

They drove past the illuminated Statue of Liberty standing by the center of Grenelle Bridge. Michelle told him it was the model for the big one in New York. She explained that she used to come see it when she was a little girl, that she'd heard the story over and over: how the people of France gave the statue to the people of the United States, but when it got to New York the lady didn't have a pedestal to stand on. A newspaper asked children to give pennies and nickels for a foundation. That was how the Statue of Liberty finally got a brick base. Paul remembered the drop he made to the skyscraper office on the hundredth anniversary of the statue and all the fireworks in the sky.

Paul wasn't surprised when Michelle told him she was born in Paris. There was no reason to be surprised. Why should being born in Paris be a surprise?

Paul was infatuated by the story of the Eiffel Tower illuminated at night. Michelle was so patient when she told him things. Patient the way his parents were.

The tall buildings with lights made him think of New York. Only they didn't push each other like trees in a forest. Illuminated sightseeing boats were moving on the river Seine like ferry boats crossing the Hudson.

His father had told him about Lafayette, who helped George Washington fight the British in the American Revolution.

He had never asked his father why Lafayette left his country to help George Washington. One day he would ask Michelle. She would explain it simply. He'd understand. He felt comfortable with her. When she looked at him, she never looked through him.

He saw barges and tugs moored on both banks like back home. Some of the barges had lights. Michelle told him to pull off the main road. He stopped near trees and bushes.

She had a plan they'd begun to carry out. She didn't trust the woman at the farmhouse. That was the kind of woman who would, for money, tell the French police what kind of sedan they bought. Or she would tell Eddie. Paul hadn't forgotten that Eddie had sworn to kill them. Or she would tell whoever Pegasus sent after them. That woman would tell anyone who paid her.

He opened the trunk, pulled out the bulging backpack and rucksack. She got out with the baby. He tossed the sedan key into the Seine, fitted the rucksack on her back, placed the sleeping baby in it, hoisted the backpack, followed her. She was carrying the blue bag of diapers and her shoulder-strap bag.

It was a refreshing feeling of safety to abandon the sedan as they walked along the Seine. The moon was full. Security was here right where they were. Who would ever look for them on the waterfront in Paris?

She stopped at a stone ramp leading down to the moored tugs. He waited. She descended to the tugs and slowly moved along the water, trying to locate a specific one. After a few minutes out of Paul's sight, she returned, swiftly ascending to where Paul waited.

Michelle pointed. "He's in one of the two bars up ahead."

They walked toward them. Paul had never asked the name of the friend she trusted. Paul had confidence she knew what she was doing. He had confidence because she had confidence. Paul felt a good partnership between them. She came up with Paris. He came up with Johnson's forged passports.

He again thought about Johnson. What a good friend to have. Like her Paris friend, he supposed. Only Johnson was the only friend Paul ever had. The word trust between them had never risen.

Suddenly Paul felt sick. He had had another friend, too. The Boss. But she didn't understand his desperation and fear. Johnson helped without any hesitation. The Boss had put business before friendship. Johnson had not.

He felt shame for comparing them.

It was a new emotion for him. Hard to figure out. He felt shame for having any bad thought about the Boss. She had told him she had a boss over her. Maybe she couldn't do what he demanded because her boss wouldn't let her do it. He stopped questioning her friendship. She had done so much. One day he would tell Michelle more about it. Maybe Michelle would think of a good explanation why Eddie wasn't hit in the street by the Boss' men.

What kept moving around in his head was his own shame. He'd never felt any before. He carried blood money, dope money, murder money, but in his mind, he only delivered the mail. The word shame never could make sense to him, not in his most secret feelings. It was possible, he thought, that he really was mentally retarded. That might explain it. No sense of guilt. No capacity for it. Even when he shot that kid, how long had the guilt lasted? Not long. Of course, he had killed in self-defense. But he had still killed, a kid, and hadn't felt a twinge over it in years.

Stealing? He hadn't stolen. He was going to make delivery to Railey after the hit. Things had happened fast, he'd done what he had to do. If he hadn't, the murder of Michelle and the baby would have brought guilt for sure. But he would make it right in the end.

They reached the first bar. Michelle looked through the window.

"Not there," Michelle said. "He must be at the other."

They walked toward it. Three waterfront bums came lurching ominously toward them. Michelle quickened her pace, advancing toward them belligerently. She shouted at them in French. Her hand was outstretched.

The trio staggered past her. Not a word from them. As they passed Paul in the moonlight, he saw fear in their faces. The three vanished. Paul reached her.

"*Clochards*," Michelle said. "Bums."

"What did you say?"

"I told them we needed money for a fix."

He admired her.

They could hear singing coming from the Anchorage. Michelle peered through the window.

"There he is."

As planned, Paul lifted the baby out of the rucksack. She unwound herself from it. He placed the rucksack in the shadows near the entrance, gently put the baby down on the ground beside it, but kept the backpack on. She went into the Anchorage.

It was crowded with people and smoke. Captain Lafitte was standing at the bar, big as ever and only slightly grayer, rugged-faced under his battered seaman's cap, leading the lusty singing of a French bawdy song with his tugboat friends. Michelle, near the entrance, tried to catch his eye. But she couldn't. She thought she could push through the crowd, but what use would it be? She had to talk to him privately. Better to wait. He had to come out sometime. She turned to leave when she heard a drunk's voice boom:

"*Lafitte!*"

Lafitte turned his head into a massive fist, sending him crashing against his friends, taking three of them down to the floor with him.

Startled, he looked up at the stranger: a bearded King Kong who pulled a trembling woman out of the jam. She looked about forty, tubercular, drunk. She wore horrid red makeup to fake health. She coughed as the man hauled her up and pointed accusingly down at Lafitte.

"You tried to rape my woman!"

He lifted one foot high. The shoe, big as a tennis racket, came down on Lafitte's face, but in the last instant before it smashed his nose to splinters, Lafitte flipped the tennis racket, throwing the assailant off balance. Lafitte stiff-legged a savage kick into King Kong's groin.

The man doubled over.

Lafitte seized him by his long beard, got his other hand under his knees, and lifted him off his feet. The crowd around him made room as Lafitte carried the man to the front door and dropped him heavily to the sawdust. With one foot against the man's backside he shoved him out into the street.

The crowd roared its approval and spilled out after them. Michelle followed.

King Kong lay sprawled on the street, groaning. Lafitte pulled him up to his feet, shoved him face-first against one wall of the bar. Paul was nearby, the baby still on the ground. The baby started to wail.

"See what you've done?" Lafitte shouted. "You see? You not only accuse me of something I would never do, which is insult a woman, you have made that fine infant cry."

Paul had picked the baby up, was attempting to soothe him.

Lafitte turned to the tubercular woman, who was trembling beside him. "Did I try to rape you, angel?"

The woman wept, coughed. "I don't know him, Anatole! It was to make you jealous!"

"Anatole?" Lafitte laughed. "With a beard like that?"

The men around him laughed.

"You want to apologize?" Lafitte said, twisting the giant's arm behind his back.

"I apologize. I apologize!"

Lafitte cracked him hard on the back. "Take your woman and get the hell out of here!"

The man staggered off down the street. Lafitte turned to the bar.

"Drinks on me!"

The crowd roared again, headed inside. Lafitte let them go first, then put a foot over the threshold himself. Over the din, Michelle made herself heard:

"*Zozo!*"

Lafitte wasn't sure that he heard it. But it did make him stop. He looked around for the source of the voice.

Lafitte saw her in the moonlight. Stepped toward her, squinting. "What did you call me?"

"*Zozo!*"

It took him time to recognize her.

"*Michelle?*"

"Yes." She pulled him over to where Paul had finally gotten the baby quiet. "I need your help."

In the wheelhouse of the tug chugging through the night, Paul was on a bench, his back propped against the wall. He felt as much heard the throbbing of the engine. He watched Lafitte's broad back at the wheel, and Michelle holding the sleeping baby beside him. He looked around him. Where was the backpack? He'd had it when they'd boarded, had set it down to help Michelle with the baby, had sat for a moment to catch his breath and drifted off, come to with a start… Where had he put it? It couldn't be lost, it *couldn't*—

Paul panicked. He heard the flute.

The brainquake hit. In pink he was dragging Eddie by the hair, both walking on the Seine. The baby was dancing on the river, playing Frère Jacques *on the music box held above its head. Michelle was running along the Seine. Machine guns were firing red bursts.*

The brainquake only lasted a few seconds. Gone was the flute, the color of pink. The red lights he saw were from a passing sightseeing boat. And in their glare he saw the backpack, tucked in a corner where he'd left it. He stared at it, slowly forcing himself up, stumbled, lurched against Lafitte who, glancing over his shoulder, spoke in English. "You doing okay there, Hank?"

Michelle had introduced them on the way back to the river:

"Captain Lafitte. My husband, Henry Smith."

"Yes. Sorry," Paul said.

"You sound ragged. A snort'll help." Lafitte reached over to a cabinet, offered him a bottle.

"He doesn't drink," Michelle said.

"Bad liver?"

"Yes," Michelle said.

Lafitte took a drink himself instead, a long slug. They could see it go down his throat, his Adam's apple bobbing like a buoy in rough seas. "Smith, eh? Every Smith I met in the war from Normandy to Paris said they were family to Captain John Smith. What I don't understand is why an American like him fought us French."

"Zozo, Captain Smith was British. They were fighting the French."

"See what school does?" He put the bottle away. "You know, Hank, people think I'm related to Jean Lafitte. I wish the hell I was. I'd've inherited enough loot to own a fleet of tugs. As a kid, I used to see myself with Lafitte, the greatest pirate of them all. Me and Lafitte fighting for Andy Jackson in the Battle of New Orleans!"

Paul vaguely remembered his father showing him a fat book with pictures about Andrew Jackson getting help from Lafitte when America was still fighting the British.

The tug tied up behind Lafitte's barge, moored solidly in a secluded area.

33

Paul dropped the backpack on the floor rug of the massive living room. Michelle placed the sleeping baby in a leather armchair. The windows had curtains. Through them penetrated lights from the other bank. A huge round mahogany table was in the center with matching chairs. In one corner an antique rolltop desk. Near the entrance on a clothes tree hung old slickers, an umbrella, an oilskin hat.

Paul glanced at framed photographs on the wall of Lafitte as a boy with his parents, as a teenager with DeGaulle, with some Resistance leaders during the war, Lafitte in his tug pilot house, Lafitte and a five-year-old blond girl on the barge.

"That's me," Michelle said.

Paul had to think about it. Hard to imagine this little girl growing up to become Ivory Face. He glanced at the galley, equipped with stove and fridge. A bar with whiskey, Calvados, vodka. A small wine rack.

On the other wall a battered lifesaver with the words: JEAN BOURGOIS.

Paul watched Lafitte carefully pouring a green liquid into three glasses, then adding water. The mixture made the liquid white. He gave each a glass, clinked his against theirs.

"Happy to have both of you aboard."

"I told you he doesn't drink."

"This is not just a drink, Michelle."

She smiled. "I know."

"Then you should know this moment calls for absinthe."

She glanced at Paul. He sipped his drink. Felt it in his throat, his chest. He coughed.

"Absinthe's been illegal in France for many years, Hank. Like Prohibition in Al Capone's day. Wormwood's in it. Made with white and yellow flowers. Drink too much, you go blind—they said. Who said? Joy killers. I take a sip every day. My eyes are like a hawk's. And poets wrote about absinthe. Take another sip while it's alive. Don't let it die."

Paul didn't let it die.

"Bravo, Hank!" Lafitte pointed to a bedroom. "My bunk." He lifted the bulging backpack, carried it into the bedroom across the way. "Your bunk."

Michelle carried the baby into their bunk.

It was a comfortably furnished room. Rug. Big double bed. Bureau. Two armchairs. A table. More curtained windows.

"Hope you'll like it here, Hank. There's no phone. No TV. No radio. No neighbors. No friends dropping in. Anyone I need to meet, I meet them at bars. I live like a hermit, and so will you. Hope that suits you?" He didn't wait for an answer. "Michelle will show you the john. I'll keep my door shut so you won't hear me snore. You can sack down here as long as you want."

He kissed Michelle on both cheeks. She kissed him on both cheeks.

"Good night, Michelle."

"Good night, Zozo."

He slapped Paul on the shoulder. "Good night, Hank."

"Good night."

Lafitte stared at him. "Got throat trouble, Hank?"

"Just the way I talk."

"Whiskey's good for a sick throat. Help yourself."

Lafitte left, closing the door behind him. They closed their door. Michelle placed the baby in the middle of the bed. They spoke in whispers.

"How do you like him?"

Paul nodded.

"Any more attacks?"

"Short one. On his tug."

"Bad?"

"Pink was redder."

In the Brobant farmhouse near Omaha Beach, the woman screamed.

"*Citroen!*"

"Price?"

"*Twenty thousand dollars!*"

"Color?"

She passed out. What kept her from falling to the floor was the spike through her palm that had been driven into the wall.

Father Flanagan spotted a bottle of Calvados, poured it down her throat. She was still out. He pulled her head back by the hair and emptied the Calvados on her face. Her head dropped at a weird angle.

She was dead. He hammered the second spike through her palm, the third spike through her feet. The spike hit a bone. He kept hammering until it was deep in the wooden wall.

He folded his collapsible hammer that became six inches long, put it in a small bag in which he also kept his spikes, slowly removed his black kid gloves, neatly placed them into the small bag, and stared at her.

But his thoughts were not of her.

Where the hell could they have driven to? Paris? Berlin? Their forged passports could take them anywhere from Rome to Brussels or Helsinki or Madrid. It was so goddam easy to get lost in a big city—especially with ten million dollars to buy protection. They could buy it for the rest of their lives.

Once he'd tracked a bagman who took off with four million, lived very quietly in Dorset, got bored, began to spend money in London.

Paul had the widow and baby with him. He could pay an old lady to take care of the baby. A nice old lady in Caen or even Deauville who would be very happy getting a fat fee every week.

Since it was the closest, he started with Paris.

34

Lafitte had, in his own fashion, shut out the world. That intrigued Paul. In a way, Lafitte was like him. Lafitte's barge was Paul's shack in the Battery. Paul felt comfortable. They had something in common.

The sun breaking through clouds warmed the faces of tourists on the upper deck of the sightseeing boat moving down the Seine. The river was alive with more sightseeing boats, tugs pulling barges, barges moving on their own steam.

Through Lafitte's powerful binoculars, Paul enjoyed studying the faces on the upper decks. A boy crying. A child laughing. A young couple kissing. An old lady sleeping. An old man taking in the sights. Couples there for the music festival, judging by their clothes and hair, the peace symbols on their canvas shoulder bags. Some with kids. A few with babies. It wouldn't be hard to keep Michelle and her baby from standing out. Until the festival ended. Then what?

Michelle and Paul were in yellow deck chairs finishing coffee and baguettes smeared with butter. The tablecloth was blue. Under the red-striped awning the baby was dozing in a yellow hammock. Potted plants and boxed flowers made the wide deck of the old barge look like the deck of a houseboat. It was peaceful. Everything had the feeling of safety. The seclusion was perfect. Thick bushes and trees on both flanks hid their hideout. They were sitting in the open, but they were part of the landscape. Like sitting on the front porch of a mountain cabin.

He could watch many faces. None were watching his.

"Hank…?"

He lowered the binoculars, found Lafitte looking at him. "I asked if gambling's a tough racket, Hank."

"Yes."

"Cards?"

"Horses," Michelle said.

"How about going to the track one of these days?"

"Sounds good, Zozo."

"It *is* good. You said you changed the color of your hair to change Hank's luck?"

Paul heard Michelle talking about the ups and downs at the track for a professional gambler. Why had she told her friend that that's what he did?

"How'd you get the bug?" Lafitte said.

This time Michelle did not answer for him. Paul knew it would be better if he answered.

"My father loved the horses."

"Ever make a killing on a long shot?"

"Yes."

Paul lifted the binoculars again, spotted a Harbor Police Boat, saw the faces of two cops as they passed. Behind them, a tug was pulling a barge loaded with coal. Going upriver, another barge loaded with lumber was on its own steam.

"Every day more barges are putting in their own engines," Lafitte said. "But tugs'll never be put out to pasture as long as the big ships need us to tow them in or out of harbors."

"Why don't you retire, Zozo?"

"I'm going to. The day after I'm pronounced dead." Lafitte laughed. "Hank, that tug you've got your glasses on is about to tell me what time I haul a cargo today."

Paul kept watching the tug. Its horn blasted twice as it was passing. Lafitte stood up, waved with both hands. The tug's horn blasted once. Lafitte glanced at his watch.

"Two o'clock. We've got plenty of time, Hank."

"Don't want to be a bother."

"Bother?"

"Don't need to get us anything."

"I'm glad to, Hank. I want to. Michelle's baby—that's like family to me."

Paul turned to Michelle who shared his worry. The barge was their safest place. But clearly it would make Lafitte happy for them to go with him. And they were his guests; they had to keep him happy.

"Okay." Paul stood up. He left the deck, went to their room.

Michelle came in. "He always locks up, Paul. No one's going to get in here."

He felt strange, not liking the idea of trusting the backpack alone. But carrying it around in the street was worse. Michelle picked up her shoulder-strap and blue diaper bag.

"Should bring money," Paul said.

"He wants to buy everything."

"I'm no freeloader."

Paul swiftly dropped on his knees, crawled under the bed, dragged himself back with the backpack, opened it, clawed under the clothes, opened his bag, dug inside until he'd pulled loose a handful of bills, closed the bag, stuffed it back under the clothes in the backpack, shoved it under the bed until it reached the wall, rose, gave her the money.

Lafitte poked his head in as Paul was picking up the rucksack.

"Don't need it, Hank. Takes the fun out of carrying little Jean."

They trailed Lafitte off the plank to the stone quay. Paul looked behind the barge at the tied-up tug. Then back at the barge. It was the first time he had seen it in daylight, the first time he'd been able to read its name: just like on the life preserver, *Jean Bourgois*.

"Named after Michelle's grandfather, Hank. He was a hero in the French Resistance."

"So were you, Zozo."

Paul didn't know what they were talking about, but didn't ask. Later, Michelle could tell him. Carrying the baby in his arms, Lafitte led them the four hundred yards along the riverfront to a cement ramp, ascended it to a phone booth on a street crowded with people strolling and fast two-way traffic.

Lafitte phoned for a taxi, listened, hung up. "No taxi for twenty minutes. Let's enjoy the walk to the bridge. We'll flag a taxi there."

Dressed in the faded, secondhand clothes Johnson had supplied, they made a strange contrast to the tug skipper in his dark suit, collar open, and his sea captain's cap. They could only hope they remained anonymous, wouldn't attract too many glances. Michelle caught Paul's eye, saw the fear there. She squeezed his arm to reassure him. There were plenty of people walking in both directions along the low stone wall facing the Seine. Plenty dressed the way they were or worse. Even one or two with babies. And they wouldn't stay out long. Lafitte had to be back before two.

As they walked, Lafitte enjoyed telling the baby all about the wonders of the Seine, pointing out different barges and tugs and a passing sightseeing boat.

"Hank, I want to thank you for letting Michelle name the baby Jean."

"He liked the name the minute he heard it," Michelle said.

"Didn't know it was her grandfather's, did you?" Lafitte bent his head to coo at the baby. "Your grandfather would have loved seeing you." There was an undertone of sadness in his voice.

A car slowed down abreast of them. The driver shouted.

"Want a ride into town, Captain Lafitte?"

"No thanks, Jacques. Need the exercise."

"Who're your friends?"

"Visiting from the States!" Lafitte shouted back.

The driver waved, stepped on the gas. Paul and Michelle looked at each other with renewed apprehension.

In the plane taking her to Paris, Zara wasn't getting any rest. She ate little. She spurned the drinks. The photos of Spikes' latest killing clung to her. Paul was a mob man or Spikes wouldn't be hunting him.

Bagman? No bagman was stupid enough to get himself involved in the gun-in-the-carriage/bomb mess triggered by somebody owing somebody $10,000. What was Paul's real role? Collector of cash on its first step to laundering? Or he worked in the laundry? Or in Receiving? That made more sense. He would know the time and place for the drops, the code number of the bagman. Or a mole in Receiving? Or he knew a mole in Receiving. That way it might add up. Paul got the info from the mole, hijacked the bagman, killed him. $200,000 for a plane ride was nothing if he pirated millions.

But Spikes wouldn't be assigned to find a pirate. There were plenty of enforcers for that kind of hunt. Spikes only went after people who knew names—people threatening to turn state's evidence, people who could say too much. Crucifixion was for important betrayers, to silence and to punish and to set an example. A bagman gone rogue would be worth his attention. To keep the other bagmen in line and ensure the police got nothing from this one.

So let's say Paul was a bagman. Using taxi driving as a cover. Nothing new about that. Paul's isolated shack in the Battery. A loner. Didn't say much. All that was a bagman's brand. And they carried millions in cash day and night.

They must have trusted him. And he'd evidently been trustworthy, until he got a hard-on for Michelle. He must have been carrying a loaded bag the night Al came over and wound up dead. Had Paul shot him, or did Michelle do it with Paul's gun? And how did Al fit into the picture? Maybe Paul's last drop was the link that made the mafia assign Spikes, and Al was just collateral damage.

Either way, Spikes was after them now. The money was incidental. No matter how big the sum, they replaced it with more within days. Even millions could be lost without seriously hurting their bottom line. What couldn't be tolerated was betrayal.

Her head became heavy and pain came, behind her right eye. Migraine. She rubbed it with the heel of her hand, willing it to go away. She was wasting time trying to figure out the details. This was a simple manhunt. They could worry about the details after she had Paul safely in custody.

But the puzzle haunted her and her headache got worse. From the day she put on her badge, she learned that it was almost impossible to nail a bagman. So little was known about them. But this time it was a must—she had to nail Paul before Spikes could.

The Commissioner had faxed Interpol in Paris. Half of France was sweeping for clues, from the Brobant farm to St. Lo, Caen, Dunkirk, Lilles, Nantes. She was headed for Paris, at the Commissioner's instruction. They were probably countries away by now but she had to start somewhere. And maybe they'd stayed put—Paris was easy to get lost in. At least she knew they'd flown to France. That was a start.

Why her? She'd seen them, both of them, could recognize them if she saw them again. Even through a disguise. They needed her there. And frankly she'd lobbied to go. Not just to keep Paul from the crucifier's hammer, but to bring down the man wielding the hammer himself.

Spikes had been on her radar for years. Not just hers, but as long as he insisted on plying his trade on her streets, she took it personally. Would she shoot Spikes on sight? Never! Would she torture him? She sure as hell would. She wanted the name of the man who gave Spikes his assignments, and she'd break every rule a cop has taken an oath to uphold. To get the name of that man out of Spikes, she would make the Spanish Inquisition, the KKK's bonfire lynching parties and Hitler's concentration camp methods look like child's play.

She found the Interpol man waiting for her at Charles de Gaulle Airport. Driving through heavy traffic toward Paris, he showed her the photo of the crucified woman at Brobant's farmhouse.

She filled him in with more details. He wasn't optimistic. By this time, Paul must have had a cosmetic job.

"Maybe," she said.

And of course Michelle's blurred photo was of little help. Probably they'd deposited the baby somewhere, making the search for them more difficult. Interpol was checking every hotel, every recently rented furnished or unfurnished apartment, every rented or purchased house in the Paris suburbs.

The Interpol man asked her about Spikes.

"What does he look like, Lieutenant?"

"Nobody knows."

"You have no informer in the organization?"

"Sure we do. But none of them know what he looks like either."

"But he knows what you look like."

"Yes."

"No offense, but they sent the wrong detective."

"I insisted. If they ordered me not to go, I'd have come on my own."

They were approaching the Champs-Élysées. The Interpol man honked his horn to wake up a slow-moving driver ahead of him.

"There are still some moderately priced hotels here."

"I hope so."

"On a tight expense account?"

"Tighter than a drum. I've got to produce receipts for every bribe."

The Interpol man sighed. "That's the song we have to sing every day. Last week I bribed a smuggler with Dom Perignon. How could I ask for receipts? How could I convince my superior I did not drink all that champagne with the girls at the Crazy Horse? Even murder calls for a receipt."

The shop on the Champs-Élysées was crowded with tourists, parents with children, grandmothers out shopping to spoil the next generation as they'd never spoiled the previous one. Eight clerks weren't enough to handle the crowd. The shelves were piled high with pink and blue clothes for infants, colorful prints for older children, all kinds of toys that made the children in the store shout and squeal. Many languages mingled with the crying of babies. It was Babel without the tower.

Lafitte wanted to buy everything for the baby. Pants, shirts, shoes the baby would grow into. His enthusiasm was contagious. Boxes were piled high on a table for him near the counter. And through it all he never gave Paul the baby to hold.

Michelle came out of the change booth across the street, all the American hundreds turned into francs. She pushed through the crowd, waited for the green light, crossed the wide street to a phone booth that had three compartments separated by windows.

In one compartment three teenage fans from the music festival were jammed in, all trying to grab the phone to talk to their friend in San Francisco. In the second compartment a young woman was telling her husband why she couldn't stand the sight of him and refused to tell him where she was calling him from.

In the third compartment Michelle was talking to Eddie.

"We're in Paris. That's right. Trying to blend in. He's wearing a beard. Zara still on your ass?" He said something meant to be reassuring. She could only make out every other word. "Grab the first plane here," she told him. "Check into the Trainee Hotel in Montmartre. Stay glued to the phone. Everything's got to be handled in steps. Steps. *Steps*. Yes, that's right. Trainee. T-R-A-I— That's right. I'll tell you the minute you get here."

Across the street Zara cried, "*Stop!*"

The Interpol man braked hard. The angry driver of the car behind them swerved wildly, missing the Interpol car by an inch. Cars further back began to honk. Zara ignored it, strained her eyes on the dark profile in the phone booth. The hair was black. She wore a ratty torn shirt like some of the kids Zara had seen on the street, in town for the concert. But that profile—she remembered Michelle gazing out the back of the ambulance. Zara hopped out, zigzagged through the fast two-way speeding traffic. The green light for pedestrians came on. The horde swarmed at Zara. She reached the phone booth.

Michelle was gone.

Zara scanned the street for a glimpse of her. She hopped up and down, giving her height an even better view, hoping to spot that shirt, the hair. She was wasting time. She broke into a sprint, shoved through people. More were in front of her. She elbowed her way and spotted Michelle headed into the shop.

Zara charged in after her but couldn't get through the people without physically shoving them aside. Already she was drawing stares, hissed curses. There were disadvantages to being a six-foot-tall black woman in Paris—anywhere, but worse here than in New York. Already she saw a uniformed policeman plunging through the crowd toward her. Now came the explanations, the showing of credentials, the countless apologies. But meanwhile Michelle would get away. She searched faces. No Paul. No Michelle. Damn it. But at least she knew they were here.

Zara crossed her arms over her chest and walked toward the French officer.

Lafitte was grimly holding the baby flanked by Paul and Michelle in the taxi headed toward the Seine. The open trunk was jammed with his purchases.

"You're not freeloading!" Lafitte growled. "You're not spongers! It was my idea! I wanted to pay because I'm selfish. It would have made me feel good. Picking out all those things made me feel good, goddam it! And I was feeling great until you picked up the tab behind my back!"

"We're sorry, Zozo."

"At least let's split what Hank spent."

"We're not broke, Zozo."

"You're not staying at the Ritz, are you?"

"I wanted to stay with you, Zozo."

That calmed him down a bit. He managed a smile.

"Okay. Hank dropped a wad. We'll go to the track and you'll win some of it back. That'll make me feel better."

Lafitte told the driver to stop at the newsstand for an *International Herald Tribune*. "Maybe you'd like to read how the horses are running in the States, Hank."

Paul took the paper, but didn't turn to the racing pages. He flipped through the front pages instead, to see if his picture was there, or Michelle's. He was relieved not to see them. But then under WORLD BRIEFS a story caught his eye. He read:

BODY IN PHOTO STUDIO
VICTIM OF MAFIA SLAYING (NY, AP)

...the mutilated body found in the back room of the studio was identified as William Johnson, 61. His tongue had been cut out gangland style, customarily a punishment for betrayal...

Paul's head rumbled with pain. He waited for the playing of the flute. It came.

In pink Johnson was crawling through giant ice cubes... reached for his opium pipe, lit it with a giant torch, took a puff. The pipe dropped. His tongue fell from his mouth, pink lava spilling down the ice. The lava turned red. The ice cubes melted. Red lava smothered Johnson's death cry, yelling for Paul.

The brainquake was over. Gone was the sound of the flute and gone was the color of pink and red. The words of the news item danced. Paul took a moment. He made out the words and read on:

Johnson, who had a criminal record, was believed to be involved in the international drug trade. His testicles were also amputated.

35

Lafitte opened boxes and packages in the big living room in front of the baby. The baby kept crying until a toy monkey was placed in his hands. When Lafitte took the monkey away and replaced it with a toy giraffe, the baby cried. Lafitte put the monkey back in the baby's hands.

The baby stopped crying and kept pulling the monkey's tail. Paul and Michelle watched. The baby couldn't understand. No music came from the monkey.

That night in his room, Lafitte was asleep and snoring.

In their room the baby was asleep in his new crib, the monkey held close to him. Moonlight washed through the curtains. Michelle was in the chair, staring at the baby. Then she glanced up at Paul standing at the window, his back to her. The silence was heavy. She knew, without his showing it, how hard the news had hit him.

"He didn't tell them," Paul said quietly.

"We don't know that. Sometimes they cut out your tongue after they learn what they want to know. It's a mafia trademark."

"He told them nothing."

"But if he did, they're in France now."

"He told them nothing."

"I'm just saying if…that's all, Paul…if. I'm not saying we should do anything different. It's no good to run. We'll find nothing as safe as this barge."

"He told them nothing."

"We'll keep inside. We'll hang the baby's washing in this room. We'll keep the carriage in this room."

Paul said nothing. Then, after a few moments:

"You're right. No place safer than this."

She changed the subject. "Was the attack bad?"

"How did you know?"

"Your face in the taxi…sweating."

"It was bad."

"What did you see?"

"Johnson. Ice cubes. Opium pipe."

"Ice cubes?"

"To pack on his balls."

"Why?"

"They help."

"How do you know?"

"I packed them on his balls many times."

"You did?"

"That and milk."

"Milk?"

"They helped him stay alive. When the drug made him sick."

"You never told your boss?"

Paul said nothing.

"Johnson owed you."

Paul said nothing. She rose and went to him, held him close. His back still to her. She turned him around slowly, and caught a flash of tears glistening in the moonlight. His face remained a cipher.

"I'm sorry, Paul. I'm sorry he's dead." Michelle was surprised because she meant it. She led him to the bed. They undressed in silence.

He got in bed, couldn't sleep, stared at the ceiling. Then he looked at her. She was looking at him. The sleeping baby in the crib gurgled.

"I wish Lafitte hadn't bought that monkey," Michelle said.

This time he changed the subject. "What is the Resistance?"

She lay back against the pillow and told him about the French Resistance. The stories Lafitte had told her as a girl, about fighting in the underground against Nazi soldiers when Hitler's German troops occupied Paris. About Jean Bourgois, about how brave he was. And how one day the Nazis captured him and executed him by firing squad.

"How did he fight them?"

"Blew up bridges and factories making guns and shells and other things to kill people. He and his men ambushed Nazi soldiers in the streets, in the parks, on the riverfront."

"Jean Bourgois was your grandfather?"

"Yes, Paul."

"Michelle Bourgois is a beautiful name."

"It's my mother's name. Mine's Borcellino. My father was with the mafia. He was a bagman too."

It took a long moment for Paul to absorb it. She went on.

"My father was born in New York. His family was from Sicily. That's an island off Italy. The mafia was born there. It was called the Black Hand. They shook down shop owners and factory owners in cities and in towns for protection."

"Protection?"

"Protection against the Black Hand." She was sure he didn't understand. She had to make it plainer, so that a child would understand. "If a shop owner paid them money every week, it was protection against the Black Hand blowing up their shops."

"Like gangsters in the bootleg days."

"Yes."

"My father told me about them."

"You said he was a bookie."

"My grandfather was a bootlegger. He wouldn't hurt a saloon if they bought his whiskey and beer."

"That's it."

"He hijacked whiskey and beer from other bootleggers."

"Like pirates."

Paul nodded. "There are pirates today who hijack bagmen."

"Were you ever hijacked?"

"A hijacked bagman is killed." There was a long silence. "Tell me more about your father."

"You really want to know more?"

"Yes."

"He got a job driving for one of the mafia families when he was seventeen. My grandfather repaired shoes down in Little Italy. Ten hours a day, hammering nails into soles, polishing rich men's boots. He was angry and ashamed because my father was giving the Italians in America a bad name. When my father became a bagman, his father never spoke to him again.

"My father was a lot like you, Paul. He kept to himself, never talked much, knew he was in the wrong business but it was too late to quit. If he quit, he would be killed. He knew what kind of money he was carrying in his bag, and he hated it. In that way, he was not like you. You told me that for ten years you slept nights. He never slept. He would wake up and feel sick about what he carried. But I understand you, Paul. You were doing nothing wrong. You had nothing to do with what that money represented. You were delivering the mail like a mailman. You didn't ever think where it came from."

Paul eyes slid shut. She read his silence.

"You were born with three strikes against you, Paul. You had no reason to feel guilty, for doing what you had to."

"I did once. Feel guilty. I shot a boy who shot at me."

"You thought he was going to hijack your bag?"

"Yes."

"Then it was self-defense, Paul. That's not the kind of guilt I'm talking about."

Michelle slipped out of bed, slowly paced. Her bare feet on the rug made no sound.

"One day an informer who hated my father gave his name to the police. His bosses found out. He knew they would never believe him that he'd been loyal. He got a forged passport under the name Valour and he flew to Paris, to his old friend, Captain Lafitte."

The baby woke up crying. Michelle changed its diaper, and went on with the story in a low, soft voice. "Years before, my father had been in Paris on business. That's when he first met Lafitte. They met at a bar, I guess, went drinking and whoring together. Lafitte told him he was trying to track down an old Resistance fighter. He gave my father the man's name. He'd heard he was in New York. When my father returned to New York, he made it his business to find the man. He sent Lafitte the address. Lafitte and his friend wrote letters to each other until his friend died."

The baby fell asleep again with the monkey held very close. Michelle sat on the side of the bed. "My father hid on this barge. Lafitte never asked him why. No visitors ever came on the barge until one day Lafitte introduced my father to Camille Bourgois, his old comrade's daughter. They fell in love. Lafitte brought a priest to the barge one afternoon, another former Resistance man, and quietly they got married.

"Then my father heard, through the only man he trusted in America, his lawyer, who grew up with him, that on his deathbed the informer had cleared my father's name. All was forgiven! His bosses wanted him back, wanted him to work for them again. My mother was pregnant. They needed the money. The lawyer advised my father to return without his wife and to never mention her name. If the mafia learned about her...well, you know what they expect from a bagman. No attachments. Anyway, that's what my father did. He went back to New York and for very good pay became a hit man."

Michelle stretched out next to Paul. "Every week he sent

money back, for me. I wasn't born yet, but he wanted to take care of me. My mother wrote him every week, through the lawyer. I was coming early. My mother was hysterical. No time to call a doctor. No time to get a midwife."

Michelle paused.

"Lafitte delivered me."

She sat up, propped the pillow behind her head.

"My mother died a year later. Cancer of the kidney. She was young, but that's what happens. I grew up on this barge. When I was five, Lafitte brought me by bus to the school every morning and picked me up every night. Lafitte had no trouble explaining me to the authorities. He told them my father was dead and he didn't want to put me in an orphanage. He was a Resistance hero, I was the granddaughter of one. The authorities blessed him for giving me a home.

"When I was eighteen, my father stopped sending letters, but the money kept coming. Every week. Less and less, but always something. I couldn't reach him. Lafitte had a telephone number, but his phone had been disconnected. I was frantic. I phoned his lawyer but the lawyer wasn't reachable either. Lafitte arranged for my passport. I flew to New York. Found the lawyer in the hospital—he looked terrible, like a corpse, maybe ninety pounds. Said it was pneumonia. Didn't want to say AIDS. He gave me the address where my father was living, a cheap room in Chinatown, no phone, nothing but a bed. Sick, he was of no use to the mafia anymore. He made a little money stealing, sent me every penny, kept only enough for his room and one meal a day. I found a small furnished apartment, got a job as a cashier. Bought him medicine, food. I had to give him back some of what he had given me all my life.

"That was when I met Frankie Troy. My father met him, didn't like him. But Frankie had money, more than we had, and he promised he'd get a bigger apartment if I married him. I did. My father lived with us at the Saint Charles, without ever saying a word to Frankie. The same week I got pregnant, my father had the stroke that killed him. Frankie said, 'About time.' When my baby was six days old, we left Frankie."

36

Happily piloting his tug into the rising red sun, the engine throbbing, Lafitte blew three sharp whistle blasts. Michelle and Paul
waved back from the barge deck. He was off to pick up a load
of soft drinks. He wondered why the baby favored the monkey
above the other toys. He dreaded the day they would leave him.

Paul and Michelle watched the tug become a silhouetted
speck against the sun, then sat down to have more coffee. They
glanced at the baby in the hammock. The awning shielded him
from the sun. He was pulling on the monkey's tail.

Paul looked through the binoculars, but his mind wasn't on
the faces he saw on the upper deck of the approaching sightseeing boat. The pace of events in Michelle's story last night
crowded his brain. Her bagman father hiding on this same
barge…Lafitte delivering her…her mother's death…her father's
death…Frankie Troy…running away with her baby…Frankie
shot by the gun in the carriage…bomb under the baby…Al and
Eddie…all had led them here. How? And where was it leading
now?

The question brought gigantic pressure. Yet he had no brainquake.

Throb of engine getting weak. Craft in the Seine becoming ghosts.
Banks of the river vanishing. Rays getting cold.

Then Lafitte saw him.

Red sun became the red face of General Petain, hero of Verdun
in the Great War of 1915, traitor of World War II in 1940. For
decades, the Petain nightmare had ravaged Lafitte's sleep. He

had challenged Petain to explain his treachery, never got a response.

Now Petain was haunting him in the sun.

Lafitte had gotten used to the Petain nightmare like he had gotten used to his own nightmares as a youth fighting the Nazis occupying Paris. Led by Jean Bourgois, he fought Nazis drinking French wine with French collaborators, bombed them and ran. He shot Nazis eating French food at sidewalk tables with French Jew-haters and ran. He shot Nazis fucking French whores and ran. He saw swastika flags flying from the Arc de Triomphe and ambushed Nazi soldiers in side streets. He saw Nazis escorting Hitler down the Champs-Élysées to the Tomb of Napoleon and that night grenaded a truckload of Nazi soldiers.

The recurring Petain nightmare and his own recurring nightmares as a youth were linked. The linkage enraged Lafitte.

Now, he and Petain were alone. Everything was silent as a coffin. Petain's giant face was saintly in the sun. His eyes of compassion met Lafitte's eyes of contempt. Then Lafitte's fallen idol broke decades of bitter silence.

Captain Lafitte, it's time we had a talk.

General Petain, what is your defense?

Let me remind you, first, that I fought the Kaiser.

You were a Frenchman then. You stopped being a Frenchman when you went over on Hitler's side.

I was never pro-Hitler.

Why didn't you fight him?

It was wiser not to.

That's traitor talk!

I was never a traitor.

Then why did you order us to stop fighting Hitler?

Two million Germans were about to invade Paris.

We were at war, goddam it! In war we fight the invaders. We should have died fighting Hitler. Foch would have died fighting him. Joffre would have died fighting him. Were you afraid to die? Were you too old and wanted to live? Is that why you kissed Hitler's ass? To live?

It was mass killing season for Hitler.

You should have died fighting him.

Then millions of French corpses would have been swept into Hitler's ash-heap of history.

You shamed us!

I saved you.

Saved us? You became Premier of France under Hitler, goddam it! You had a big office, a big desk, hundreds of guards to protect you. You lived like a dictator. You lived like Hitler! You posed with Hitler while Frenchmen were put into concentration camps. You posed with Hitler knowing French would fight French as you signed the surrender truce!

Those French casualties would be small. I had to prevent France from becoming a nationwide graveyard.

You collaborated with Hitler!

Wrong. I knew one day he would lose. All dictators in history have lost. I had to save France.

You are saying what you did was heroic?

Yes.

You are saying you saved France?

Yes. I alone saved France.

Then goddam it, General Petain, tell me why you were convicted of treason against France when Hitler lost the war in 1945?

The face of Petain vanished. His tears remained, streaks of yellow along the red face of the sun.

The baby was still playing with the monkey's tail. Michelle was reading the *Herald Tribune*. Paul was looking at the faces on the upper deck of another sightseeing boat.

He suddenly shook.

Sitting alone in a rear seat, in a brown jacket, smoking a cigarette, was Eddie.

His hand holding the binoculars shook and he lost Eddie. Forcing the glasses hard against his eyes, he focused to the limit.

Eddie's face was big as life.

Paul waited for the sound of the flute. It didn't come. He waited for the brainquake. It didn't come.

Not a touch of pink in Eddie. Binoculars moved to other people. All natural colors.

Binocs went back to Eddie sitting there.

"Eddie's on that boat."

Michelle put down the newspaper. "Brainquake."

"No brainquake."

"Did you hear the flute?"

"No flute."

"Is he pink or reddish?"

"He's for real on that boat. Alone. In the last seat."

Michelle looked at Paul tensely. His cipher face showed no panic. But something in his eyes did. She stood up. Paul stared at her, saw the fear in her face. She grabbed the binoculars, looked through them, saw Eddie in his brown jacket sitting alone on the last seat.

Eddie was looking directly at her as she kept the binoculars on him.

"I don't see him, Paul."

She held out the binocs to him. They slipped from her hands, fell. Eddie saw Paul bending down to pick them up. Eddie stretched out on the last three seats and out of sight. Paul looked through the binoculars.

"He's gone."

"He was never there."

"I saw him."

"So did I. In Normandy."

Paul's head began to ache.

She went on. "I saw Eddie in the baby shop, too. I saw Eddie's face on the Champs-Élysées when I went to get francs. I see Eddie's face everywhere."

The ache grew painful. Her words sounded far away.

"Paul." She gripped his shoulders. "Fear makes me see his face everywhere. Fear made you see his face on that boat. It wasn't a brainquake, but it wasn't real either. Fugitives see men pursuing them. It's normal."

"Normal," Paul repeated.

"Yes, Paul. Normal."

She read his face, watched his eyes as he thought about the word.

"You'll see Eddie's face again, Paul. The fear will be with us until he's dead."

That night Lafitte returned with another gift for the baby. A bowl of fish. He placed it on the table near the crib in their room. He pushed a button on the bottom of the bowl. Next to it was a tiny music box. The music began to play *Swan Lake*. He held the baby up close to the bowl.

The baby was infatuated.

Lafitte smiled. "He thinks the fish are making the music." The baby reached his hand out. Lafitte moved the table closer. The baby felt the bowl, watched the fish dart. Music played.

Michelle stood, hands clenched. "I need to take a walk."

Paul understood. It was the music. He nodded.

Michelle walked up the cement ramp to the phone booth, called Eddie in his hotel room and gave him the next step.

✿

Early next morning the sun threw Father Flanagan's huge shadow across the crowded yard of the orphanage. He was sweating under his holy garb. Sweat not from his clothes or the sun. Sweat from memories. On the outskirts of Paris, he had found the 14th-century monastery that had become an orphanage. Mentioned last night by a young whore in her bed. She had heard it was the biggest one in France. She was right. It covered six acres of ground.

He had never seen so many happy children. He watched them play near the stone fountain. The nuns were there, and the children clearly adored them.

He concentrated on how they treated the kids. The Mother Superior was his guide. His knowledge of the Carthusian Order impressed her.

The Mother Superior had shown him where the babies slept. He observed no scarcity of nuns taking care of the infants. Observed how children in the cloisters and in the yard were handled.

He didn't find an unhappy child.

He saw the children's library, and their classrooms that were once the monks' workshops. All the children were dressed well. He noted how the older ones showed respect for the mausoleum. He watched them play games.

They loved their home. It was not a prison.

Back in Paris he drove his rental car through streets, satisfied about the future of the baby he was going to make an orphan.

Suddenly he pulled up to the curb. *Jesus Christ!*

The advancing black flagpole towering over everyone was Zara. From New York, it was, it could be no one else. It was the first time he'd seen her in person, but he knew her instantly, recognized her from countless appearances on television and in newspapers, magazines. Lieutenant Zara, here, no doubt pursuing the same people he was. Or pursuing him.

She strode past him. Every click of her high heels deadly without missing a beat.

He got out, followed the tall dead cop heading across the street toward an eight-story stone building fronted by a high black iron-barred fence. Atop each bar, a huge spike was painted in garish gold. There was no gate. She pushed the buttons on the door code box, went in. He caught the door before it closed. She went into the elevator. He stepped in behind her.

Pushing 6, she nodded at the priest. He nodded back, pushed 8. Door slid shut. As they ascended, he knew where he was. A few years ago he had found a room in one of the same official-looking structures that had been converted into apartments. No hotel. Rooms rented by the month. Cheap. Concierge to clean stairs, rooms and take care of the mail.

Elevator stopped at 6. Door slid open. She took one step out.

He rabbit-punched her from behind. She slumped in his arms. Before she could move or catch her breath, he slammed his fist into the side of her face—once, twice, three times. One more. Her leg stopped the door from closing. He stepped back, pulled her in. Door slid shut. He wiped his prints off the elevator button.

The door slid open on the eighth floor. He poked his head out. Corridor empty. Sound of a phone could be heard ringing. He dragged her toward the stairs, opened the door, hauled her up the stairs to the roof door, opened it.

Across the roof. He carried her to the edge. Placing her down, he studied the distance of fence from building, waited until the sidewalk below was clear of pedestrians, picked her up, biceps straining under her weight, teeth gritted, and flung her away from the roof.

As he hurried back to the door, he heard screams from the street. He wiped off prints on both knobs, noiselessly flew down the stairs, wiped off prints from the eighth-floor knobs, continued down the stairs to the basement door, opened it, wiped off prints from knob, exited to the alley behind the building, walked around to the front.

A shocked crowd had already collected.

Zara lay across the spikes.

Father Flanagan noted that one spike had penetrated her neck.

Blood and gold on the spike's tip sparkled in the sun.

37

He murdered her sure as hell. The fact clawed inside him. He stared at his lamb chops on the plate. He was at his favorite outdoor table. Fouquet's luncheon crowd was buzzing. Around him horse talk. Everyone had a favorite.

Father Flanagan didn't use the word murder lightly. Zara was not on his death list. She was an obstacle. He'd had to act fast. He'd had to make sure the bloodhound wouldn't find the two fugitives before he did. Had she, Mr. Hampshire would have been furious at him. He knew the importance of nailing that bagman.

All the same, Father Flanagan felt like vomiting on his empty stomach. He should have bypassed Zara. He should have cornered the two fugitives alone.

Never had he hit an obstacle.

It was not a hit but a murder. And in murdering Zara he had become emotional. It degraded him.

He couldn't think himself out of that emotion.

He had to cut that emotion out of his system or throw in the towel.

He attacked his lamb chops, watched the women at nearby tables. A blonde, a brunette. Forced himself to see them nude. Rarely did he have to force himself. Normally it happened naturally, and it always gave him comfort, seeing the women around him as naked. Often just picturing them naked in his mind was more satisfying than actually seeing them naked in a bedroom. This one, the blonde, in the flower-print dress, with the heavy breasts and prominent chin—what would she look like undressed, her brassiere unhooked, her breasts released to swing freely?

And her friend, slightly older, her hair cut short as a man's, no ass to speak of, barely any bosom, would she look boyish underneath, or did that shapeless dress hide a woman's shape after all, a quivering wet snatch and gem-hard nipples? His mind traveled over this imagined landscape and his breathing slowed to normal, his feelings of shame forgotten, quelled.

He was roused from his reverie by a taxi, forced to brake not far from his front-row table. The driver honked angrily for the traffic jam up ahead to clear.

Father Flanagan heard the driver telling his passengers the worst drivers in the world were Paris drivers. One of his passengers laughed, a huge gray-haired man in sailor's cap and jacket.

The woman by the window, holding a baby, was darker-skinned, looked Mediterranean. Black hair. Giant earring. Funky black-and-orange striped blouse. The baby was holding some kind of toy. Next to the woman was a bearded man with his hair in a ponytail. Next to him was the sea captain.

The impatient honking of the taxi driver was joined by a chorus of honks and shouts behind him. The toy fell from the baby's hands and it began to cry. The beard bent down, picked up the toy, gave it to the baby.

The toy was a monkey with a long tail.

The murder in Central Park crossed Father Flanagan's mind. He saw the beard looking at the baby, who had now stopped crying. The man's eyes startled Father Flanagan. They looked familiar. They were strange, lifeless eyes. Looking into them was like looking at gray clouds.

Father Flanagan tried to imagine the face without the beard, the way he'd imagined the women without their clothes on.

What he saw was the picture of Paul Page on the front page of newspapers and on TV.

The beard was the bagman.

The disguise made sense. Paris was exploding with music fans for the festival. Smartest thing the two fugitives could do was blend in with the sea of ex-hippies and young people in funky gear.

The traffic jam broke. The taxi lurched forward. Father Flanagan memorized the license number, threw a handful of francs on the table, dove behind the wheel of his rental, and tailed the bagman, widow and baby.

He would wait until they were alone. He didn't want to kill the old sea captain as a witness—no collateral damage this time. He kept a couple of cars between them. Traffic was thick. They couldn't go fast to lose him.

He ruled out crucifixion. He never used a gun on the job. He didn't trust guns. They often jammed at the wrong moment, like a condom breaking at the wrong moment. He'd have to use the switchblade he detested. It had no class. A knife was so goddam amateurish. Messy. Used only in an emergency.

But that's what this was.

In the taxi the baby kept tugging at the monkey's long tail. Michelle regretted she couldn't find a moment to phone Eddie. The crowd at the track would have been a perfect place for Eddie to do his act. Perfect and safe.

Staging Eddie's performance today would have helped the momentum in her plan. But tomorrow night's event would make up for it.

Lafitte was worried. "Hank, if you score on that long shot in the third race, are you going to move on?"

"No. We like the barge."

"You're welcome to stay as long as you want."

"Thanks."

❖

The track's parking lot was packed. Father Flanagan joined the line of cars, each hunting for a space. He spotted Paul and Michelle getting out of the cab. Without being obvious, he studied their clothes. Her black-and-orange striped blouse would be as easy to follow as Paul's faded red shirt hanging over rumpled Levis. Both were wearing beat-up sneakers. Lafitte slipped the rucksack on his back. Paul put the baby in it. The baby was hanging onto the monkey.

"Pardon me, Father." The cop saluted. "It's illegal to park here. You'll find space over there."

"Thank you, Officer."

The cop saluted again.

Father Flanagan found a space, locked the car, moved swiftly through the crowd swarming toward the ticket booths. In the distance he spotted the tall sea captain and the baby on his back.

Then he lost sight of them.

He pushed through to the ticket booth. Spotting the priest, people stepped aside to let him pass.

"Thank you," Father Flanagan said. "I've got to find a lost soul…a parishioner of mine…if he loses today, his wife will leave him."

He bought a ticket, plunged into people. All kinds. Teenagers. Couples. Elderly. Young gamblers. And plenty of people from the music festival. The colors worn by the young music fans made him dizzy. Many were dressed like the fugitives. Some carried babies and guitars on their backs.

The first race was announced. A roar from the crowd blasted Father Flanagan's ears. He lost his targets. Several times he thought he located them. Located a couple, anyway, but on second glance they were not dressed quite the same as the fugitives. Orange and black, red over blue…

Horses thundered toward the home stretch. The crowd went wild. He spotted the sea captain again.

Then, not far away, Paul and Michelle, backs toward him.

He knifed both of them. They fell. A woman's scream was drowned out by the roar of the crowd. Another woman screamed. She was heard. People pushed the priest aside. He was close enough to make sure they were dead.

But the ponytailed man in jeans and the woman beside him were not the bagman and the widow.

38

That night in drunken shock Father Flanagan wandered through Place du Tertre in Montmartre. People were blurs. The long flame blown out of the mouth of an entertainer was a blur. Hands seized the priest, pulled him away as he came close to walking into the second blow of flame.

He slumped into a chair outside a café, asked for a whiskey, planted his arms on the table, dropped his head on them. The glass of whiskey was placed in front of the sleeping priest. The sleep was short-lived. Sleep couldn't alibi that he had fucked up. The first time in his life he had hit the wrong targets.

Christ!

He had washed himself out of his trade. He was a goddam amateur. He had lost his mind. He had lost his vision. He had lost everything. The noise around him made him think that he was still at the track.

He raised his head enough to see the blur shimmering in front of him. The café neon brought out the color he had known for years. He slowly moved his fingers toward the blur, closed them around the glass without raising his head higher, downed the whiskey. He blamed Zara.

She had shaken him up, invaded his timing, aborted his caution. He was never that impatient. He should have walked in front of the beard, looked into his eyes. But he didn't. He had never jumped the gun before, never acted until he was certain.

He shouldn't have murdered them. Now he had murdered himself. He shouted for two more whiskies, saw two more shimmering blurs placed in front of him. He drank one, dozed off, fingers still clutching the empty glass. Through his semi-doze, he faintly heard a woman's voice:

"That's better, Skipper."

Father Flanagan slept.

Lafitte, holding the baby on his lap, tilted back the peak of his cap, which was half-hiding the baby's face. A sketch of the baby was being made by an attractive artist.

"You're American," Lafitte said.

"I'm an international omelet," Jacqueline said. "So you won at the races today?"

"Not me. My American friend here won on Red Comet in the third. The only long shot in the field."

Jacqueline glanced at Paul. Next to him was Michelle. Both were still shaking about the double-murder at the track. They knew they were the targets. The victims were dressed like them. Lafitte holding the baby was close to them when it happened. The killer was either Eddie or the mob.

Jacqueline said, "You were there when that man and woman were knifed? I heard it on the radio…"

Lafitte shrugged. "It was a shock, but the races had to go on."

"Hold still."

Father Flanagan stopped dozing long enough to pull the full glass to his lips. He sipped the whiskey and with one eye saw the blur of a baby, the blur of Lafitte, the blur of Paul, the blur of Michelle.

Father Flanagan's gaze rolled back to Jacqueline's pencil sketching the face of the baby.

Then his eye rolled back to Paul. Slowly, through the blur, Paul's eyes came into focus. Only for a second, but that second was enough to recognize Paul's eyes. Father Flanagan tried to raise his head higher, tried to get his arms off the table, tried to stand up.

His head dropped back on his arms. He saw the bagman's eyes. But Father Flanagan was drained of strength. He fought passing out. Whiskey won the bout. He fell asleep. But in his sleep he hung onto his last thread of knowing he had seen the bagman.

A couple hours later Father Flanagan woke up. A young man was sitting at the table. He was being sketched by Jacqueline.

"Does it look like me?" the young man said.

"Coming along," Jacqueline said.

"Coming along," Father Flanagan said, waving for another drink, "isn't enough, Rembrandt."

Jacqueline took the barb in stride. She smiled. She was polite. "I never charge for a portrait until it *is* right, Father. I'm no bluenose, Father, but I think another whiskey'll put you back to sleep."

Father Flanagan smiled. She was friendly. She liked to talk. Attractive, too. Not hard to handle. "What's your name?"

"Jacqueline. What's yours?"

"Flanagan. New York."

"Midland, Texas."

"You don't sound like a Texan."

"Find me a Texan who does."

They laughed. The young man was annoyed.

"Are you concentrating on my sketch?" he said.

"All the time," Jacqueline said. "Just about finished."

She added a few strokes and produced it. The young man beamed, paid her and left.

"How about you, Father?"

He nodded. She turned her chair around enough to face him.

"You're the first priest I've sketched. I had a rabbi, two ministers, and a baldheaded religious leader of some new sect."

"And babies."

"Some."

"One earlier tonight."

"How would you know? You were asleep."

"Not the whole time."

"Close enough."

She worked for a bit in silence.

"I like your work, Jacqueline," Father Flanagan said. "What I saw of it."

"This is nothing," she said, sketching. "This is to pay the bills. Give me an hour to do a proper drawing and you'll see something you'll like."

They heard the cash register ring in the café.

"Know what that bell just rang up, Jacqueline?"

"A sale."

He smiled. "I've got an hour if you do."

"You really want to, Father?"

"Why not?"

"I'd have to charge you more."

"I'm not rich, Jacqueline, but art is the best use of money. Think of the great frescos commissioned by the Church."

She glanced up from the sketch. "I would have thought you'd say charity was the best use."

"They're equal. Food sustains the body, art the soul."

"Fifty dollars?"

"All right."

She swiftly gathered up her equipment. "Let's do it in my place. You'll be more comfortable."

Her place was a one-room apartment on Impasse Trainee, around the corner. It was a very small street.

"Even smaller than the street named after Cezanne," Jacqueline said as she continued to sketch him.

From where he sat for her, he had a fine view of paintings and sketches hanging on the walls. She glanced up now and then, pleased how he studied each one.

He turned his head slightly to admire the bust of a baby on a pedestal.

"You sculpt, too?"

"I wish I could. Bought it at the Flea Market, cheap, brushed it up. It was so dirty."

"What did you pay for it?"

"Three hundred francs."

"Who made it?"

"No name on it."

"I'm reminded of the baby you sketched earlier tonight. Do you know I thought his parents looked familiar?"

"Could be. They were American, too."

"That would be extraordinary. I've been looking for the father. He was in my parish some years ago."

"You should have come over, said hello."

"I should. I should."

"Paris is a small town in some ways, Father. Maybe you'll run into them again."

"They didn't say anything, did they, about where they were staying?"

Jacqueline thought for a moment. "They didn't, but the old man…it was his idea to sketch the baby, the parents wanted to go home. The old man said he wanted the sketch to hang it up on his barge."

"Barge? A sketch for a barge?"

"Oh, many barges have become houseboats. People live on them. Deck them out nicely: real bedrooms, nice furniture. Haven't you ever dreamed of living on a boat?"

"Not a barge."

"Don't be a snob. A boat's a boat." Jacqueline changed her

pencil for a softer one, began shading his eyelids and around his cheekbones. "It's a dream I've always had. To live on a boat that's a real home. Plenty of space. And paint and sketch on the deck."

"Did the old man say which barge?"

Jacqueline squinted, trying to remember. "He did… Damn it, I can't remember…oh sorry, Father…"

"That's all right. I've heard worse swearing in the confessional." He smiled warmly. "But are you sure you can't recall?"

"What was it? Jules? No. Jacques? No. Jean! It was Jean something…two names…I should remember. It rang a bell when I heard it. Jean Bourgois! Of course! The Resistance guy, the one they made that documentary about. That's the name of his houseboat, the *Jean Bourgois*."

Father Flanagan stood up, smashed her head in with the bust of the baby. Saw the baby's eyes tilted on the floor staring up at him through her blood and hair.

He ripped the sketch of himself from the pad, crumpled it, wiped his prints off the bust, used his handkerchief to place it back on the floor near her. With the handkerchief, he opened the door and closed it behind him.

39

At midnight Lafitte was asleep in his room. The moonlight coming through his window illuminated the sketch of the baby on the wall. It was signed by the artist: *J Sterling—Montmartre, Paris*.

Lafitte tossed in his bed. Sweat began to cover his face. It was his recurring nightmare.

Jean Bourgois was facing the Nazi firing squad. The air was tinged with yellow. Bourgois turned his unmasked head and his eyes met the eyes of young Lafitte. It was high noon. Lafitte was standing with a large group of French civilians forced to watch the execution of the enemy of the Reich. Behind the civilians stood armed German soldiers, their Schmeissers ready to blow apart any civilian that turned his head away from Jean Bourgois. Lafitte heard the order: "Ready, aim—"

Lafitte cringed as he heard the word "Fire!" He heard the squad firing. Jean Bourgois, lashed to a pole with his hands tied behind his back, was riddled by the automatic machine gun bullets. His head slumped. The officer of the firing squad shot one bullet from his revolver into the head that hung already dead.

Lafitte pulled the blanket over his head, crying like a baby.

In their room the baby was asleep in the crib. Its tiny fingers held the monkey close. Michelle was in bed staring up at the ceiling. Paul was at the window staring at lights on the bank. Silence hung in the room.

Each knew how close they had come to death.

Whatever they had to say about it had been said. Now, in the quiet of a tomb, thoughts of survival crowded their minds.

A soft blue light was on. Its softness conveyed tranquility. And safety. It never kept the baby from sleeping.

Paul knew there was only one way to relieve the agony Michelle was going through. He would go back to New York, surrender to Pegasus, return the money, what was left, and throw himself on their mercy. If they let him live, he would go to the cops and explain to them why Michelle shot Al. It had been self-defense. They wouldn't pursue her for defending herself.

He turned around very slowly to tell her what he'd decided when he heard the sound of the flute and the rumble in his head.

He tried to hold it off, but the brainquake came. In reddish pink color he saw Eddie suffocating the baby with a pillow.

Paul suddenly seized the fishbowl and held it high above the baby in the crib. Like a bullet, Michelle sprang from the bed and knocked the bowl out of Paul's hands. It fell and shattered. Fish fought for their lives.

The brainquake ended as quickly as it had come. The crash had awakened the baby. It began to cry.

"Goddam it!" Michelle shouted. "You're crazy!"

"Eddie was…was suffocating the baby."

Michelle slapped him across the face, the full force of her rage behind the blow. "Eddie's not here, Paul. I told you that. You're just seeing things!"

"Brainquake…"

"I don't care! I don't care what it is. I've had enough of your goddam attacks. I can't have you in the same room as my baby. I can't risk his life around you."

Paul looked down at the shattered bowl and the dead fish. He looked down at the crying baby he could have killed. He'd

been lost in his brainquake. He didn't know what was real anymore and what was hallucination. If she hadn't knocked the
bowl out of his hands...

"I'll go," he said, and reached under the bed for the bag.

Michelle was breathing hard, holding the baby now, stroking
its head. Her face paled as she realized he meant it. Swiftly
Michelle ran to him, seized him, turned him around, held him
close with her free arm.

"I'm sorry, Paul. I'm sorry. I know you have no control over it."

"But you're right. I have to go."

She put her hand over his. "We're both on the brink after
what happened today. I've got to help you, Paul. I want to help
you."

"Nobody can help me."

"I can, I promise."

"It'll happen again. I'll see Eddie, and I'll hurt the baby.
Might kill him. Can't take that risk."

"Eddie's in New York." She gripped him hard. "Just keep
telling yourself that. He's not here. He's probably dead already.
Your bosses killed him, back in New York, like they killed those
two people at the racetrack. There's danger here, yes, but it's
not from Eddie!"

The baby kept crying. Paul was staring through the baby.

Michelle set the baby down in its crib, gave it the monkey,
came back to Paul. "Please, don't give up. You can sleep in
another room. Or I'll stay with you every second. I'll watch you
close. No matter what you see, I'll stop you from hurting the
baby. I'll be there to stop you from hurting him no matter what
you do."

She led him to the bed, sat him down on it, dropped on her
knees and clenched his hands.

"You're not crazy, Paul. That jackal in your brain is, but you're
not. Paul, please listen to every word I say and fill your brain with

those words. Eddie is not here. He'll never find us. Believe
that! Say it!"

"Eddie will never find us."

"Eddie isn't here!"

"Eddie isn't here."

"Say it again, Paul!"

"Eddie isn't here."

She kissed his hands, then his face, then his lips.

"Michelle…" Paul said very softly.

"Yes, Paul?"

"Thank you for trusting me."

Tears rolled down his cheeks. It was the second time she saw
him in tears.

40

The morning was turning out to be the most enjoyable hunt in Father Flanagan's career. He loved boats. All kinds and sizes, sail or engine. Now he was a kid steering his small rental outboard, slowly passing at close range a world of its own in the heart of Paris.

He was on a joyride. No strategy, no complicated tactics this time. So he took his time. Why rush? Why not take advantage of put-putting past all the faces and enjoy them? The bagman and the widow were smart to hole up on a moored barge. But a barge with a name on it wasn't smart.

Except for the one he was looking for, the French names on the barges didn't interest him. Though the funny ones amused him. All over the world owners of boats had a sense of humor.

The decks of the houseboats all had individual touches reflecting the owner's taste. The extremely long and very wide holds once filled with various cargoes were now arch-roofed. In the holds that now had windows with curtains, the inhabitants lived.

He saw no one on any of the roofs.

But the wide decks were bristling with life.

He didn't care much for naming a barge *Jean D'Arc* until he saw a topless beauty in a bikini on its deck taking a sun bath. She heard his outboard, turned, smiled at him.

"Good morning, Father."

"Good morning."

He passed more barges moored close to each other. Sometimes he had trouble seeing the name on the stern, but he always got the name on the prow. A few barges looked unoccupied, their decks victims of decay. But the majority of decks had had incredible facelifts, were painted in different colors, boasted all kinds of box flowers and a variety of plants. There were deck chairs, wooden chairs, rocking chairs, hammocks, even a small wreck of a car used as a chicken roost.

Aboard the deck of *Left Bank Lovers* a husband and wife were arguing. On *Amour* two boys were riding tricycles. On *Cezanne III* an aged artist at his easel was working on a seascape. On *French Fry* a man playing the harmonica to his dog. On *Best Seller* a woman typing. On *Mare Nostrum* three teenagers playing guitar and singing to an older couple, presumably their parents.

He gave little thought to retiring, as a rule. But Jacqueline's comments had stayed with him and he thought now about the idea of spending his declining years living on a barge like one of these. He could buy one, moor it somewhere isolated, and spend the rest of his life on deck writing a book on hit men. He'd name no names. He'd prove, with examples, that all victims were informers or thieves and deserved to be hit.

Aboard *Angel* twins were crying in a hammock. The red-haired mother began to swing the hammock gently. The babies stopped crying. Their daddy appeared.

"Leave the baby in an orphanage." Hampshire's last words had been tossed away like a crumpled pack of cigarettes. Father Flanagan bristled as he remembered those words. How callous of Hampshire. The cardinal sin was the abandonment of a baby. It was criminal to have a baby dumped and for the baby to grow up knowing it was unwanted, unloved, unnamed. Anyone dumping a baby deserved to be crucified.

Father Flanagan suddenly felt absurd nursing such thoughts. What the hell! He had been an orphan-maker for years and it had never bothered him.

But this time it did. Up to now it had never been a baby he'd orphaned. A grown child was different. A baby...

He went back to contemplating his book. He would tell how things had changed since the days of Murder, Inc. He would point out that today only the elite like him were on annual retainers aside from the big fee for making a hit. He would tell the reader the majority of hit men were good, but not top quality. He would tell how crude they were; how careless; how innocent bystanders were shot.

He had heard that Zara's grandfather, the first black to command the Vice Squad, was also the first victim of the newly patched-together Murder, Inc. A picture of her grandfather hung at Police Headquarters.

The thought brought back the Zara sickness. It wasn't just her death that displeased him, it was his method. Zara deserved a far more noble hit. He would miss hearing about her on the news, in the papers, imagining that powerful black body of hers naked.

The idea of her in bed seemed like a better idea when she was alive.

Now the idea made him feel unclean.

War broke out within Paul. The enemy was himself. He was no longer just fighting the jackal in his brain for his sake. He was also fighting not to have another attack and hurt the baby. Or hurt Michelle. Or hurt them both.

He had no appetite for breakfast. She did. It confused him. How could she be enjoying it, sitting there laughing with Lafitte? Last night he could have killed the baby and now Michelle had forgotten all about it. She knew that he was more danger to them than Eddie or the mob or Paris cops.

Maybe she wasn't really enjoying the breakfast. That's what

it was. She didn't want to let Lafitte know what happened last night.

He met her eyes on him, aware that she had been studying him.

Michelle had noted something different about Paul's eyes. Something new. Something strange. The gray irises remained gray. But something had changed, and it made her nervous.

Lafitte was still laughing about the broken fishbowl. It must've been very cheap glass. He'd get another bowl, new fish.

"Better yet," Lafitte was enthusiastic, "I'll find some toy that plays music! They were sold out at the shop, but I'll find one. A nice music box inside that will play a nursery rhyme." He laughed. "And he'll think the giraffe or lion is playing the music!"

Lafitte didn't notice the lines at either side of Michelle's jaw tightening as he spoke. He carried on, oblivious, barreling through the remains of his own fears, the burden of his own memories. He was wearing the jubilant mask he had worn every day for the nearly fifty years since the war ended. His persona of a lusty, happy, two-fisted brawler with an explosive passion for life had fooled everybody. Even Michelle, who had lived with him for eighteen years. Some days he even fooled himself. But not today.

It was getting too dark to read the names on the barges. The sun was down. Father Flanagan checked his map. He had quite a distance to go yet before he reached the end of that bank. He had enjoyed the ham-and-cheese baguette and coffee from the thermos he had brought along for lunch. Now he was getting hungry again. He turned back. There was no great rush. They had nowhere to go. He found a landmark from which he would continue his boat ride first thing in the morning.

He increased speed as night fell, anxious to shower and enjoy dinner watching the beautiful nudes at the tables at Fouquet's. He passed an illuminated sightseeing boat packed with passengers and roared past Lafitte's tug without a glance.

The tug began to buck like a bronco. Michelle was holding the baby close with one arm. The other hand hugged the edge of the pilot house entrance. Paul was holding onto the opposite side of the entrance. Both were wearing a new set of old clothes, still from the pile Johnson had provided.

"I told you we'd buck when we hit the estuary," Lafitte said. "Same as in the U.S.A. Hauled barges there for a couple of years —you didn't know that, did you? I did. But New York wasn't for me. Streets were too dangerous. Coffee and crime for breakfast and street fighting every night. You know, Hank, I still don't understand you Yankees. I never saw such *life* in American faces until they talked about violent death…and today… holy smoke!…New York's a battlefield." He glanced at his watch. "We'll just about be in time for the beginning of the fireworks. You know, Hank, you ought to raise young Jean in Paris. There's no shoot-ups in the streets here where babies are killed by a stray bullet. If George Washington came back right now and saw the blood in the streets of New York, his hair would really turn white! Why, today they have kids on crack and kids in street fights and they've even got fan clubs, I heard. When nailed, they have their own TV in their prison cells, so they can watch themselves on the news. They're celebrities. Hell, Paul, even your hamburgers are happy grave-diggers." He laughed. "And I'm a sucker for them!"

The tug bucked more. Paul and Michelle held fast to keep their balance until at last the restaurant hove into view and the bucking stopped.

✿

Miniature American and French flags were standing on every outside and inside table at Lafayette Restaurant. The tables were crowded with happy diners. Waiters in Uncle Sam suits with high hats were busy popping champagne corks. At the piano, another Uncle Sam was playing *Yankee Doodle Dandy*, then other American favorites, such as *God Bless America*.

Champagne made every customer a Caruso.

The baby, with its bottle and monkey, was rigged high in a child's chair. On the attached plank in front of him was his baby food. He was sitting between Lafitte and Michelle. Facing them was Paul. Candles on outside tables were flickering in the soft wind. On the inside table, the candles remained subdued.

The main course was strictly American-style with spare ribs, mashed potatoes and gravy. The first of the lights in the sky burst red, white, and blue as Uncle Sam played *The Star-Spangled Banner*.

Lafitte nudged Michelle, tapped Paul's ankle under the table. They looked at the baby seeing the explosions in the sky, rockets coming from all directions, crossing each other, sputtering into blackness.

The baby was hypnotized by the sight. He reached up with his tiny fingers trying to grab the falling sparks. He laughed. Then awe wiped his face clean. Then he laughed again.

During a lull, the owner made a brief speech in French and in English about the historic friendship between America and France. The diners applauded.

More champagne corks popped through the restaurant. Paul was on his second glass of champagne.

"I don't believe you, Zozo," Michelle was saying.

"We've been rehearsing. Honest!"

"Prove it."

Paul and Michelle watched Lafitte lean closer to the baby.

"Young Jean," Lafitte said, ignoring the hum of voices around and the piano playing George M. Cohan's *Over There*.

The baby stared at him, waiting, as if he understood.

"You Jean, what do you think is the world's greatest invention?"

The baby stared.

"The telephone?"

The baby stared.

"Electricity?"

The baby stared.

"Diapers?"

The baby farted and laughed.

Michelle burst into laughter. Lafitte proudly kissed the baby on the nose.

On the piano Uncle Sam was playing *Roll Out the Barrel*.

Slightly dizzy, too much to drink, Paul excused himself and rose.

"In the back of the bar, Hank."

Paul nodded, moved through waiters and tables, went into the john, relieved himself, washed his hands with warm water, then his face with cold. It made him feel better. But he had a kind of bitter, mustard taste in his stomach. There must be a reason people drank alcohol. Then he shrugged. Must everything have a reason?

He opened the door and heard the flute.

In increasingly reddish pink Eddie fired a gun at him. The gunshot exploded, flame spitting. Paul slammed the door in his face.

An instant later a diner opened it, brushed past Paul. Paul was rooted to the floor. The red around everything's edges was redder than ever. Dazedly he walked like a robot between the tables. He knew what had happened. The second time he had almost killed the baby had brought him closer to that red explosion, the one that would end his illness the way it had ended his father's. In his mind, moving like lava, the brainquake tore through healthy tissue, left devastation in its path. For an instant he wished last night's attack had been the final one, the big red one. It was a plea for escape from the illness.

If he died like his father, right here, now, in this restaurant? Michelle and the baby would be safe from him. Alive, what good was he?

He found their table and sat down very slowly. Michelle knew at once from the sweat covering his face.

"Another one?" The words came out uncontrollably.

Paul nodded. "Eddie fired at me."

"Who's Eddie?" Lafitte asked, concerned. Paul's face was so wet. "He fired at you?"

Michelle was quick. "He has terrible headaches."

"Migraine?"

"Worse," Paul said. "I see things. People who aren't there. All in pink."

"So do I," Lafitte said, astonished.

The statement hit Paul like a hammer blow.

"You do?"

"Not in pink," Lafitte said. "In yellow."

"Do you hear a flute?"

"Just gunshots, and everything colored yellow."

Paul was speechless.

"We're visionaries, Hank," Lafitte said, attempting bluster, a hearty joke. But the air went out of him like a punctured tire. "We're visionaries," he said softly. "God help us. Better than He helped Joan of Arc."

Michelle was staring at Lafitte. "What people do you see in your visions, Zozo?"

"Your grandfather."

Michelle reached out and squeezed Lafitte's hand.

"When Jean died in the war, I died with him. When the bullets went through him, they went through me at the same time. He bled. I bled inside."

"You've had those hallucinations all these years, Zozo?"

Lafitte nodded, withdrew his hand and turned to Paul.

"Hank, a helluva lot of people have visions. In all different colors. And they hear a lot of crazy things like thunder or an ear-busting waterfall. Hell, some of the greatest brains in history had hallucinations. They're terrible, but you learn, a man can live with all sorts of terrible things."

"Or he can die," Paul said.

No, no, don't be foolish! Lafitte wanted to say. *Buck up! Another drink for my friend!* The old bluster. But what he said was:

"Or he can die."

41

Michelle felt she was walking a tightrope. One more bad attack where he thought he might hurt the baby and Paul would run off. With or without the bag? Christ! Either way was disaster. With, and she was left with nothing. She'd come too far to be left with nothing now. But if he ran without the bag it would be even worse. Stuck with those millions was the last thing she wanted now. The mob would never call off the hunt for the bag until he died, and only if he died exactly *when* and exactly *how* she had planned.

She had to keep him close to her until D-Day.

She said, "It was healthy you talked about Eddie in front of Lafitte."

That confused him. Good.

"Yes, Paul...talking about Eddie was very healthy."

He turned his head. Her eyes were in moonlight. She was right that he was thinking about Eddie. But he didn't know why it was good to talk about him to Lafitte.

"Paul, talking about Eddie made you realize he wasn't real. *I* saw Eddie tonight in the restaurant. It was a waiter with Eddie's face. Know what I did? I laughed. Not out loud. Inside, Paul. I laughed at his damn illusion. You know what else I did? I shut him out of my mind for good. So can you, Paul. In childhood you had the willpower to learn to talk...to read...to write... Know why you didn't stay a vegetable? One word, Paul. *Willpower*. It means strength of mind. Say it."

"Willpower." He thought of his mother making him repeat words.

"Use it, Paul, like you did when you were growing up. Laugh

at Eddie. Don't let him help the jackal kill you like it killed your father. With me you'll have double willpower. Never run away from me. Double willpower will knock the hell out of that jackal. Alone you will be weak. With me close to you, your willpower will be strong."

She held him close.

"And our real enemies…in time, Paul, all bloodhounds lose their scent. Even the ones that carry guns."

She let that take root.

"And when the right time comes—and it will come, like it did for my father—we'll go back."

She detected even in the moonlight a slight spark in his eyes.

"You'll return the money. You'll explain. Your boss will understand."

The spark in his eyes remained.

"I'll tell the cops why I had to shoot Al. They'll understand I ran away because I was frightened of Eddie. Time will make them believe the truth. Time changes people. Time makes enemies friends."

There was a long silence. He broke it.

"And Eddie?"

"He's dead. I'm sure of it. But if he's not, the cops will change his mind, too. He thinks I shot Al in cold blood. He'll feel like a shit when he learns why I really shot him."

The morning sun shimmered on the Seine. After a night of sound sleep, Father Flanagan was guiding his outboard along the opposite bank of the river. He knew he was nearing the end of the hunt.

Today he would spot the *Jean Bourgois*.

He passed all kind of moored craft. On the deck of the *Gorby* an elderly man was wearing a sea captain's cap and an old sweater with a huge anchor emblem, pouring hot milk from an old kettle into a big glass and listening to the radio news. He heard the outboard and grinned at the priest.

"Fishing for sinners, Father?"

"It's a fine morning to catch one."

Even as he laughed, Father Flanagan thought about the skipper of the *Jean Bourgois* and wondered if he was always with them. He didn't want to kill another innocent bystander. It was a matter of pride and a hit man's most degrading fear. It was unpardonable.

Memory brought back an old story about how the Eleventh Commandment—"Thou shalt not hit an innocent"—was born…

Al Capone's two hit men disposed of four rival gangsters at midnight in a closed restaurant…but accidentally killed a young couple sitting in the corner partially hidden by a big plant. The papers crucified Capone. Nobody cared when gangsters killed gangsters, but when innocents were killed…it was very bad public relations for Capone. He wanted people to like him and to keep buying his hijacked whiskey and beer. So he had the bodies of his two hit men dumped in front of Police Headquarters the next night, and people went back to liking Capone and buying his hijacked whiskey and beer.

But those two Capone hit men were young amateurs.

He was an old pro. And he had already killed two innocents.

Of course he believed it was because of Zara. What bullshit! She was no innocent. She was after the same targets. But she'd rattled him…

Way down deep, Father Flanagan knew he was blaming the wrong person. The fuck-up was all his. His reflexes were getting shabby. His eyes were no longer twenty-twenty.

Was it time for him to retire?

He thrust out one hand, studied it. Steady. Firm as Gibraltar. Retire, my ass! Zara was to blame for his shaky concentration at the track!

He immediately felt ashamed of himself. It was a cop-out to make her the patsy.

He had to take the rap. And he did.

He pushed the boat onward. It was early. He would find them.

It hammered Lafitte. Soaked with sweat, his blanket had been kicked on the floor near his pillow. He'd been running through yellow smoke, chased by gunfire. He opened his bloodshot eyes, felt the horrible taste in his mouth, tried to get his bearings. There was no smoke. He was in his bunk. Schmeisser machine guns hadn't burst his eardrums. But they might as well have. The nightmares were getting worse by the day. Each morning, he woke wondering if he could take one more night of it. And today of all days. There had been too many.

Crawling out of bed in rumpled blue pajamas, he poked around, found his slippers under the blanket on the floor. He swayed to the window, stared at musicians rehearsing a free show for the benefit of early birds on the sightseeing boats.

He shuffled to Michelle and Hank's room. Empty. He shuffled to the door, poked his head out toward the deck.

Alone, with the binoculars trained on the musicians, Paul was keeping time with their monotonous beat with one tapping foot. On the table a cup, baguette and butter awaited Lafitte.

"Morning, Hank."

"Morning."

"Where's the family?"

"Stroll along the waterfront."

"About time they baptized that carriage. Any coffee left in that pot?"

"Plenty."

Bringing him the pot, Paul saw Lafitte's agonized wet face. He looked like death. Like Paul's father had just before he died.

"Another rough night, Hank." He looked at Paul at the railing and seemed to reach a decision. "Join you in a minute," he said.

Lafitte shuffled to the galley, put the pot on his electric stove, turned it on. A red light appeared. He shuffled back into his bunk, dropped on his knees and opened his war chest on the floor.

He rummaged through his war mementos…trench knife given to him by an American infantry dogface…GI hand grenade from a sergeant on D plus four days…old Resistance clothes…Nazi potato-masher grenade…SS helmet…French bayonet…Mauser rifle…photo of Nazi truck burning…lethal knives…photo of a blown-up bridge with Jean Bourgois and young Lafitte posing before it…wire to strangle Nazis from behind…crumpled maps …and the Luger given to him by Jean Bourgois.

He picked up the Luger and stared at it. Opened the German pistol, checked the ammo, made sure the safety was on, closed the chest.

Wearing his seaman's cap, he slumped into his deck chair, poured hot coffee, ignored the baguette. He stared at Paul. Paul was watching a distant speck through the binoculars and then made it out. A small boat with an outboard motor. Paul was thinking: why were Lafitte's attacks in yellow, and his in reddish pink?

"Hank."

"Yes?"

"I need to tell you something. This is only between you and me, you understand? You can never tell Michelle. Can never tell anyone."

Paul nodded, pulled his chair to the table, watched Lafitte pour coffee.

"In the war," began Lafitte, "a yacht packed with high-ranking Nazi officers was moving down the Seine."

Lafitte spoke very quietly, but Paul heard the tremor in his voice.

"Jean Bourgois was at the wheel of a tug loaded with high explosives and a mine rigged to blow on impact. Hidden behind a barge, I was waiting in a speedboat to fish him out when he jumped off the tug."

Lafitte sipped his coffee. His cup trembled. The pot hadn't trembled when he poured. He put the cup down, placed his arms on the table, locked his fingers. His eyes never left Paul's.

"Bourgois jumped when he was supposed to. Off the tug, into the water. He began swimming away from it. A Nazi officer on the yacht saw him, pulled his pistol out and aimed just as the tug hit the yacht and blew it up. Fire and smoke. More explosions. I saw SS soldiers on the bank shooting at Bourgois swimming toward me. I shit in my pants. If I raced out to help him, they'd see me and I'd be dead before I could reach him. I crawled out of the speedboat, hid behind the barge, grenaded the speedboat. I heard them stop firing at Bourgois. I saw a Nazi launch haul him out of the water."

Paul glanced at Lafitte's interlocked fingers kneading each other.

"The SS picked up a hundred civilians. I was one. They marched us through Paris to the execution yard. Standing there was Bourgois facing the firing squad, but not with rifles, with Schmeisser burp guns...machine guns! I was in the front line of the civilians. He was looking at me. He knew I had betrayed him. I could have drawn fire from the SS on the bank until he could get closer to me. I know I could have saved him but I had no balls. I wanted to live. He kept looking at me. In his eyes was no hate. In his eyes was compassion for me. He had saved my life twice. I never made a move to try to save his. They shot him with twelve burp guns. His head, his body, the yellow pole…all splattered. Every night I see the execution again. Every night bullets splatter my head, my body and the yellow pole…"

He pulled the Luger from his pocket, forced it into Paul's hand.

"It's called mercy for a reason. I've come to the end, Hank. It has to end. You of all people can understand."

Agony swept Lafitte's face as Paul sat, silent, his own face showing no expression.

"For God's sake, Hank, say you'll do it. You don't have to do it now. Do it sometime when I don't know it's coming. Make it a surprise. I don't want to know."

His eyes begged.

"And you can never tell Michelle."

Father Flanagan spotted the *Jean Bourgois*, saw the Luger in Paul's hand, passed them wondering if the old skipper had a gun, too. He spotted a landmark: a phone booth at the top of the cement ramp leading to the street.

Paul was still holding the Luger, hypnotized, when he heard the voice behind him.

"Good morning, Zozo."

Michelle was carrying the baby onto the deck. The baby carriage was on the quay nearby.

Paul shoved the Luger into his pants pocket.

Horror was in her face as she stared at Lafitte.

"Are you sick?"

"Bad stomach."

Paul left the deck to get the carriage.

She had never seen Lafitte so old. Agony in his eyes. It was like he was dying in front of her.

"I'm running late for a sugar haul," Lafitte said.

He left for his bunk.

Paul was wheeling the carriage into the living room.

"He looks like death," Michelle said, following him. "Did he say anything to you?"

Paul shook his head, parked the carriage near the galley.

She began to change the kid's diaper on the table in their room. Paul wanted to tell her what the trouble was, but he couldn't. He'd given his word.

Lafitte emerged from his bunk dressed for work in a windbreaker and wearing his seaman's cap.

"What time will you be back, Zozo?"

"About nine."

He left. She put the baby in the crib and they went on deck to watch Lafitte start up his engine and pull away in his tug.

A pall hung over the deck.

"It's Zozo's birthday, Paul. Let's surprise him with a party. I'll get a cake right now."

She left.

He could stop Lafitte's pain. It was the finest, the kindest thing one person could do for another. But doing it that way... he had to think about it. The more he thought, the more stress pumped into his brain.

He heard the flute, remembered Michelle's words. He used willpower against the flute. Felt the struggle. Sweated. Fought the fire aching in his brain. The flute stopped. The brainquake didn't come.

It was his first victory against the jackal.

En route to the bakery, Michelle stopped in the phone booth on the top of the cement ramp, instructed Eddie to rent a car immediately, told him how to get to the barge.

42

Dark was the living room but for moonlight through the curtained window. In half-shadow the baby in the highchair played with the monkey on the attached tray. Sitting next to the baby was Lafitte waiting for the surprise Michelle had promised. The door of the room was flung open by Paul silhouetted in soft wavering light as Michelle appeared with a two-decked cake, every candle burning.

Paul couldn't sing. He spoke the words.

Michelle carried the cake in, singing

> *Happy Birthday to you,*
> *Happy Birthday to you,*
> *Happy Birthday dear Zozo,*
> *Happy Birthday to you!*

The fascinated baby gaped at his mother's face through the forest of flickering flames advancing to the table set for dinner. Song ended. Michelle embraced Lafitte, kissing him on both cheeks. Her smile at Paul spoke. He found himself kissing Lafitte on both cheeks. Lafitte kissed the baby, the monkey, then sucked a long deep breath preparing to blow out the candles. He caught the baby hypnotized by them.

"Dining by candlelight's more fun, eh, little Jean?"

They drank champagne, dined by candlelight and Lafitte opened a bottle of absinthe. Paul and Michelle were relieved. The party worked. Lafitte felt and looked better.

But the reason was not the party.

Lafitte was in top form because Paul hadn't returned the Luger.

Michelle was in top form because her plan was progressing on schedule. She kept pouring absinthe for Lafitte.

Paul was in top form because his willpower had stopped the flute.

For the party, Lafitte was in the old brass-buttoned, double-breasted sea captain's jacket he had bought in the Sixties when he became owner of his own tug. Black tie on a white shirt.

Michelle was in a blinding orange T-shirt with a pirate skull and crossbones that said *CAPTAIN BLOOD FOR PRESIDENT* in blue. Her green shiny leather jeans were ass-tight. Where had Johnson found these things?

Paul was in the secondhand white turtleneck that read *I ♥ Paris* on the front. He'd chosen the baggy coffee-colored pants because they had very deep pockets. The pressure of the Luger against his thigh kept him prepared to act when the right moment came, to shoot Lafitte by surprise and ease his pain.

Demolishing nearly half the bottle of absinthe, Lafitte was the life of the party, singing a bawdy song to the baby, crooning a romantic tune, executing long gliding steps and dips, dancing the tango with Michelle. Paul and the baby watched them. Paul wondered how much it took to get Lafitte drunk. He certainly seemed to be, but Paul had a feeling it might just be a pose.

It would be a blessing if Lafitte dropped dead from an OD of absinthe. But that was too much to hope.

Making a sudden whirl, Lafitte lost his balance, crashed against the tables, fell with bottles, dishes, glasses and flickering very short candles in the remains of the cake. The crash frightened the baby. It began to cry.

Michelle quickly switched the light on as Paul helped him up. Lafitte was in fact too drunk to recognize him and shoved him away, staggered into his room, kicking the door shut. They heard a thud and the ringing of the alarm clock. Michelle swung his door open.

In the soft blue light, Lafitte was sprawled on the bed. Michelle switched on the overhead light. He lay on his back, his shoulders and head against the wall. His eyes were shut. Out of his sagging open mouth came the growling snores of a man dead to the world. His eyes under their lids looked untroubled. No nightmares were hounding him now.

Michelle picked up the ringing clock from the floor and turned it off. Paul picked up the big stone ashtray and straightened up the overturned night table. Michelle put the clock back on it as he put down the ashtray. Paul reached to help Lafitte out of his grotesque position.

"Don't touch him. He likes sleeping off absinthe like that."

She switched off the bright light.

In the soft blue light she said, "When I was ten, I tried to move him and he took a swing at me."

She pulled Paul out, closed the door, glanced at her watch.

The baby was crying louder. Paul carried it from the high-chair to their room. The baby squirmed violently and was difficult to keep from wriggling out of his hands. Paul placed the baby on the small table. Michelle put the monkey on the table and held the baby's flailing hands as Paul removed its diaper. The baby promptly stopped flailing and crying. Paul reached for a clean diaper.

Michelle picked up the trash bin, threw the dirty diaper in and again glanced at her watch. She carried the trash bin to the window in the galley, pulled aside the curtain. Eddie was waiting.

She swiftly moved to the front door, unlocked and opened it. She pointed at her room, then at Lafitte's room. Lafitte's door was still closed.

She returned to the living room, dumped broken dishes and glasses in the trash bin, carried it back to the galley, glancing into their bedroom on the way. Paul was gently placing the baby in the crib. Paul stroked the baby's belly. It giggled.

Eddie entered with a life-sized rubber baby doll, diapered and swaddled in a blanket. He stole along the wall, keeping out of Paul's line of sight, waiting for a signal from Michelle. Standing in the galley, she could see Paul readjusting the blanket, then holding up the monkey by its tail, lowering it. The baby's hands reached for it. Paul raised the monkey again, lowered it. The baby seized it.

Paul was too close to the baby. Michelle wanted space between them. She didn't want to chance the baby getting hurt when all hell broke loose. She waited.

Eddie waited.

43

The Luger was burning Paul's thigh as he stood close to the baby, staring at how happily it was sleeping with its monkey. But Paul wasn't happy. He felt sick. He hated to do what he had to do. The burning became red hot. He had made up his mind to commit the mercy killing, but he was beginning to have doubts. He couldn't share his terrible decision with Michelle. He couldn't betray Lafitte.

He dropped on his knees and kept looking at the baby. He had to talk to someone. He spoke in a whisper to the baby for reassurance.

"I've got to do it."

Don't.

Barney's voice was an echo a million miles away.

"Pa?"

Don't do it, Paul.

"Pa?"

Yes.

"Is Mom with you?"

I'm with him, Paul.

He hadn't heard her voice in twenty years. His tears burned as much as the Luger.

"I've got to ease his pain, Mom…"

It's wrong.

He felt a strange pressure in his brain. He was confused. He had eased her pain. Why was it wrong to ease Lafitte's pain? Why must everything have a reason? He had to know.

"Why is it wrong?"

Think.

He didn't hear their voices anymore. He thought hard. He thought harder. The reason it was wrong was the reason. It was that clear now. It was wrong to murder in cold blood. Lafitte was good but what he did against Bourgois to save his own life was bad. Killing him likewise would be bad, even if he wanted it.

He knew now what to do. He stood up and paced away from the baby and felt relieved. He'd throw the Luger in the river. He felt the strange pressure in his brain go away.

He turned and saw Eddie holding up the baby by one foot.

No flute.

No rumble in his brain.

No tremor.

The brainquake came without warning. The flute shrieked. In brighter reddish-pink Eddie was smashing the baby against the wall. Paul whipped the Luger out and pulled the trigger. It was frozen. Safety on. The baby was shrieking louder than the flute. Paul clicked the safety off and fired point blank and the room shook and spun and pictures fell from the walls and his brain cells were pulling the baby into the crevice and Eddie vanished but Michelle lunged at him, raking his face with her fingernails and tearing the Luger out of his hand and the flute stopped, the brighter reddish-pink gone, the brainquake over.

But the baby was crying.

"You shot at my baby!"

"Eddie…smashing baby…against…wall."

She pulled him to the baby crying in the crib.

"Do you see a smashed baby? Do you?"

The room spun. The floor moved. Part of this was brainquake. Part was not. No blood on the wall. No blood on the floor. She pointed at the bullet hole in the crib.

"You missed my baby by a hair!"

He started toward the door. She spun him around. "You're not running anywhere, you bastard! Out there alone you'll shoot at another baby and you'll kill it!"

Holding the gun in one hand, she beat his face with the back of her fists, the barrel just missing his eye. He stood there, took the beating, knew she had the right to do it, the right to shoot him if she wanted. But she was no killer. Blood covered his face.

Michelle stopped suddenly, the hand holding the gun raised, poised for another brutal swipe. Her manufactured hysteria boomeranged. *He had a gun.* He'd been waiting for Eddie. Who'd prepared him? She stared at the gun, recognized it. Her plan collapsed.

"Where did you get his Luger?"

"Lafitte."

"Why did you steal it?"

"Gave it to me."

"Why?"

"To shoot him."

"Why?"

"Stop his pain."

"What pain?"

"…Cancer."

"Oh, my God!" She broke into tears. "Oh, no! Did he tell you that? He's sick?"

Paul said nothing.

She put the Luger on the table, lifted the crying baby, comforted it, put it back in the crib.

They both stared at the gun. Paul reached for it, but she got it first. "No, Paul. He's my responsibility, not yours. I'll stop his pain."

He followed her out into the galley, but she stopped him at the sink. "Here." She ran water over two towels, wiped blood from his face, stuffed the blood-splotched towels in the cardboard cake box on the counter. "You stay here. Please, Paul."

She went into Lafitte's room, closed the door.

In the soft blue light, Eddie and his gun were shaking.

"The bastard's armed!"

"Shh! Keep it down, Eddie. Pocket your gun."

He did. She thrust out the Luger.

"Use this one."

Eddie took it. A snore from Lafitte made Eddie jump.

"Dead drunk," Michelle said.

"Where'd he get this Luger?"

"From him. It's a godsend. What're you waiting for?"

Eddie pointed the Luger at Lafitte. Eddie couldn't fire.

"Shoot him!"

"You shoot him."

Through dizzying fog of pain, Lafitte heard:

"He's like my father. Goddam it! Haven't you got any feelings? *Shoot him!*"

Eddie shot him.

The bullet impact in his chest shook Lafitte. Blood covered his brass buttons. His hand spasmed. Eddie stared at Lafitte's open eyes.

"He's looking at us!"

She felt for a pulse under Lafitte's ear.

"No. He's dead."

"What makes his eyes stay open?"

Lafitte saw the fuzzy Michelle staring at him.

"Reflex," Michelle whispered.

"They give me the willies."

She opened the door calling out "*Paul!*" She picked up the big stone ashtray from the small table, positioned herself behind the door, raised the ashtray high.

How hard should she hit him? He still had the wig on, which

would soften the blow. He might come out of it too soon. But too hard a blow could kill him. *Jesus Christ, how hard should I hit him to keep him alive?*

Lafitte saw the white turtleneck sweater opening the door. Paul hesitantly walked in. Smashed on the back of his head with the ashtray, he fell, hitting the edge of the chest, and crashed to the floor. She dropped the ashtray next to him and ran out.

With handkerchief around the barrel of the Luger, Eddie wiped off his prints from the butt, fitted it into Paul's hand, pressed hard on the fingers, made sure one was on the trigger. He wiped the barrel clean.

Where he lay, his vision fading, Lafitte saw the shadow that was Michelle reappear, carrying the baby, a cardboard box and the leather bag. Eddie scooped up the baby doll from the floor, took the bag from her. They vanished.

A thousand miles away, Lafitte heard a car starting up and roaring off.

In the car driving down the waterfront road, Eddie was still sweating. She felt good.

"I still can't forget his open eyes," Eddie said.

"Maybe a muscle snapped. I heard about a man shot in a steam room…fell naked on his back and his cock stood up and saluted after he was dead."

The car roared up the cement ramp, braked at the phone booth. She got out. The car waited. She called Police HQ and asked for Inspector Sainte-Beuve in Homicide.

"Your name, please?"

"Michelle Valour."

"He's on the phone. Can I help?"

"It's urgent. A man's been shot!"

After ten seconds Sainte-Beuve was on the line.

"Michelle! Last week Lafitte told me you were in New York!"

"Lafitte's been shot. Just minutes ago, on his barge. A man broke in. He's unconscious. I hit him. Please come. You must come!"

"We will, stay there," he said, and she heard him shout something to someone in the room with him. "The man? Do you know who he is?"

"Yes. It's Paul Page, the taxi driver wanted for murder in New York. They want me for the same murder, but it's not true, he did it. My baby is with me! I need help!"

She hung up to sell panic, jumped in the car. Eddie backed down the ramp and returned her to the barge.

"Dump that cake box in a sewer, Eddie. Stay glued to the phone in your hotel. After I get a clean slate from the New York cops, I'll phone you in Paris."

She got out with the baby, slammed the door, ran aboard the barge. Eddie drove away. She found Paul still unconscious, put her baby in the crib, pushed the backpack under the bed, flopped on the mattress, still tasting the miracle that Inspector Sainte-Beuve had been there, not out on another case. From the start she had planned to use him, and only him, as her unwitting ally. He was an old friend. He'd question her gently. How did she get mixed up in murder? She would never mention Paul's brainquake. She'd give him the facts she wanted to and no more. Lafitte was dead, and Paul couldn't talk, especially under the stress of a police interrogation. Nobody would be able to untwist the facts she presented. Sainte-Beuve had dealt with homicidal maniacs. He'd grill Paul, hoping to drag out a coherent phrase to bring before a judge. With the blow on his head and under pressure of questioning, Paul would have a brainquake, convict himself. Sainte-Beuve would buy her story. She had delivered the first blow.

That was half the battle won.

44

After Michelle hung up abruptly, Inspector Sainte-Beuve searched for Interpol's "Wanted List." Nine fugitives, including the baby.

My baby is with me! Whose baby was it? Her husband's? Paul Page's...?

Staring at Paul's photo, he saw a cipher face, eyes opaque gray, unmemorable.

He looked at Michelle's blurred face in the photo taken through the ambulance doors in Central Park. Would he have recognized her if he hadn't known her years before? He doubted it. *Michelle Troy.* He certainly hadn't recognized the name when Lieutenant Zara had told him about the case she'd come across the ocean to work on.

Alerting his team to get to their cars immediately, the Inspector swiftly went over the report as he rose, slipped one arm into his jacket, then the other, shifting the report from hand to hand as he did so. Poker-cheating husband shot by gun concealed in baby carriage...bomb...$10,000 involvement with some black psycho...the gunshot murder in her apartment, the flight with the taxi driver...

He's unconscious! I hit him!

A week after Lafitte delivered baby Michelle, Sainte-Beuve had toasted him as the absinthe-drinking midwife on the Seine. *Help me!* How? The New York police said she had murdered a man and run. The child he had picked up after school whenever Lafitte was working had grown up to be a wanted murderess...

In his car, followed by horns clashing with sirens, the Inspector was speeding along the Seine toward the *Jean Bourgois*. He was behind the wheel himself. He hated being driven. It made him nervous, he felt he wasn't in control. Of course, how could you feel in control when you were driving into a nightmare involving dear friends? He idolized Lafitte. He loved Michelle as a daughter.

He checked his rear-view mirror. Tailgating him with blinding headlights through traffic were the ambulance, mobile lab, lab crew van, and minibus with eight cops. A year ago at the Anchorage Bar he'd told Lafitte about his idea to speed up investigations and cut down red tape. He requested a fully equipped mobile crime lab with him in the field. He got it.

Now it was racing to help Lafitte.

The Inspector had bought Zara's story that Page was connected with organized crime, probably as a bagman. He had to have some shady connections to raise $200,000 in cash for the charter pilot to fly them to France. The pilot's partner had been tortured and killed in the manner of a known organization hit man. And now Zara's brutal murder in Paris before the police could find the fugitives...

What the Inspector couldn't buy was Michelle fleeing the country with her baby and a homicidal maniac. Unless Paul only became one tonight. He thought back to the photo of Paul and to Zara's description of him. The Inspector hated stone walls. He knew how tough it was going to be to pull anything coherent out of Paul.

The Inspector was not a desk psychiatrist. He was a cop. Paul was just another fugitive, wanted for questioning about murder. If he was insane, that wasn't the Inspector's problem.

But of course it was. And it was Michelle's, too. Her husband dies and she runs away with this man...had he somehow convinced, mesmerized, romanced Michelle? How, if he was the man Zara had described?

And why, if he had been the one to pull the trigger, did the murder gun also have her prints on it?

And how could this Paul have gotten the drop on Lafitte tonight? If Lafitte had suspected Paul was dangerous, he would have shot him himself, or held him at gunpoint while Michelle ran to phone the police. Lafitte had no shortage of guns on his barge.

The Inspector hoped that through the cracks of the stone wall a few words would slip out from Paul…a few lucid words…but rarely, in the Inspector's experience, had those words, when pieced together, been worth anything.

Lafitte was the Inspector's only hook. Lafitte would fit the pieces together. If he was still breathing.

"How long have you known him, Inspector?"

The Inspector glanced at the man sitting beside him: the police surgeon who had already saved several lives in emergencies in the mobile lab's operating room over the past year.

"Known whom?"

"Captain Lafitte?"

"Thirty years."

The Inspector was back with them again, grateful to the surgeon for having broken into his thoughts. Behind them sat a young forensics man, Gautier, the whip of the mobile lab crew. With him was the surgeon's top assistant, an ex-paratrooper medic named Rensonnet.

"My son," Rensonnet said, "has a picture of Bourgois and Lafitte on his bedroom wall."

"You think that's something," Gautier said, "my niece wrote a school play about the Resistance. Her little friend was Bourgois."

"Does Lafitte still live alone on his barge?" Rensonnet said.

"Yes," said the Inspector.

"Is it true he has no phone, no TV, no radio?"

"Yes."

"How can he live in Paris without them?"

"He doesn't understand how we can live *with* them."

They exchanged wry smiles at the old man's eccentricity.

"Was he wounded in the head, Inspector?"

"Why the head?"

"To live like that, like a hermit…"

"He was wounded three times but not in the head. He was hit in the balls. Lost one. He told the Resistance doctor it was all right. He could live with one ball. That was why they gave us two of them."

They laughed.

"I saw that in an American film," Rensonnet said.

"American—French—balls are the same all over the world," the Inspector said. "All men could live with only one ball. Lafitte's all iron inside. No bullet's tough enough to kill him."

"How long's he been living like that?"

"Since the war. But it's wrong to call him a hermit. Hermits don't go drinking and brawling in waterfront bars." The inspector weaved between two slow-moving cars in front of him, saw the convoy in his rear-view do the same. "He likes to brawl and he likes to drink and that's got nothing to do with liking to live alone after a day's work on his tug. His barge is his castle. I'm one of the rare ones who's been on it. There's nothing strange about living in privacy."

"Don't you think the war made him a little crazy?"

"Hell, no. Just suffering from battle fatigue."

"After forty-five years?"

"Time has nothing to do with it."

Rensonnet snorted. "My father fought with the Free French in North Africa. Infantry. Close combat. Saw men's faces shot off. Enough to drive him insane. Wounded twice. Lost a leg.

But not a single sign of battle fatigue forty-five years later."

"He wore a uniform," the Inspector said.

"Of course he did! He was a sergeant!"

The Inspector glanced at Rensonnet in the rear-view mirror. "A captured soldier knows he'll live. A captured Resistance fighter knows he'll be shot. The man who fights with a gun has got to know he has a chance to survive. Without that chance, he is dead every day he fights. Lafitte is suffering from that kind of battle fatigue."

There was silence in the car. Only the horns battling the sirens as they rocketed toward the waterfront. They weren't far now.

"I never thought about it that way, Inspector," Rensonnet said. "It makes sense. He must be a sad and frightened man."

"Sad? No. I've never known someone with a bigger joy for life, or a better sense of humor. Mischievous. We'd go out drinking and he'd toast everyone with a quote, he'd say it was from Balzac, and everyone would say, 'Yes, yes, Balzac!' But it was just something he'd made up himself. 'You know that line?' he'd ask. And some snob would say, 'Oh, yes, yes! My favorite line!' And he'd say, 'From such a wonderful play, no?' And the poor sap would crawl further onto his own sword: 'Oh yes, one of his best!' 'The one about the duchess and the gardener?' 'Yes, yes, I think that's right…' He could keep it up for an hour. Then finally he'd drop the blade: *Balzac never said it, I did.* And as often as not the sap, trying to salvage his dignity, would insist: 'No, no, I'm quite sure I remember reading it…' "

"Sounds like a scene Balzac would have loved," the surgeon said.

"Now don't you start," the Inspector said.

"Why'd he do it?" Rensonnet asked. "Just to have a laugh at their expense?"

"That," the Inspector said, "and because it was a line he was proud of. If they thought Balzac said it, they'd take it seriously. Who'd believe a tug captain hauling coal and Cokes should have his words listened to respectfully?"

"What was the line?" Rensonnet asked.

"Later," the Inspector said, stepping on the gas as he swung onto the quay. "Pray he can tell you himself."

45

Two-way speeding traffic in the isolated tree-lined Seine area came to a sudden, head-jerking, angry, jarring halt amid sirens, horns, and blinking police lights, punctuated by sounds of bumpers striking bumpers.

Careening off the road, the Inspector's car lunged past the phone booth, charged down the cement ramp, whipped along the dirt waterfront road, led his noisy team to the barge.

All its lights were on.

The Inspector jumped out of his car, saw the wild-eyed black-haired woman in funky clothes and huge gaudy earrings streaking toward him like an arrow, kissing him, hugging him, clinging to him, her body shaking with panic.

He did nothing. He hadn't kissed her, hadn't hugged her. He stood as stiff as a telephone pole. Horns and sirens died, to the relief of awakened birds in their nests. The distant, haunting, lonely whistle of a tug horn could be heard.

Crew and cops erupted from their vehicles. Their lights kept blinking.

The Inspector could almost hear her heart, feel it hammering against his chest. Slowly, he stepped back and stared at her made-up face and her jet black hair. The only recognizable thing he saw was the unforgettable blue of her eyes, gleaming in the blinking lights.

He was aware he hadn't greeted her as she'd expected, hadn't flung his arms around her to comfort her. She needed to see he was not going to be on her side in murder. He saw the fear now filling her eyes, and made the smallest gesture he could: he took her arms in his, held them gently.

She burst into tears. They were the same tears she'd shed when she was nine and he had removed a painful splinter from her toe.

"Let's go."

They crossed the plank. She led him to the room. She stayed in the doorway while he went in.

Reacting more to Lafitte's staring eyes than to the abundance of blood glistening all over his jacket, he didn't—he couldn't—examine him. The surgeon would do it any moment. With four citations for bravery as a street cop, the Inspector lacked the courage to see if Lafitte was dead. He had seen many victims of sudden death staring up at him with popped eyes, and none had been revived to life.

Michelle watched his glances swiftly take in the baby sketch on the wall…the raked, bruised face of Paul, still prone on the floor…the blood-matted thick hair on the back of his head… blood-smeared ashtray on floor…red gash on his temple… Luger in his hand…blood on the bed, on the blanket, on the lid of the chest.

The Inspector knew the tale behind every memento in that memory chest, including the Luger that Jean Bourgois took from a Nazi he had killed and gave to Lafitte for courage on the youth's seventeenth birthday. Unlocking Paul's grip on the gun, he recognized the trench-knife-scratched initials on the Luger's butt.

CL for Christian Lafitte.

He looked up at Michelle framed in the doorway, her blue eyes riveted on his, her dark makeup smeared with tears on her cheeks.

"You know how this bastard got Lafitte's Luger?"

She nodded.

"We'll have a talk, Michelle. Go clean your face."

She nodded but before she could move a cyclone slammed her aside. The surgeon blasted in, trailed by Rensonnet carrying a stand and two medical boxes, the ambulance doctor, Dr. Sully, with his intern carrying medical kits, and Gautier, the forensics man.

The surgeon stared at Lafitte's chest blanketed with blood.

"X-ray!"

Gautier bolted for the quay.

Michelle didn't allow herself to feel anxious. She knew the Bomb Squad had used an X-ray machine to save her baby's life, but she didn't believe any machine would save someone dead, and Lafitte was stone dead.

Watching the surgeon feel for Lafitte's pulse with his hand on Lafitte's neck, under his ear, she felt a strange but exciting spasm shoot through her. She was in control of all this. The surgeon would never feel a beat.

The powder-blue shoulder of a lab technician in a smock shoved her aside and jarred her thoughts.

The technician stood by Rensonnet, who was taking a specimen of Lafitte's blood in a small vial. The vial was handed to the technician, who carried it out to the mobile lab parked twenty feet from the water.

Michelle watched as the surgeon pulled up the lid of Lafitte's left eye. Rensonnet adjusted the stand next to him, checking the long tube attached to it, checking the syringe.

The surgeon struck a match, held the flame against Lafitte's hand. Michelle felt the pain. There was no reaction from Lafitte.

Rensonnet opened both medical boxes, placed two metal cartons on the bed. One filled with balls of cotton absorbents, the other empty. Also on the bed he placed a plastic bag containing surgical gloves, and a headband with a lamp attached, like coal miners' helmets.

Her gaze shifted to Dr. Sully listening to Paul's heart on his stethoscope.

She was shoved aside again, this time by two females.

One was a cop in uniform. On her right hip hung her holstered gun. On her left hip hung a batch of pressed cellophane bags with attached cards. On the top bag, stamped in blue: POLICE/NATIONALE. She went over to the Inspector, who was watching the surgeon examining Lafitte's eye.

The other female, not in uniform, was a police photographer with a dead panatela in her mouth who began to take flashbulb photos of Lafitte and of Paul. She turned to the Inspector, who indicated other articles to photograph. She took pictures of the Luger, the blood on the back of Paul's head, the blood on his temple, the blood on the chest, the blood on the ashtray on the floor.

Then she left for the crime lab's developing room.

Michelle watched the surgeon slipping out of his jacket, rolling up his sleeves, slinging stethoscope round his neck, adjusting the headband.

The lab technician in powder-blue smock returned with a bottle of blood and left. Rensonnet hooked it on the stand, jammed the needle into Lafitte's arm, switched the flow open.

Michelle watched blood moving down the tube into Lafitte.

The surgeon, the Inspector and Rensonnet watched.

The blood clogged.

She knew it would. There was no heart to pump blood anymore.

She watched Rensonnet tear open the plastic bag, blow into the two gloves, hold them out. The surgeon thrust his fingers into them.

Rensonnet turned on the bulb on the headband.

The surgeon pulled apart the top of Lafitte's jacket, ripped off his tie, ripped open the shirt. Rensonnet repeatedly sponged blood, tossing red balls into the empty box.

The surgeon moved his stethoscope in the blood as he hunted for a single faint beat.

Michelle knew he was wasting his time, so she watched Dr. Sully examining the blood-soaked hair on the back of Paul's head. His intern held out scissors. Dr. Sully began cutting away the hair and stopped. Exploring the matted hair, he pulled off Paul's thick wig, handed it to the Inspector, then began cutting Paul's real hair away.

The female cop ripped off a bag, opened it, wrote on the tag as the Inspector said:

"Wig. Paul Page."

He gave her the wig, initialed the tag. She placed the wig in the bag, clamped it, ripped off another bag, opened it.

Dr. Sully examined the gash.

"The wig softened the blow."

The Inspector ripped off Paul's beard.

"Beard. Paul Page."

The female cop wrote it on the tag. He initialed it. She placed beard in bag, ripped off another bag as Dr. Sully dabbed antiseptic on the head gash, then moved to check the temple gash being dabbed with antiseptic by the intern.

Dr. Sully examined the second gash, then glanced at the smear of blood on the edge of the war chest, then back at the gash.

"An inch higher, he'd be dead."

The Inspector picked up the Luger. The female cop wrote as he said:

"Murder weapon. Luger. Paul Page."

He gave it to her barrel-out, initialed the tag. She placed the

Luger in a bag, clamped it, dug another, larger bag out of her pocket as he picked up the stone ashtray. She wrote as he said:

"Assault weapon. Stone ashtray. Michelle Troy."

He initialed the tag. She placed ashtray in bag, clamped it.

Without a word, Michelle pulled off the black wig she was wearing, handed it to him, stepped back in the doorway. The female cop ripped off another bag, wrote on the tag as the Inspector spoke:

"Wig. Michelle Troy."

He gave her the wig, initialed the tag. She placed it in the bag, clamped it.

"Wait in the other room."

The female cop with bagged exhibits brushed past Michelle. The Inspector beckoned to someone behind Michelle. A burly cop pushed her aside and entered, followed close behind by a moustached cop.

"Put him on the big table out there."

The two cops lifted Paul up. The intern gathered his gear, followed Dr. Sully out past Michelle.

"Want him cuffed, Inspector?" the burly cop said.

"Not yet. When Dr. Sully patches him up, don't move him to the ambulance. Keep him on the table. When he comes to, I'll talk to him. If he wants the WC, stick with him."

They carried Paul out to the living room. His limp arm struck Michelle's body as they passed. She turned, watched them place him on the big round table where they'd had the birthday dinner.

No sound from the baby in the crib meant he was sleeping peacefully. One blessing.

Gautier returned, powering toward her like a runaway locomotive.

"Don't block the doorway!"

She stepped out of the way and he dashed past, followed by two lab technicians. They slid the adjustable metal table across the bed as Rensonnet swiftly picked up the two boxes. Metal legs on each side of the bed were adjusted firmly.

Michelle moved back slowly, peering in to see Rensonnet placing the two boxes on the metal table.

"Don't block the doorway!"

She moved away like lightning as four lab technicians carried in the big X-ray machine and, under Gautier's supervision, placed it on the metal table. All the technicians left.

Gautier switched the machine on.

Her view was blocked by the surgeon, the Inspector and Gautier. Again she reassured herself that the machine would be useless…but she started to get a sickening feeling. She forced the feeling away. She hated herself for even permitting the feeling to hit her gut.

She stepped to one side so she could see. Through the X-ray, the region of the heart clouded by blood was brought into view for the surgeon, the Inspector and Rensonnet. Between flashes of Rensonnet's skeletal finger bones mopping blood, the surgeon caught a glimpse of the bullet.

"See the bullet?"

"No," the Inspector said.

The surgeon pointed out the spot on the window. When the blood was mopped away:

"I see it!"

"Slightly deflected by that brass button."

"I see no button."

"You will."

Two more balls of cotton filled with blood…then:

"I see it!" More blood was sucked up. "Did it pierce the heart?"

Michelle tensely waited for the affirmative.

"No."

The floor under her reeled one way, she the other. She fought to maintain her balance. Her mouth was dry, her body shaking.

"The bullet smashed the edge of the sternum."

"It bruised the heart?"

"Can't tell yet. I want the heart to fill the window!"

Gautier adjusted.

"That's as close as we can get."

"Perfect."

The stilled heart filled the window.

The Surgeon's finger tapped the spot. "Looks like a hair distance between bullet and heart." They stared. Veins and arteries could be faintly seen now.

The Inspector moved. An instant later the flattened bones of his hand came on the window. They were pressing down hard on the heart, lifting abruptly, pressing down hard, lifting abruptly, pressing down hard, lifting abruptly, and the procedure never stopped as they watched.

"Hold it!"

The Inspector did.

The surgeon's eyes glued on the heart saw a single, very weak movement. It could have been the flash that he wanted to see. But now the heart was still again.

"Keep going."

The Inspector did. Every time he abruptly lifted his hand, the surgeon and Gautier felt their own hearts jump. But there was no movement at all.

Suddenly they saw the Inspector's bone fingers clench into fists. He beat down on the heart and, with a steady rhythm, kept beating, pounding, furiously, steadily. When blood gathered it was sponged up by Rensonnet who kept his eye on the blood in the tube.

Still clogged.

"Want me to take over?" Gautier said.

"Hell, no!" the Inspector said, breathing heavily. "I'll beat him back to life myself!"

Like hell you will, thought Michelle. The strain was tearing her apart. *Can't they see he's dead? Don't they know? They're experts. Don't they know? They couldn't hear it beat! They can't see it beat! Are they crazy? Why are they doing this to me? Eddie fucked up! He should have jammed the muzzle against his chest and fired! He should have fired twice! Three times! I felt for a pulse, there was none. So I fucked up, too. I should have made him fire three times. Four.* The sickening feeling in her gut became a fist that seized and squeezed hard and twisted. Then she realized it wasn't her gut being twisted. It was her heart. She felt it stop beating. She felt it as still as Lafitte's.

"Hold it!" the surgeon shouted again.

The Inspector stopped. This time the surgeon was sure. He caught another weak movement…and another…and another.

"Good lord. You've done it."

The Surgeon moved closer, bent to give Lafitte mouth-to-mouth. The Inspector kept up the compressions.

"I see a very slow beat," Gautier said.

Who said that? Is he crazy? He's imagining it! He saw nothing! He saw nothing!

"Getting stronger…"

They continued, their rhythms matched, laboring over the old man's bloody body.

"Stronger!"

In the color of blood shrieking mutely, she heard Lafitte's heartbeats growing louder…

Michelle was ashamed of herself. Sweating. Shaking. Hysterical like an amateur. She was not Paul. She was not sick in the head. The situation had made her lose her grip for a second. Lafitte alive was a monkey wrench, an unwelcome development. But who could say how long it would last? Or if he'd ever regain consciousness? She was in control again. She would make it through, as she always did. So Lafitte was coming back from the dead. It would be very brief.

She took a long deep controlled breath. She knew exactly what she had to do. The Inspector expected it from her.

"Heart's pumping!" Gautier said.

"*Thank God!*" Michelle screamed.

And she collapsed.

46

Tonight. It would be tonight.

The stroll to his car parked off Étoile was enjoyable. Sober as a corpse, not a drop of wine with his late dinner at Fouquet's, Father Flanagan was pleased he wouldn't have to dodge death like a lunatic on wheels around the Arc de Triomphe to maneuver out of that traffic merry-go-round that had become second nature to drivers in Paris.

For no reason at all, a thought crossed his mind: how much was a hit man paid in the old guillotine days? They must have had them from the time the hill of Montmartre poked its head out of the ocean that covered Paris. The run of kings wouldn't have made first base if not for the killers they employed.

Hit men helped make history.

That absurd word "assassinate" brought a smile. A king or president was assassinated. Any lower human was killed. Rank in death always amused him. He frowned, unable to believe what some hits went for today. He'd read of a wetnose paid by a jealous girl to hit a high school football hero who had cheated on her. Fifty bucks! It was insulting. The killer was a student. What kind of education had he gotten? Just by reading history you should know that hit men got money, land, castles. Or perhaps the wetnose couldn't read.

After the double hit tonight he'd leave the baby in that orphanage and get his ass out of Paris. This hit had put a strain on him. It was the only job he could remember that had done that. Once it was over, he would need a vacation. He reached his car and opened the door.

"We beg your pardon, Father."

At the sound of the woman's voice he spun around. Two nuns smiled up at him. One about fifty, the other in her early twenties. He had noticed in the last few days how their teams were made up of contrasting ages. For an instant, he saw the older nun nude. Not the younger.

It worried the hell out of him.

"May I help you, Sisters?"

"You're American," the older nun said.

"How did you know?"

"You have the American look. We saw you leave the restaurant and we followed you."

Jesus! If a pair of nuns could follow him without his noticing, he was further gone than he thought. He'd have to take extra care tonight.

"We are taking a poll," the younger nun said, "of what American priests find the most memorable about Paris…"

He glanced at his watch, frowned. "Forgive me, if I had time we could enjoy a cup of tea and discuss the matter, but I'm afraid I am late for a meeting with a member of my parish—a twentieth-century Mary Magdalene—I swore to her parents that I would meet with her and usher her back to the fold. It's taken me several months to find her, and…I'm sure you understand?" He didn't wait for an answer. He climbed behind the wheel, started the motor, closed the door, rolled down the window. "Good night, Sisters."

He sped down Avenue George V.

Framed in black, the young nun's face had been ivory…like the widow…the bagman called her "Ivory Face" in those poems he had written; the poems dug up at her apartment by Zara, God rest her soul; poems published on page one of the New York *Post* and *Daily News*; poems read aloud on news programs on TV and radio; poems analyzed by psychiatrists, grandstanding politicians, angry Op Ed bloviators.

He had read the poems, too. They were silly. Juvenile. But the wave of coverage they'd spawned was even worse. He'd heard one Sunday-morning commentator who'd unearthed a statement attributed to Al Capone: "*Love makes a bagman a poet or a madman*"…bullshit…love could never make a bagman a poet. Though it sure as hell could make one a madman.

Only a madman would open the bag for a woman.

He drove along the Seine, keeping an eye out for the landmark he'd sighted earlier. It was going to be difficult to spot the right phone booth with so many blinding lights hitting him in waves from the opposite lane. How many phone booths were there atop those goddam ramps? He had neglected to check. He drove slowly, angering the cars behind him. He was sure he hadn't passed one on his left yet.

He should have started out at dusk. He shouldn't have lingered to enjoy that dinner. When he found the phone booth, he would find it impossible to buck those lights. He'd have to keep driving until he found a way to make a U-turn.

Out of the corner of his eye, he spotted the phone booth. It was the one. To his amazement he saw a gap coming, eased into the middle suicide area between the two-way stream of galloping monsters and waited, deaf to the screeching brakes and strident horns behind him. The gap was two seconds away. He sharply turned the wheel, charged between two cars, flew past the phone booth, down the cement ramp, and then braked abruptly, almost snapping his neck. He stopped inches from the French cop's giant paw, raised high in his beamlights. In the glare the cop with wrinkled face and pendulous ears stepped up to him, saluted politely, spotted the collar, said:

"This road is temporarily closed, Father."

A cop in this isolated wilderness meant only one thing: they had nailed his targets.

"I'm American. I'm lost." He said this in French that he deliberately pronounced wrong. "I can't find the gallery."

"Gallery *here*?"

"The Church Architectural exhibition."

"Oh, yes, Father, the one near Passage Pont Neuf."

As the cop patiently gave him directions back to an exhibition he'd already passed on his way, Father Flanagan looked past him at the blinking police lights, the ambulance, the crowd of cops and vehicles in front of the barge, and all the barge's lights on. No surprise. He was on their turf now. They had beat him to the punch. But how heavy was their punch?

"Thank you, Officer. I'll find it now. Was it a bad accident that happened here?"

"Bad, Father, but no accident."

"I'm willing to help if I can, Officer. I have delivered the last rites in many emergencies."

The cop showed no reaction.

Father Flanagan didn't give up.

"When a person is dying, it makes no difference whether a Catholic, Protestant, Jew, Muslim or Buddhist is praying for his soul."

"That's how I feel about it, Father."

"Catholic?"

"Yes, Father, but when my time comes, I wouldn't give a damn if a Martian was praying for me."

"Amen." He cracked his door, got out. "Please. Don't deny him the love of God."

The cop waved him toward the barge. "Come along."

47

Twenty minutes after having thanked God for the miracle of Lafitte's revival, Michelle astonishingly found her aborted time-table back on schedule.

She had been carried into her room by the burly cop, revived by Dr. Sully, and comforted by the Inspector, who remained alone with her near the sleeping baby. Michelle had answered his questions with hushed clarity after he brought her coffee and aspirins.

In those crucial twenty minutes, he had left her alone briefly three times at five-minute intervals to check with the surgeon and return with the hopeless news:

Lafitte was dying.

In those three intervals, she had sat on the bed ready for more questions and stolen glances at Paul's gashes being treated out in the living room, his head being bandaged while Dr. Sully and the two cops waited for the criminal to come to. Paul had not been cuffed. This made the burly cop nervously whisper to his colleague: "Maniacs have animal strength, you know!"

In those twenty minutes, the Inspector's questions were often out of context, disjointed. At times, he felt it was like in-terrogating his daughter. Then at times his questions were very professional, fast, impersonal. Those moments forced her to keep her guard up.

Disjointed as it might have been, she was coming to the end of her story—just as Lafitte was coming to the end of his. She had never mentioned Paul's brainquake. She gave the Inspector their forged passports.

"One thing isn't clear to me, Michelle."

She didn't show fear. Before she could ask him what wasn't clear, an older cop appeared in the doorway, saluting.

"Excuse me, Inspector, I took it upon myself to bring an American priest to you. He got lost looking for a gallery. He saw the ambulance, offered his help. To give last rites. He's waiting in the other room."

"You did the right thing. Thank you. Tell him I'll be right with him."

The cop beamed, saluted, left.

"Michelle, try to remember exactly when Page first showed indications he was capable of murder. I'll return in a minute."

"I could tell you right now."

"In a minute, Michelle."

She watched him approach the priest standing near the exit door as the cop who'd brought him left the barge.

"Inspector Sainte-Beuve, Police Nationale." He thrust out his hand.

The priest shook it. "Father Flanagan."

"I hope you understand my English."

"I speak French."

"I prefer English when I get the chance to use it."

"Your English is okay, Inspector."

"We might need you, Father. Thank you for offering to help." He led him a few steps to the open door. The priest could partially see Lafitte. "A bullet's close to his heart. We're fighting to keep him alive. If that fails…Christian Lafitte will be in your hands. You understand why I'm not bringing you in right now, don't you?"

"Perfectly, Inspector. A dying man often dies sooner if he sees a priest. So as not to keep God waiting."

"Exactly." He indicated the black leather chair across from Lafitte's room. "Make yourself comfortable, please. And excuse me, Father."

"Of course, Inspector."

Father Flanagan sank into the leather chair, his eyes following the Inspector rejoining Michelle in the doorway. She immediately began to whisper something to him. Father Flanagan tried hard to make out her words. He couldn't. Evidently the baby was asleep in that room, and she didn't want it to wake up.

She wore no handcuffs. Odd. Or maybe not so odd. Enough cops out there to keep her from running. And it would be tough to hold the baby with hands in bracelets. He watched the Inspector nod, whispering a few words back.

Quicksilver flashes jumped through Father Flanagan's head, explanations and hypotheses…the widow, no black wig on anymore…blonde…cool…looking nothing like a captured criminal wanted for murder…could she actually be an innocent in all this?…the man out here, no beard, bandaged…had a bullet grazed his head?…bloodspots on his white turtleneck sweater… on the deck he'd had a Luger on the skipper…had the skipper wanted a bigger fee for hiding them?…the shootout cut their deal short…with both out of action, she'd run off with baby… but then who called the cops?…or maybe the cops tailed them here, shot both men, took her without a scratch…the Inspector was grilling her right now, then he'd work on the bagman when he came to…if the skipper died right now, it meant last rites… thank you, Father…and then he'd have to leave…he prayed for Lafitte to die *after* the bagman was grilled…he would sit ringside, hear every word…he had to hear what the bagman would say…

He saw Paul's fingers twitching.

A moment later, Dr. Sully saw Paul's hand reaching for his bandaged head.

"Inspector!" Dr. Sully called out.

✻

Michelle watched the Inspector help Dr. Sully gently move Paul up to a sitting position. His back was to Michelle. If he turned his head toward her, she knew the face she would wear when their eyes met. But he didn't turn his head.

The Inspector was in luck when Paul said, "I'm all right."

The sandpaper-scratching rasp was the sound Michelle had described when they talked. At first it would be irritating, but he would get used to it. She'd also told him sometimes Paul was coherent, other times he wasn't…but that he had always been so gentle when they first met, so willing to help her…

She watched them help Paul off the table. On his feet he reeled. Their grip was firm.

"I'm all right," Paul repeated.

"Is your head spinning?" the Inspector said.

"Worse on my back."

They helped him into a chair.

"Want some water?"

Paul shook his head, rested his arms on the table. The Inspector pulled a small tape recorder from his pocket, placed it between Paul's arms.

"We're recording everything you say."

The Inspector sat on the table edge close to Paul, bending over so that his words would be recorded, too. He looked at Paul's dead gray eyes. They were rooted on him but felt like they were looking through him at the priest in the chair behind.

The Inspector was hypnotized by those gray eyes. Not a movement. Not a muscle in the face moved.

"I'm Inspector Sainte-Beuve, Police Nationale." His voice was gentle, but not too gentle. He kept the tone of a cop about to question a fugitive. "Feel well enough to answer questions?"

Paul wondered where Michelle was. Slowly, as he took in the room, things came into focus. He didn't see her. She must be in the bunk with the baby. He had to make sure she was all right. He started to turn his head. Pain stopped him.

"Is Michelle all right?"

"Yes. Feel well enough to answer questions?"

Paul nodded.

"I didn't hear you."

"Yes."

"You feel well enough to answer questions."

"Yes."

"Is my English good enough for you to understand every word I'm saying?"

"Yes."

"Good. I'm not comfortable when every word has to be translated. What is your name?"

"Paul Smith...no...Henry Smith."

"Anyone suffering from a blow to the head—multiple blows—might get mixed up. But we believe your name is Paul Page."

Blows to the head? Father Flanagan was confused. *Then he wasn't shot by the cops? Who called them?*

"Paul Page—have you ever been in a mental institution?"

Though his face remained blank, Paul reacted to the words, remembering the institution his parents kept him out of as a boy. He began hearing the flute playing far away and knew what was coming. It was a different tune than usual. A strange one. He waited. He heard no rumble, felt none. Was he using willpower to stop that rumble from coming? He was sure it was willpower. He had stopped it once before, thanks to Michelle. But the flute kept playing, far away, the same strange tune.

"No," Paul said. "Never an institution."

"Not even for a few days under another name?"

Paul shook his head.

"Please say yes or no."

"No."

"Perhaps overnight in the Bellevue psych ward in New York?"

"No."

"Were you born in New York?"

"Yes."

"How old are you?"

"Thirty."

"Any family?"

"No."

"Live alone?"

"Yes."

"Any friends?"

"Ivory Face."

"You mean Michelle?"

"Yes."

"How long have you known her?"

How to answer? Where to start counting? "Two months."

"Where did you first see her?"

"Central Park."

"And you didn't talk to her for how long?"

"Two months."

"What kind of work did you do in New York?"

"Taxi driver."

"For how long."

"Ten years."

"And before that?"

"Learned to drive a taxi."

"Drive for a fleet?"

"Indie."

"Your reflexes have to be good to get a taxi license in New York."

"Yes."

"Are your reflexes good even when you're not driving?"

"Sometimes I get headaches."

"What kind of headaches?"

Michelle stiffened. *I said nothing about Paul's headaches to the Inspector. Nothing! Absolutely nothing!*

"All kinds."

"What would you call your specific kind of headache?"

Good God! He was going to find out about the brainquakes! And if he learned about the brainquakes…

"Migraine," Paul said.

"You get visual disorders?"

"And nausea."

"I'm familiar with migraine, Paul. I get them now and then, too. On the right side of my head."

"Mine's on the left."

Michelle came up for air, stopped sweating. *God bless you, Paul! And you, too, Inspector! Now get on with the show.*

"How long have you worked for organized crime?"

The hammer hit her heart. *What was the Inspector doing?*

"I drive my own taxi."

"You're not a bagman for organized crime?"

"No."

"Would you tell me if you were?"

Paul remained silent.

"Do you know what a bagman is?"

Father Flanagan leaned in. Only one person could have tied Paul in with the organization or guessed that he was a bagman. Zara. She had a hunch or knew, and must have shared it with this inspector. He shouldn't have crucified that goddam smuggler in the hangar. That was why she had come to Paris. Not just to find the bagman and widow, but to find him.

"Do you know what a bagman is?" repeated the Inspector.

"Yes."

"What does he do?"

"Carries a bag."

"What is in the bag?"

"Money."

"Mafia money?"

"Yes."

"How much does he carry?"

Father Flanagan's balls were in the Inspector's hands and he was turning them in any direction he wanted. It would be easy to silence the bagman and widow right now with two bullets. But suicide didn't come with his job. All those cops would gun him down with a hundred holes in him. His job was to walk away from a hit, not to be carried to the cemetery after it.

"Enough," Paul said.

"Who does he carry it to?"

The pressure on the priest's balls tripled.

"People."

A steamroller crushed his balls. What the hell would he tell Hampshire? That he wasn't here at the grilling? The cops beat him to the targets. He'd have to go to ground with that story. But for how long? This nightmare would hit the *Tribune*. It would be in all the New York papers, on TV, on radio. Hampshire would hear about an American priest named Father Flanagan who had been there to give the last rites… who had sat through the grilling…who had heard every word…

"What people?" the Inspector asked.

Paul closed his eyes. "People waiting for food."

"Food?"

The sound of the flute was still far away as he remembered the fish in the Boss' office and the lady drop's shop.

"Food for fish. If you don't feed them, they die."

The Inspector put a hand on Paul's shoulder.

"You are wanted for murder in New York."

Michelle was relieved. *Stay on that! Don't wander off. Stay on that murder*.

"I know," Paul said.

The Inspector looked at his cipher face. Never had he seen such lifeless eyes, such a frozen face.

"Did you do it?"

"Yes."

"Who did you murder?"

"Boy in the Battery. Thirteen years old."

"What was his name?"

"Al Cody."

"That's the man who was found dead in Michelle's apartment. Not a thirteen-year-old."

Paul suddenly felt awash in confusion. Clung to something he knew: "He was going to kill the baby."

"Michelle's baby?"

Paul nodded. "Gave her my gun."

"She shot him? With your gun?"

"Yes."

"What kind of a gun?"

"Saturday night special."

"Why didn't you stay with her?"

"They demanded money."

"How much?"

"Ten thousand before midnight."

"Who wanted the ten thousand before midnight?"

"Al Cody."

"He said she owed him the money?"

"Her dead husband."

"But he wanted her to pay?"

"Said he'd kill the baby if she didn't pay before midnight."

"So she shot him to protect her baby?"

"Yes."

"Did you get the ten thousand?"

"No."

"Who did you try to get ten thousand cash from so late at night?"

"Boss."

"You told me you were your own boss."

"Boss of floating crap game."

"You couldn't get ten thousand from him?"

"No."

"Who gave you the two hundred thousand in cash to fly to France?"

"Tom."

"Tom who?"

"Tom Jefferson."

"Where?"

"Battery graveyard."

"Who forged your passports?"

"Capone."

"Where's your bag?"

"In the backpack under the bed."

The Inspector sent a cop to fetch the backpack.

The cop returned with the backpack. The Inspector opened it. Empty.

"Where did you hide the bag?"

Paul winced. "Don't remember."

"Do you remember your name now?"

"Yes."

"What is it?"

"Paul Page."

"Then you must remember where you hid that bag."

"I don't!"

"Why did Michelle run from the police?"

"Shot Al. Self-defense, but cops wouldn't believe her."

"Why didn't you tell the police what you told me—you gave her your gun to protect the baby while you went to try to raise the money?"

"Wouldn't believe me either."

"You have no record, Paul. You were not on any rap sheet until a few days ago. You drive a taxi, pay your taxes, offered to help her. She was alone. Her husband had been murdered. She was hounded for money he owed. Nobody gave a damn about her. Only you. A good solid American citizen. The police would believe you."

Paul remained cipher-faced.

"Besides the police, who else was she afraid of?"

"Eddie."

"Ed Cody? Al's brother?"

"Told police he was going to kill her."

The ache in the back of his head meant nothing. The ache on his temple meant nothing. Sudden pain came. The flute was closer. The tune stranger than ever. Was that a rumble?

"Paul, the police would have protected her."

"How long? He'd kill her when they stopped."

"Who took you to the charter plane?"

"Friend."

"What does this friend do for a living?"

"Makes drops."

"What kind of drops?"

Father Flanagan felt his heart stop beating.

Paul whispered: "*Tear drops in the Seine, Ivory Face in the rain.*"

"Talk to me, Paul. Focus."

"*Ivory Face's pain. Tears are in vain.*"

"Focus!"

Paul struggled to.

"How'd you get to Paris?"

"Flew."

"Was it your idea?"

"Hers. She was born here. On this barge. Lafitte delivered her."

"So this barge was the safest place you could hide?"

"Yes."

"Lafitte welcomed you as a friend?"

"Yes."

"Did you tell him you were fugitives?"

"No."

"And because of how he lived, he didn't know. No TV, no radio, no phone. Did you feel safe here?"

"Yes."

"Then, in heaven's name, why would you shoot him?"

Paul ached to say, *He asked me to!* But he'd given his word.

"Your bag," the Inspector said. "Who was the money in it for?"

Zara had told him if Paul was a bagman, he'd never talk. Bagmen were trained to be fanatically closed-mouthed. It was drummed into them. But then they were also trained to be loyal. And when a crack appeared in the dam...

"Who, Paul? Who?"

If Paul mentioned one name that the police could work on, it would lead to more names. Names involved in dope, labor, politics. It could be the biggest coup in the history of the Paris police.

"We just need one name, Paul."

Michelle was all mixed up again. She had never mentioned the bag to the Inspector. She made sure Paul's job was never known. She'd counted on the Inspector pounding away on Paul about shooting Lafitte. Nothing else. Just Lafitte. She counted on the surgeon bringing in the news any minute that he was dead. *Goddam it, the plan depended on Paul's shooting Lafitte dead!*

"Just one."

Paul remembered so clearly the Boss telling him to pick out a bag and he picked the black one and he didn't deliver the mail to Philadelphia and he wondered why because he had always delivered the mail right on schedule.

"Who, Paul?"

The strange tune was getting louder. The rumble stronger.

"Shelley…"

"That a first or last name?"

"Last."

"What's his first?"

"Percy…"

The Inspector had lost Paul again. He shoved aside the bag, picked up the sketch one of the cops had pulled off the wall and brought to him. He held it up in front of Paul, who stared at the baby.

"You remember this, Paul?"

"Yes."

"Do you like it?"

"Yes."

"Then why did you murder the woman who drew it?"

Paul blacked out for several seconds. The strange tune got louder inside his head. Light made it sparkle. When he could focus again, the Inspector was holding a plastic bag up in front of him. The Luger was in it. For a flash, the Luger became Lafitte's face, begging.

"Recognize this Luger?"

"Yes."

"Where did you get it?"

"Lafitte."

"Did you steal it?"

"Gave it to me."

"Why?"

"To...to..."

"Why?"

"Stop his pain," Paul whispered.

"What?"

"Stop his pain!"

"What pain?"

"Cancer."

"You're lying."

"No."

"If he gave it to you, *when* did he do it?"

"Today."

"Where were you?"

"On deck."

"Just out in the open, he handed you his gun and asked you to shoot him?"

"Yes."

"I don't think so, Paul. I don't believe that. I think he showed you where he kept his war trophies, and when you needed a weapon, you went there and took it."

"No."

"Maybe you were too drunk to remember."

"Don't drink alcohol."

"I see empty champagne bottles, Paul, looks like you had a real party here. Are you telling me you didn't drink any of it?"

"Maybe some."

"A lot?"

"Don't remember."

"How much did Lafitte drink?"

"A lot."

"He got drunk?"

"Yes."

"Michelle helped him to his room?"

"Yes."

"You know what I think, Paul? I think you all had too much to drink. I think she did tell him why you came to Paris, that the two of you were wanted by the police. And then you didn't feel safe anymore."

The flute, the strange melody, louder. Closer.

"You stole the Luger. You were angry. First you shot at the baby."

Now he could identify the tune. It wasn't strange at all. It was *Frère Jacques*. He didn't like it. It had killed the baby's father. It had made Ivory Face alone in the world, except for her baby.

"You were afraid Lafitte would tell the police in the morning when he was sober. Michelle trusted him, but you didn't. Is that right, Paul? Answer yes or no."

He could barely hear the question. *Frère Jacques* was hot lava slowly filling his ears. He tried to marshal willpower to stop the lava, but it kept coming. He wanted someone to stop the tune. He saw the Boss and she spoke gently, *Paul, do you want me to kill that tune before midnight?* Yes. Yes. Yes.

"Yes," said Paul.

"So you decided you'd kill Lafitte and started toward his room. Michelle tried to stop you. She hit you, scratched your face, trying to stop you. Is that right?"

He'd never felt her nails or punches. Whatever she did was to help him. She was always there to help him. Hoppie appeared and said, *Paul, tell them she was there to help you. She was there to help you, wasn't she?*

"Yes," said Paul.

"You pushed her away and went into his room. She hung onto you, trying to stop you. He was still in his clothes, dead drunk, snoring."

Lafitte was in such a terrible position on the bed…a twisted scarecrow's head against the wall, feet spread out across the bed, still in his uniform…

"Yes," Paul said.

"You aimed the Luger at him. She tried to wrench it from your hand, she pounded your hand. You pushed her away, hard. She picked up the ashtray from the table. She hit you on the head as you pulled the trigger and shot Lafitte. Paul, listen to me: Do you remember pulling the trigger of the Luger?"

It terrified him. *Do you remember pulling the trigger of the Luger?* He saw the bullet hole in the baby's crib.

"Yes…"

Michelle's fists clenched. This was it.

"*Inspector!*" the Surgeon called out.

48

Lafitte tasted blood trickling from his mouth. Eyes saw only blackness. Ears heard silence. But he hadn't lost his sense of taste. He had tasted his own blood before. Always warm. Now it tasted cold. Cold meant fear. Fear to face Jean Bourgois again. Fear to ask forgiveness.

Gray shadows moving in the black. It was Bourgois.

Lafitte spoke through the blood: "Jean."

But Lafitte went cold. He couldn't hear his own voice.

The Inspector entered the bedroom. Blood and sputum were trickling from Lafitte's mouth. His eyes were still open.

"He's going," the surgeon said.

"Father," the Inspector called out.

The priest rushed in, stepped back to make room as Gautier left with his crew and equipment.

Father Flanagan began:

"*Dóminus vobiscum…dóminus noster Jesus Christus, Filius Deu vivi…*"

"Jean…" Lafitte gurgled faintly.

"Hold it, Father! Please!" The Inspector sprang to Lafitte's side, called out through the doorway: "Bring both of them in here right away!" He bent over, looking into Lafitte's eyes. "*Lafitte, can you hear me?*"

"Jean…Jean…"

Michelle and Paul were brought in, a cop on either side but both keeping an eye on Paul.

The Inspector spoke into Lafitte's ear, his voice catching:

"Wasn't it Balzac? Who said, The heart of humor lives long without guilt?"

A weak movement of the dying man's mouth, covered with blood. Lafitte's lips curved into the ghost of a smile.

"Sainte-Beuve," Lafitte gurgled.

Michelle was horrified. She prayed that these would be his last words.

The Inspector pushed in very close.

"*Lafitte—can you see me?*"

Like shifting smoke, the grayish fog slowly formed into a blur...and slowly the blur began to take shape and he saw the face of his old friend. Lafitte managed a tiny nod.

Swiftly the Inspector positioned Michelle so that her face was in front of the old man.

"*Do you see this woman?*"

She saw her face reflected in his glassy eyes.

Another tiny nod.

"Michelle...Jean Bourgois...granddaughter..."

The Inspector pulled Paul in front of Lafitte. The two cops anxiously kept hold of his arms.

"*And this man?*"

Lafitte looked into Paul's gray eyes...saw Paul's bandaged head...like a nightmare saw Michelle hitting Paul on the head with something...and Paul falling...

"Hank...Smith."

"*You met him through Michelle?*"

Lafitte shifted his gaze and in her blue eyes for the last time he saw her grandfather swimming for his life...saw himself abandoning the man he loved...heard the bursts of the Schmeissers ...and remembered the kind, forgiving eyes of Jean Bourgois, as blue as Michelle's. He pushed the word out of his mouth:

"Yes."

"*They threw you a party?*"

Lafitte's smile was more pronounced this time.

"Yes."

"*You got drunk.*"

"Yes."

"*Did Michelle bring you into this room?*"

"Yes."

The floor under Michelle undulated. She knew what the next question was and she couldn't stop it.

"*Lafitte—did Michelle tell you that she and Hank Smith were wanted in New York for murder?*"

Her plan, so carefully constructed and reconstructed, engineered and improvised, teetered. The Inspector was double-crossing her. He had known all the time she was lying. He was going to get the truth out of Lafitte. For the baby's sake she prayed to God to make Lafitte die before he could answer. God heard her.

In pain, Lafitte closed his eyes and said nothing. He looked dead. *Oh thank God!* thought Michelle. *Thank you!*

The Inspector shook him. "*Lafitte!*"

Lafitte was silent.

The Inspector shook him harder, then even harder.

Slowly Lafitte opened his eyes. Michelle gasped. He wasn't dead. She was.

"*Lafitte—hold on!*" the Inspector shouted. "*Just for a few seconds! Did Michelle tell you they were wanted for murder? Michelle and Hank! Did she tell you they were wanted for murder? Is that why he shot you?*"

Years of guilt flooded Lafitte's heart because never had there been a way to atone for his betrayal.

His last word before death would prevent the desecration of Jean Bourgois' name:

"Yes."

He closed his eyes.

God bless you, Zozo.

The surgeon made it official after a moment.

"He's dead."

Michelle screamed, throwing herself on Lafitte, and weeping.

Paul looked down at the body. He was glad Lafitte would never have any more visions in yellow. But why did he say...?

"Dóminus vobiscum...dóminus noster Jesus Christus, Filius Deu vivi..."

Father Flanagan continued the chant. The Inspector slowly brushed a hand over his old friend's face, closing Lafitte's eyes, and kissed him on the brow.

As she lay sobbing on the body, Michelle's mind had never been so clear, so alert. She knew that the Inspector would testify for her. She would wear a black veil all the time in New York, especially in the courtroom. She would make sure no news photographer got a picture of her face. The only photo of her in existence would be the blur of her taken in the ambulance in Central Park. She would change her name, leave the country, be safe for the rest of her life. Her baby would grow up without ever knowing his mother had been tried for murder, even though she had won. Her baby would never know that.

Gently she reached out and caressed Lafitte's bloody mouth, kissed him on the cheek. She mustered her strength, knowing the stage was set, knowing now all she needed to do was bring out a brainquake in front of the cops.

Now it all depended on Paul's jackal.

She wheeled and lunged like a wildcat at Paul, yelling:

"You killed him, you bastard!"

With her fists she pummeled Paul's face like a trip-hammer. Father Flanagan halted his chant. The Inspector grabed for her wrists but she tore them free.

"If you had to kill someone, you should have killed Eddie!"

She ripped open Paul's cheek with her nails.

Paul stammered: "I…I saw him…I tried…"

"It was Eddie who wanted to hurt us! *Eddie!*"

Another slap.

"Eddie!"

The burly cop seized her. She screamed.

"Paul! Help me!"

*The brainquake came with rumbles and flute, loud and louder.
In reddish-pink Eddie pulled out a holstered gun. Paul butted
him in the stomach, seized the gun, shot him—shot Eddie.*

The burly cop dropped dead.

Eddie whipped out a second gun. Paul shot him.

The moustached cop dropped dead.

Eddie grabbed Paul's arm. Paul shot him in the shoulder.

The Inspector fell to the floor.

*Eddie ran out. Paul ran after him. From the gangplank, Eddie
aimed at him. Paul fired.*

A slender cop fell with his gun on the gangplank. Shots were
fired at Paul by cops near their parked vehicles.

*Bullets hit the gangplank. Paul crawled to the body, crouched
behind it. Bullets sent chips flying. Paul emptied his gun, firing
at Eddie near the mobile lab. Eddie's hand seized Paul's gun
hand. Paul slammed Eddie's hand away, saw the hand belonged
to the boy he had murdered in the Battery. Paul tossed the empty
gun away, seized the boy's gun near the body, shot the boy in
the face, saw with horror it was the Boss' face. Paul spotted
Eddie running toward him on the barge roof, took aim, fired.
To get away, Eddie jumped into the river.*

Cop bullets drove Paul back onto the deck of the barge.

*From the deck Paul spotted Eddie swimming to save the
drowning Lafitte. An illuminated sightseeing boat sent up fireworks lighting the sky with rainbow colors…red, white, and blue,
but the white was pink and the blue was purple.*

Cops behind vehicles with shattered windows got a glimpse of Paul racing along the deck, bent low. They opened fire, but he was gone.

Running through gunfire Paul was slammed down by the quake-rocking earth. He heard the flute playing much louder. The earth kept shaking and heaving. He saw the quake lift the sightseeing boat high up into the sky. The boat exploded. He watched the three-masted sailing ship against the flames. He saw a giant wave sweep Eddie back on the deck of the barge. Rain came down like nails with thousands of poetry books bombarding Paul. Pages fell out. Paul ran through the poems.

The wounded Inspector ran out of the barge's cabin, shouting at his men:

"Try to take him alive!"

The Inspector raced to the gangplank.

Father Flanagan and Michelle came running out after him, only to be hurled behind vehicles by cops.

Paul ran to tell his mother the ship in the sky was a miracle. He spotted Eddie on the barge roof again. Paul charged at him, knocking deck chairs to either side. He smashed into Michelle pushing the baby in the carriage in Central Park. Paul saw the baby shoot Frankie Troy from the carriage. Paul saw Lieutenant Zara on the police horse galloping at him and he ducked out of the way. A bullet zinged past his foot as he climbed up on the barge roof and saw Eddie disappear. Paul heard the flute, turned, saw Eddie moving slowly behind the front of the ambulance.

Slowly the Inspector raised his gun from behind the ambulance.

Paul saw Eddie aiming the flute at him.

The Inspector aimed at Paul's knee, fired, saw Paul grab his leg, fall, then force himself up.

Paul fired at Eddie playing the flute.

The bullet hit the ambulance window. The Inspector darted back as splinters of glass flew.

Paul suddenly turned inward to look for Eddie, diving deep into his own enormous and expanding brain. Tremors increased. Pink getting weaker, red getting redder. He followed the tune, sloshing past his half-eaten sensory impulse organs...crawling past his busted transmitter motor half-buried in blood...splashing through thousands of cells...stopped. He saw the jackal tearing apart the remains of his nerve tissues...the jackal looked up at Paul, bared its fangs...a massive tremor shook the surface of his brain and showered debris of tissues, blood, nerve cells upon Paul and the jackal...Paul raised his gun and fired at the jackal.

The bullet hit the Inspector in his thigh, plowed through muscle, shattered bone. He collapsed to one knee. Michelle and Father Flanagan maneuvered to his side. They saw him raising his gun—and Paul standing like a statue on the roof of the barge.

Paul was wondering...Why was his brain eaten away by the jackal?...Why his brain?...Why his brain?...There must be a reason. He saw Eddie. Eddie changed into the jackal. Then back into Eddie, then Paul fired at the jackal.

The Inspector steadied his aim at the homicidal head.

Must everything have a reason?

The Inspector fired.

Paul's brain was blown apart by the red explosion.

49

"He's dead. No bag."

"Keep looking," Hampshire said.

"Jesus himself couldn't find it."

"Father—you ought to know the bag's no write-off just because they're dead."

"I didn't hit the widow."

"Then she's got the bag. Find her."

"I never lost her."

"What the hell does that mean?"

"I passed."

"You could've hit her and you *passed*?"

"Yes."

"You must've had a damn good reason."

"I don't think she knows where it is."

"You don't think…?"

"That's right. She's no saint, but she got swept up in this because of her husband. Just wanted to get away from the Codys. She didn't know who she was getting in bed with."

"Bullshit!"

"No. Page wouldn't talk. Even when his life depended on it. I think he physically couldn't. Not to the police, and not to her."

"You think so, Father? You're that confident? Confident enough to pass? *Why?*"

The *Why?* was the crack of a 240 mm gun. Father Flanagan knew exactly what Hampshire would say before calling him. He stood in the coffin-like phone booth, sweating. Two more ambulances roared past him to pick up more dead cops. The phone booth was suffocating him. His head choked with scrambled words Hampshire would never buy.

He felt no betrayal. No guilt at all. Then why was he sweating like a spent horse? He knew his decision to pass on the hit would only give her the briefest freedom. Eddie would find her after the New York police had given her a clean slate. But he couldn't stop Eddie. Father Flanagan was a professional and he only killed on contract. To kill Eddie was murder. That he would never do. Not even for a widow and her baby, not even to keep a baby from being orphaned.

He stayed in the booth, one hand depressing the metal tongue, the other holding the receiver. He concentrated on what he would say. The words in his head began to fit.

He placed the call. It took a few minutes for the international connection to go through, and then he heard Hampshire's voice on the other end of the phone.

He told Hampshire everything from the time he had walked onto the barge with the cop to the bloody catastrophe at the end. He explained there was no sign of the bag, no sign the widow even knew about the bag. He explained about the murder of the skipper, about the massacre of the police. He described the interrogation by the Inspector. He confirmed that Paul had gone to his death without naming any names. His voice was hoarse when he finished.

He waited. One word from Hampshire and another hit man would get the widow.

"I buy it," Hampshire said. "You did good."

"Thank you."

"Take a vacation, my friend."

"I need one."

"Take a month."

"Okay."

"God be with you, Father."

✿

Hampshire hung up and smiled, thinking about Paul.

He was proud of Paul. Bagman loyalty was stronger than any kind of insanity. Opening the bag for the widow had been suicidal thievery, but never mentioning a name under pressure… that was the apex of loyalty. The man had redeemed himself in death.

If Paul had mentioned Railey, Uncle Sam's top psychiatrists would have put together Paul's insane jigsaw under the scrutiny of a federal judge. They would've climbed the ladder and tried to get to Hampshire at the top, and who knows, they might have succeeded.

He hadn't slept well since Paul had run off with the bag.

Now he would sleep like a baby.

Yes, he was very proud of Paul Page.

50

Father Flanagan shed his uniform of God in Avoriaz, a ski resort in the French Alps he had always liked. Its quaint fairy-tale hotels and inns drew beautiful girls.

The first week he struck out. He tried hard, but couldn't get the attention of a certain gorgeous blonde. His X-ray eyes revealed her to him nude as she swept down the slopes. She made all the others also-rans.

The second week he tried to catch her eye at the bar of their inn, on the road, in a lift while it was snowing, on a slope.

The third week he even joined kids in a snowball fight and deliberately threw one that broke on her back. She scolded the boys. He announced he had thrown it. She kept walking without a word.

The fourth week he spotted her with a group at the bar watching the morning news on TV. Logs were crackling in the huge fireplace. He ordered a Bloody Mary and sat on the stone bench near the fireplace and kept watching her. He sipped his drink. She paid no attention to him.

When he heard the name of Inspector Sainte-Beuve on the news, he turned away from her to look at the TV newsman reporting:

"Sainte-Beuve's videotaped statement, made from his Paris hospital bed and transmitted to the New York police ten days ago, was said to be the decisive factor in the judge's decision to release Michelle Troy. Mrs. Troy could not be reached for comment. Paul Page, the New York taxi driver who was slain following a murderous rampage…"

The blonde shivered and switched to another station. Some sort of philharmonic performance. The others in the group showed relief. They were on a vacation. They wanted to enjoy themselves, not listen to the sort of news they'd come to the Alps to escape.

Father Flanagan left, gathered up his skis, still rueful about Michelle's Pyrrhic victory. He knew that no matter where she hid—California or Alaska—Eddie would find her and kill her. There was no statute of limitations on vengeance.

But if she was very fortunate, she'd live long enough to see her son grow up past toddlerhood.

He trudged through the snow on the road crowded with early skiers on their way to the lifts. Kids were still in snowball fights. Pictures were being taken of a family in a horse-drawn sleigh while the driver bit off a chunk of his baguette.

Taking the lift to the highest slope to see what it looked like from above, Father Flanagan watched experts in action. When the last skier queued up ahead of him asked if he wanted to go first, Father Flanagan shook his head. The skier sailed off. The way he soared made Father Flanagan's courage sink lower. He was not a brave man and viewed any steep slope with suspicion.

He was startled when the blonde got off the lift with her skis. She glanced through him, as if he didn't exist. It was his chance. They were alone.

He performed the suicidal feat. Sailing in the air, flying spread eagle with his legs apart, he made a perfect landing. He waited. She didn't follow. He waited.

She came down in the lift.

"You're wonderful!" she said. "I haven't the nerve to tackle that slope."

"How about a double lift to an easy one?"

"I'll race you," she said.

They trudged through snow to the double lift. They enjoyed the safe downhill race. She won. They lunched, raced down safe slopes the rest of the day, dined, slept in his bed.

The next day they repeated the same program.

When she learned he was only staying one more day, she was disappointed. She was staying on another week. Today they would enjoy themselves and tomorrow, his last, they would do the same. They were tired. Too much skiing.

But they slept well in his bed.

When he woke up, she was gone. The note on the floor was brief. She was going to the slope they met on, didn't want him there in case she proved cowardly and backed out once again. He was to wait for her at the bar.

He smiled. She didn't want him to see her chicken out or fall on her ass. There was no time to shower. Swiftly, he pulled a purple turtleneck over his head, thrust his legs into emerald green pants, jammed his feet into his heavy yellow boots, buckled them, put on his red skiing jacket, slung his tinted goggles round his neck, clapped on his knit cap, rushed out, grabbed his skis, hurried down the snow-banked road.

He kept his eyes on the highest slope. Deserted. No movement whatsoever. He looked for orange. Vivid orange—her jacket. No orange.

He stopped in the middle of the road. Steadied his gaze. Maybe she was still going up the lift. Maybe she had tried the slope and fallen.

He spotted orange on the top of the slope. It sparkled in the blinding sun. She stood there like an orange monument. He shared her fear. She was making up her mind.

She stood there for over a minute.

Suddenly she vanished. An instant later she appeared flying in the air. She sailed like a swan. She made a wonderful landing. Soon she would be skiing down the road to tell him all about it.

The sun burned his eyes. He put on the goggles and started along the road, waiting for her. Behind him, the approaching jingle of bells made him step out from the middle of the road as he turned toward the horse-drawn sleigh.

In it, he saw the widow. She was wrapped in mink. With a mink cap.

With her was a man. Both were laughing. On his lap was the baby pulling at the tail of the toy monkey in his tiny gloved hands.

The sleigh was coming closer. He knew she couldn't recognize him, with goggles and hat and collar pulled high. But he recognized her. He also recognized the face sitting next to her. He had seen that face on TV and in newspapers threatening blood revenge for the murder of his brother.

Edward Cody.

Eddie and Michelle kissed.

The sleigh passed. He watched it heading toward the inn. The shock was brief. He had been taken in. Because of him, the mob wasn't looking for Paul's bag. She had made a horse's ass out of him. She'd made a horse's ass out of Hampshire. She had pulled the old collusion sting and it had worked. Eddie, the avenger, was her partner. It was a setup that had fooled everybody, even the cops. Father Flanagan admired her cunning, her acting ability, recalling the way she had goaded Paul to blow his top, yelling Eddie's name. And Paul shot down by a French cop. What a goddam brilliant sting. She had the ten million and nobody was looking for it. Nobody.

His mind traveled back to his room, to the closet in his room, to the highest shelf of the closet, to the small leather satchel on the highest shelf, to the tools tucked away in a deep, reinforced pocket of the satchel. He was on vacation, he'd had no intention of working for a month, but because you never know what might come up, he hadn't traveled empty-handed.

He smiled, thinking of the hammer, of the spikes.

No one was paying him to rectify the situation. True enough. But sometimes an extraordinary situation calls for unusual measures. And this was a matter of pride. Of self-respect. Of justice.

And of ten million dollars.

A small, strained voice in the back of his head spoke then: *If you let them live, the baby won't be orphaned!*

But he silenced it. There was orphaned and there was orphaned. Most of the ten million remained, surely, and a generous fraction donated anonymously to the orphanage in France would ensure a better childhood than he'd ever have had with his mother. It would ensure a good childhood for quite a few orphans.

Through his brown-tinted goggles, the gorgeous nude on skis was approaching. She saw his smile, thought it was for her, returned one of her own. "You saw what I did? I felt so bold!" She leaned in toward him, nuzzled his cheek. "Are you up for doing something bold yourself?"

"Yes," said Father Flanagan. His eyes never left the sleigh.

AFTERWORD
By Charles Ardai

The word "hero" gets thrown around a lot these days, to the point where using it might inspire cynicism rather than admiration. But there's no other way to say it: while he never considered himself one, Samuel Fuller was a hero.

Not just a hero of mine, though he was that too. An actual, honest-to-god hero.

He'd have earned that description just for what he did in World War II, enlisting in the notorious 1st Infantry Division of the U.S. Army (known as the "Big Red One," and not just because of the red numeral sewn on their uniforms) and fighting in North Africa and Italy before landing in the D-Day invasion of Normandy. If you've seen the brutal opening sequence of Steven Spielberg's film *Saving Private Ryan* (or Fuller's own autobiographical war movie *The Big Red One*), you have a tiny sense of what that experience entailed. Some 160,000 troops stormed the beaches, where they were mowed down by Nazi machine gun fire. Thousands died. Sam survived.

He marched on to Czechoslovakia, where he and his fellow infantrymen participated in the liberation of the Falkenau concentration camp. "Participated in"—what a bloodless phrase. It was not a bloodless event. The hand-to-hand combat was horrific, and what the soldiers discovered inside the camp was even more so. Interviewed years later, Fuller said, "War is so insane...it's impossible for anybody to appreciate the word 'insanity' unless you are in combat. In war, we actually got used to seeing violence, horrible things. But we never thought that we would ever come across anything that would make that whole nightmare seem almost a holiday—except at Falkenau." Already a budding filmmaker with several film scripts to his credit, he was carrying a little handheld movie camera with him, and his footage of the camp is shocking and unforgettable.

> In Tunisia, I wrote to my mother to send me a movie camera. It took her over a year and a half, or more. That was '43...I received a 16 millimeter Bell & Howell, which you had to crank...
>
> [After the fighting ended at Falkenau, the] first man I ran into was Captain Walker. He said, "Do you still have that camera your mother sent you?" I said, "Yes, sir." He said: "Get it."
>
> I returned, with my camera, loaded it and all that, walked right into the camp. And didn't know that I was going to photograph...was going to shoot my first movie. It might be the work of an amateur, but the killings in it are very professional.

Samuel Fuller witnessed horrors. But he did more than witness them—he bore witness to them, not just through the film he shot in the moment, on the spot, but through the extraordinary career that followed. He made two dozen movies, many of them controversial, most of them deeply personal, all of them concerned with the topics of violence, cruelty, madness and suffering. He wrote and he directed. He was an *auteur* before the term existed. He made his pictures for very little money, in very little time, and sometimes it shows. But what also shows is his passion and absolute commitment to his subjects, to the telling of a story you can't stop watching, a story he believed was important to tell. A gruff, snarling, cigar-chomping figure who used to fire a gun loaded with blanks to commence filming rather than calling *Action!*, Fuller told stories like his life depended on telling them—and yours depended on hearing them. It wasn't a job. It was a calling.

The war wasn't Fuller's first taste of this calling. At twelve he went to work as a newspaper copyboy and at seventeen he became the youngest reporter in New York City history to cover a crime beat, writing about murders, suicides, executions and riots for the *New York Evening Graphic*. That experience later inspired his film *Park Row*, an attempt to convey the brutality and the glory of the newspaper business in its early days.

Through Prohibition and the Great Depression he worked as a journalist, reporting on Ku Klux Klan rallies, riding the rails with hoboes, covering the San Francisco longshoremen's strike that culminated in Bloody Thursday. He also began writing fiction at this time, starting with novels with titles like *Burn, Baby, Burn!* and (improbably enough, given that this was in 1936) *Test Tube Baby*. In 1944 he published *The Dark Page*, a classic noir crime novel later filmed (though not by Fuller) as *Scandal Sheet*.

Fuller broke into Hollywood himself as a screenwriter and script doctor, ghosting for other, better-known writers. His big break came in 1949, when he got the opportunity to direct his own script for the disturbing Western *I Shot Jesse James*, most memorable for depicting the psychological torment of James' killer, forced to reenact his crime nightly on stage to the jeers of frontier audiences. He made his name with his third film, *The Steel Helmet*, which was the first Hollywood movie about the Korean War, shot and released while the war was still going on. It, and Fuller, came under fire for the movie's realism, including a scene where an American solider shoots a prisoner of war. Fuller's response: he'd seen it done himself, and not just once.

More war movies followed, more Westerns. Also crime pictures such as the moving and visceral film noir *Pickup on South Street*. Many of the movies dealt head-on with previously untouched and untouchable themes, in particular racism, and drew criticism down on Fuller's head from both ends of the political spectrum.

The fifties were a fertile time for Fuller, who wrote and directed twelve films in ten years. Then came the sixties, and sources of funding began to dry up, both because of changes in the studio system and because of the controversial content Fuller avidly embraced. But Fuller kept making movies, including two of his greatest: *Shock Corridor*, about a newspaperman who gets himself committed to an insane asylum to investigate a killing, and *The Naked Kiss*, about a prostitute trying to start her life over in a small town. After that, it was sixteen years before Fuller cemented his reputation as a filmmaker with *The Big Red One*.

Along the way, he inspired a legion of other filmmakers who went on to do unforgettable work of their own: Spielberg, Coppola, Tarantino, Wenders, Jarmusch, Godard, Scorsese… the list goes on. Spielberg gave Fuller a cameo in his first World War II film, *1941*, and (together with George Lucas) named the scrappy young sidekick in *Indiana Jones and the Temple of Doom* "Short Round" after the similar character in *The Steel Helmet*. Footage can be found online of Coppola screen-testing Fuller for the role of Hyman Roth in *The Godfather*. Jean-Luc Godard famously cast Fuller as himself in *Pierrot le Fou*, where he filmed Fuller expounding, "A film is like a battleground…there's love, hate, action, violence, death. In one word, emotions."

Interviewed about *Raging Bull*, Martin Scorsese credited Fuller for inspiring some of the techniques he used. And Quentin Tarantino, who became a friend of Fuller's toward the end of the older filmmaker's life, owes a debt to Fuller that seems to grow with every picture he makes. Certainly it's hard to imagine the gut-wrenching WWII narrative of *Inglourious Basterds* or the provocative and violent musing on race that is *Django Unchained* without Fuller's spirit hovering over the proceedings.

So: *Brainquake*.

Where does this book fit in Samuel Fuller's extraordinary story?

Well, Fuller never stopped writing novels, and when making films became harder for him he found himself returning with a vengeance to the printed page. In 1982, he made his last American film, the anti-racist parable *White Dog*, but Paramount Pictures refused to release it, citing concerns about the movie's inflammatory racial subject matter. Outraged, Fuller went into self-imposed exile in France, where he made three final films and wrote two final novels. One of the novels, *Quint's World*, was published and distributed widely. The other, though, never was—it was only ever published in French (as *Cerebro-Choq*) and in Japanese. Never in English, and never in Fuller's native United States.

It's a book that fits squarely in the bullseye of Fuller's life-long themes and preoccupations. Paul Page's shack down in the Battery calls to mind Richard Widmark's waterfront shack in *Pickup on South Street*. The anecdote about the Statue of Liberty getting its pedestal thanks to contributions by children echoes a plot thread in *Park Row*. The depiction of underworld affairs has a precedent in *Underworld U.S.A.* And Captain

Lafitte's traumatic memories of World War II could be episodes from *The Big Red One*.

And yet *Brainquake* is very much its own animal. Written and set at the start of the 1990s, it's a startlingly modern novel for an author best known for stories set around the middle of the century (or earlier—*Park Row* and the Westerns take place in the 1800s). And while madness abounds in Fuller's universe, giving his protagonist the sort of brain disorder he gives Paul is a daring step even by Fuller's standards. Paul is not Lenny from *Of Mice and Men*, but his mental and physical abnormalities certainly make him a less-than-typical lead for a Hollywood crime story. Can one picture Widmark in the role? A pick-pocket may live on the margins of society and be despised by many, but Widmark still brought more sex appeal than pathos to the role in *Pickup on South Street*. If *Brainquake* had ever gone before the cameras, the balance would have had to have been different, more delicate.

And what of Father Flanagan, the Mob hit man who goes around dressed as a Roman Catholic priest, nailing his victims to walls and tables and picturing every woman he meets naked— even an old nun? Fuller was no stranger to controversy, but the firestorm this character would have created might have dwarfed all the rest.

But what a character! And what a book. From its piss-cutter of an opening image ("Sixty seconds before the baby shot its father…") to its sardonic view of corruption masking itself in sanctimony ("Laser beams on the Statue of Liberty were blinding as the guests sang along with the *Star-Spangled Banner* while Paul transferred $15 million in cash from his bag into the open fat briefcase held by the drop…") to its genuinely disturbing deaths ("She never tried to struggle. She showed fear in her face but didn't fight to live."), *Brainquake* is every bit as powerful and memorable as Fuller's best films. In spots, it makes you squirm; in spots it makes you wince. In a few places you scratch your head. But you never doubt the author's conviction or his vision or his unique talent.

When Christa Fuller, Sam's widow (also an actress who was featured in several of her husband's movies, including *The Big Red One* and *White Dog*), first contacted me four years ago to say that a novel of his existed that had never been published in English, I was astonished. It took some time to turn up a copy of the manuscript, laboriously transcribed by Sam's friend and literary agent, Jerome Rudes, from the nearly illegible pages that Sam had pounded out on a Royal typewriter and then marked up extensively by hand. When I read the manuscript, I was more astonished still. Why had this book lain unpublished all these years? It was not as though Fuller lacked for publishers. Bantam had brought out the novel version of *The Big Red One* in 1980. *The Dark Page* had been reissued by Avon in 1983, *Crown of India* by Critic's Choice Paperbacks in 1986. *Quint's World* had come out from Worldwide Library in 1988. It seems to me that one of these publishers would have jumped at the chance to publish *Brainquake* just a few years later.

But stranger things have happened. At Hard Case Crime we have turned up previously unpublished novels by luminaries such as James M. Cain, Donald E. Westlake (twice!), Roger Zelazny, David Dodge, Mickey Spillane and Lester Dent—why not Samuel Fuller?

Fuller returned to the United States from France at the very end of his life. He died in 1997 at the age of 85, at home once more in the Hollywood Hills. Today, his legacy as a filmmaker is better known and more widely respected than ever before, in part because of the devoted efforts of his family and friends, most recently his daughter Samantha, who directed the 2013 documentary *A Fuller Life*, which *The Hollywood Reporter* praised for its depiction of "an indelibly influential persona that combined showman-like flamboyance, old-school masculinity and die-hard personal integrity to disarming and intoxicating degrees."

That Fuller also had a legacy as a novelist is less well known. He was every bit as flamboyant and showman-like on the page as he was on the screen, and brought the same integrity and intensity, the same uncompromising, excoriating vision, to his books as to his films. It is a privilege to have the opportunity to remind readers of this, by giving his last book its first publication in the language in which he wrote it and the country he defended with his life.